Fae Ainslie grew up in the Northeast of England with her parents and two siblings. When Fae isn't reading or writing gang novels, she is studying biomedical science at university. At age 20, Fae was diagnosed with dyslexia and dyspraxia, and the diagnosis only pushed Fae even further to finish her first novel, *Gods Among Kings*, striving to shatter the stereotypes of neurodivergent people.

Mum, Dad.
My Parabatai—Ellie
And Harry Styles.

Fae Ainslie

Gods Among Kings

AUSTIN MACAULEY PUBLISHERS™
LONDON • CAMBRIDGE • NEW YORK • SHARJAH

A CIP catalogue record for this title is available from the British Library.

ISBN 9781398469013 (Paperback)
ISBN 9781398469020 (ePub e-book)

www.austinmacauley.com

First Published 2023
Austin Macauley Publishers Ltd®
1 Canada Square
Canary Wharf
London
E14 5AA

I couldn't have finished *Gods Among Kings* without the mountains of moral support and reassurance from my friends and family. Mum, Dad, Jessica, Michael, Ellie, Kat…

Austin Macauley Publishers, you made me realise how great my work was and taking a chance on a young first-time author.

At 20, finding out that I am dyslexic, dyslexic and ADHD was a huge game changer in the way I viewed my time at school and my achievements. The SPLD team at university helped me understand that the diagnosis didn't put me at a disadvantage, it meant my mind viewed the world in a different vision. When I was doubting myself the most, they picked me up and helped me value myself, and helped me knock down the Neurodivergent stereotypes.

"If there's a book that you want to read, but it hasn't been written yet, then you must write it."—Toni Morrison.

Table of Contents

Prologue
Impromptu Shootouts

Impromptu shootouts were always Link's favourite way to end the night, the rush of adrenaline that hit levels of excitement he would be left chasing—aching for. It wasn't often the small group had a day off. Their boss would say there was always something to do—and then find the most tedious, unimportant task for the four men. Which, of course, they completed efficiently and without question.

Tonight, was a very surprising change. They had finished their report and awaited tomorrow's orders. And their boss had waved them off, claiming they had earned a rest day. They waited a few moments for the man to call his own bluff and throw paperwork at them—he didn't. So, they had gone out.

Hino had been boasting a new swanky nightclub that had opened in town. The main entrance was hidden down stone steps, but the waiting line ran for half a mile down the street. They swaggered to the entrance and no one in line complained. Instead, offering a hand to send them ahead.

The boys couldn't hear the music until they stood in front of a large security man. His clipboard groaned under his meaty fingers when he had seen them. He didn't bother checking the list of A-star guests and bowed a sweaty head and opened the red velvet rope to allow them entrance. Marius, who was dressed in a lavish jade waistcoat and matching velvet shoes, clapped a hand on his shoulder and thanked him before descending into the purple hue of the nightclub.

Link and Hino held excited grins as they headed through the dancing crowd and straight to the bar. The club was unlike their usual drinking spot, a rundown dive bar that played the same loop of songs and smelled like cigar smoke and stale alcohol. At their normal hangout, they'd dress down—leather jackets and jeans. But tonight, they took advantage.

Ash followed Marius to a booth hidden in the corner of the bar. The lights above illuminated them in a deep maroon shade. Ash lay his overcoat over the booth seat and sat on it. His pinstripe light grey suit was brand new and cost far too much too dirty from the private booth. The music had no lyrics and bounced the walls enough for neon signs to shake. People dressed in expensive and revealing outfits danced seductively around the booth—their bodies moving fluidly to the music.

Link remembered ordering at the bar, he remembered Hino's sleeve riding up as he reached over the bar to place some cash into the tip jar, flashing his tattoo. And he remembered the guys next to him pulling their guns.

The four friends were ducked behind the bar counter. Ash was drinking the whiskey bottle with a free-flow pourer. Marius was reloading. Link was peeking up around the empty bar and Hino wore a wicked grin.

"Link," Ash hissed. "You're wearing a hot pink jacket. Get your ass down here before they see you."

The group was outnumbered and bullets flew back and forth across the room. Bodies of dead rivals were littered over the dance floor, bystanders stomped over them in a screaming panic—rushing to the only exit. The flashing lights from the party strobes and gunfire made it hard for the four to locate targets, but there was a reason why they were their boss's favourite.

"Marius said it looked very Gatsby," Link said. He lifted his gun up and made three clean headshots, the bodies hit the floor with a thud and Hino high-fived him.

Ash spun up as Link ducked back down and waited for the woman hiding behind a concrete pillar to pull her gun out and he fired at her hand and when she screamed in agony and clutched her wounded hand, revealing her full body, he shot again.

He passed the bottle down the line. "Have you even read the book?"

"I watched half the movie," Link confessed and took the bottle from Hino.

Marius and Hino lined their guns and shot four times around the club, their shots were echoed with dropping bodies.

"Are we really talking about fashion right now?" Marius shouted over the loud shots that dented the metal bar and the counter vibrated their backs.

"I think you look great, Link. Though with your dark hair you should try a darker shade—" Hino knelt up and fired his gun. "Like maroon. Or black, you'd look good in a black suit with a black shirt, Ya know," he shouted.

Hino was in a blood-red three-piece suit. Black embroidered roses decorated the fabric. He was always wearing loud clothing. If it wasn't an eccentric three-piece, it was high-waisted flares and a fitted sweater. The boys had been trying to dress Link since they'd met. He had been wearing a pair of dark jeans and a half-tucked white shirt—as if he going to a high school dance. They had been through some aesthetics—recently, a bold jacket was the favourite. White was too 80s cop movie orange was too 70s.

The shoot-out didn't last long after that. They split into two groups and crawled out from either side of the bar. Two guns each and bullets fired with perfect accuracy. Their polished shoes stepped over casings on the ground and they sidestepped the fallen bodies. Adrenalin fuelled their cruel smiles as they eliminated their enemies, leaving no one breathing.

They looked around at their victory. Ash wiped the blood from his suit and complained about another ruined outfit. "The fucking paperwork we're going to have to fill out," he groaned and his friends cringed.

"I'll wait for clean up," Marius announced and tutted at the mess. "Meet you at *Ethel's*?"

"Let's go, lads," Link said.

Chapter One
Strawberry Pie

Foreigner's 'Waiting for a Girl Like You' played throughout the near-empty bar for the 7th time in a row, earning quite a few complaints from the lunchtime regulars. Rory couldn't hear the repeated song over the sound of metal grinding on metal from under the dishwasher.

Like everything in this hellhole, the dishwasher had broken again. This time it wasn't rinsing and had left a pretty big puddle when the morning shift had opened the door to take out the glasses from the night before. After half an hour of lying on her back, getting sprayed in the face by dirty water and nipping her fingers on the wrench, Rory was confident that she had fixed it. She slid from under the machine using the car creeper she had stolen from the Mechanics at the end of the block. She grabbed the white tub of salt from under the sink.

She read the back of the white tub and scoffed at the label that stated: 'Once a month'. "You won't last the week," she mocked an evil laugh as she unscrewed the tog to the canister on the dishwasher.

Now the task came as easy as she breathed, unlike the first time. It was three weeks into her new job. 17 at the time, Rory spent most of her shifts behind the scenes, glass collecting and stock taking. The dishwasher started to leak out dirty brown water from the bottom and she was the only one available. Half an hour it took to find a YouTube tutorial on a model like the 80s junk and then half an hour spent pulling the metal block away from the wall so Rory could attempt to fix it.

Two hours later, she emerged from the backroom, covered head to toe in rust, grease and dirty water. Customers gave her a cheer and Nia, her colleague, clapped her back and welcomed her to the team. Now she could fix it with her eyes closed (mainly because she didn't have any goggles and one time the sink pipe burst and she saw double for two days).

Rory used the bar's old mop to clean away the grubby water, swaying to the imaginary music in her head, but the filthy mop just left a rainbow of brown swirls and her combat boots left small footprints behind her. Rory sighed and leaned the wooden mop against the sink, grabbing the towel that lay beside it. Rory laughed at herself as she got on her hands and knees, the dirt transferring onto her knees. She could picture her mother standing at the door, nagging her about standers, image and wasted potential. Her Mother would have a fit if she could see Rory right now. And her father would be on the floor with her, just to annoy her mother.

She rested her fists on her thighs and decided the floor was as clean as she was going to get it. Her wristwatch read 10:43 AM and she debated wasting the seventeen minutes left before her break by hiding in the dishwasher room. The bar wasn't busy at all; Nia could do without her for another seventeen minutes.

Nia barged through the swing door, letting it bounce back and forth wildly behind her. "If that jukebox plays that song one more time—" she threw herself on top of the bench, knocking the mop which toppled over the bucket full of dirty dishwater and Rory had to jump up out of the way to avoid it. "—it's going through the dishwasher!"

Nina Trevino had worked at *Ethel's* not much longer than Rory and was only a few months older. Nia had a thick layer of freckles that were darker in the summer and hazel brown eyes that made her appear older, so she was stationed behind the bar for almost all her shifts. She had an ease with customers that Rory admired and envied equally; Nia could talk to anyone who had ears, from the moment a customer walked through the door, she would find a common topic.

A college student on a Saturday night wearing a Gemini necklace, zodiac signs would be the conversation while she mixed a cocktail. A 40-year-old man coming in on a Wednesday night wearing his mechanics overalls, she'd ask him for advice on why her car was making funny noises whenever she changed gear.

Rory gaped at the mess on the floor and almost cried; she waved her arms around the scene, mumbling incomplete sentences while Nia vented. Rory decided to throw the wet floor sign up and leave it until later. "I'll sort the jukebox," the girl said, packing her tools up and exiting into the bar with Nia on her tail, singing her praises.

Nia slid behind the bar while Rory headed across the room to the jukebox in the corner, making mental notes to change the band posters hung on the wall that were so old, the ink had washed out and the band couldn't be identified. Giving the jukebox a once over, she assessed her tools and then evaluated the antique. Rory's balled-up fist came down hard on the top of the machine, leaving a dirty print from Rory's stained hands and the next song, 'Here I go again' by Whitesnake, jumped to a start. Both she and Nia cringed at the outdated rock music they heard on repeat every day.

Possibly the only thing in the bar older than the jukebox mumbled a comment about needing a new one with updated music (Rory and Nia had a feeling he'd still complain, no matter music they chose). Colonel, a World War II veteran, sat at the bar from opening and would likely not leave until closing. Smoke came from his cigar in clouds that reached as high as the disconnected smoke alarm on the stained brown ceiling from the years of yellow smoke. The thickest patch of smoke above Colonel's seat.

"It was a new sound system or sanitary products in the girl's toilet, pretty obvious which was more important," Nia scoffed And Rory snorted at the honesty.

A quarter of the girl's wages went to stocking female products just for the bar. Rory made a makeshift dispenser using an old mini fridge that the cafe next door was throwing away. Nia and Rory eventually convinced their boss to consider the idea of investing and he had told them that if they could find room in the tight budget, they could splurge. Rory stayed up an entire night going over budgets and finances.

"Well, back in my day, women weren't even allowed in bars." He swilled his Guinness in his glass. "Bars were for men, real men—" He cast a side-eye to the hipsters in the corner, taking selfies with the holes in the wall for their aesthetic Instagram posts. The girls didn't mind the chino-wearing customers. Sure, they looked out of place in the dive bar, but they bought a pint each for photos and then a fruity cocktail to drink. The more money that came in, the more likely the bar staff would get a Christmas bonus. "—A way to escape from the nagging of a woman," he finished.

"Oh, you mean back when you used to burn women for having their own opinion?" Rory asked sarcastically, silencing the old man and leaning over the bar to give Nia a high five.

Rory wiped the dirt off her hands with a spare cloth and Nia shot her a disproving stare at the transferred grease on her own. The toolbox was put back under the bar where it was kept for emergencies. She ignored Nia's glare as Nia bent down to wipe the bottom of the toolbox so it wouldn't leave more stains on the shelf.

"I'm going for my break; want anything?" she asked Nia.

Nia's black hair popped up from the counter, her large brown eyes wide with excitement.

"Grab me a strawberry pie, please?" Rory smiled and turned to head to the front door, Nia's loud voice stopping her from leaving, "Wait, give Charlotte these!" Nia threw an object across the bar and Rory swiftly caught it.

Chapter Two
All American

The last few days of September's wind had managed to release ginger whispers of hair from Rory's ponytail on her way to the cafe next door, which was a whole of 15 steps. A bell chimed as it opened and Rory had to blink at the change in lighting. Baby pink walls and pink and blue furniture being too bright for her eyes that had spent 4 hours in the opposite building next door. The cafe, 'All American', was packed for lunch, a mixture of hipsters born in the wrong decade, older couples reliving their decade and construction workers surviving on refilled black coffee and pie.

'All American' was third in the list of places Rory spent most of her time. *Ethel's* and the park, taking the top spaces. Every break, Rory would spend it at the cafe to escape the bar and remind herself that she was alive, healthy and young.

Hours in the darkened bar merged and felt as though the real world was miles above them. As big as they were, the windows let through a sliver of light and most customers were old and miserable enough that it appeared the building moved slower than the rest of the world. That was another reason why Rory didn't mind the clearly under-aged college students passing in and out. They reminded her that the world was still outside the brown door.

Rory's green eyes scanned the cafe and her lips pulled into a smile when they landed on her best friend. Charlotte, straight A's throughout school, long Barbie blonde hair, bright blue eyes, white teeth, sweet doll face. Charlotte managed the 'All American' Cafe on 53rd street and made it clear to people that she got the job because of her hard work, by the wall filled with framed educational certificates and not because her father was the chain owner.

Her father had just gone into business with 'A S Co.' They now owned 40% of his cafes in America, including Charlotte's, with a promise of raising profits up to 60%.

Charlotte waved Rory over to the counter where Charlotte had just finished serving a bulk construction worker who stood out in his bright orange overalls. Charlotte flashed him an award-winning smile and Rory watched as the man tripped over, flustered on the way back to a table of mocking workmates.

Just like the construction workers, Rory stuck out like a sore thumb. Black denim shorts and a black top that read 'Ethel's 1984', one side hung off her shoulders. The murky water had dried on her bruised legs and left light brown stains in splash patterns.

"I've got half an hour," Rory told her, taking a long gulp from the soda Charlotte had placed before her. The refreshing drink washed the dust from the back of her throat and she almost moaned at the cold sensation. She climbed onto the pink stool, her feet swinging back and forth, too short to reach the footrest. "Nia wants a slice of strawberry pie and here are your laces," she finished, playing with the straw in her glass.

Nia was known for her colourful laces. Her black and orange canvas high-tops were always tied with colourful laces: pink, green, blue—name a colour and she would have it. Days before, she had been sporting rainbow laces and Charlotte expressed how cool they looked.

Charlotte's blusher-stained cheeks were already pink, but a rose blush crept up her neck. "She didn't have to get me the laces," Charlotte said as she examined the bright pink laces, excited to lace them in her plimsolls and replace the plain white ones. "I only complimented her on her pride ones and mentioned how a pair of pink laces would go with my uniform perfectly."

Charlotte collected a slice of strawberry pie for Nia, placing it in a small box with bright pink napkins on top.

"Have they tried to buy shares yet?"

Charlotte offered Rory a chocolate muffin and she accepted with child-like excitement.

"Nope, haven't heard from anyone, doubt we will."

Rory watched with wide eyes as Charlotte brought the giant muffin out from the case and sat it on a tea plate in front of her.

"Don't sell yourself short, *Ethel's* has—" Charlotte paused, trying to find the right word that wouldn't insult her best friend's workplace. "—Potential."

"What would a high-class professional company like *A S Co* want with a bar that was formally a brothel and is currently a hot spot for gang activity and dried-up rockers?" Rory took a few bills from her pocket and handed them to Charlotte before digging into the double chocolate delight. "Besides, the minute they meet Davis, they'll want to back out anyway, chocolate covered her lips that made Charlotte giggle."

Davis had bought the bar in the '80s and that was the last time it had been decorated. He'd gotten it for a reasonable price, only because no one else wanted the illegal brothel. Ethel Branons, the woman who owned the structure beforehand, had sold it to the first bidder. Davis was a young fool who madly fancied the woman enough to name the bar after her. The building was located on a corner and faced the dry cleaners across the street and was one of the only businesses that 'A.S. Co.' hadn't tried to buy shares.

Rory meant it; she wouldn't be surprised if the company worked through the street getting shares in every business and just skipped past *Ethel's* as if it was a stain on the pavement. Not many looked past the crude history, peeling walls, the homeless begging outside the door and the scary-looking customers with spiked jackets and leather pants. She secretly hoped they wouldn't take an interest; of course, the bar would benefit a great deal with the help of A S Co, but currently, the entire team of three weren't even old enough to drink. Even Abel had come to his senses and walked away.

Abel.

Rory's mood dropped and she began to shift pieces of her muffin around her plate with her folk.

Her friend noticed her sad expression, which Rory had worn so often the past few months; "I'm sure he'll come back soon; this is Abel." Charlotte placed her hand over Rory's and gave it a small reassuring squeeze. She continued with a positive tone, "He's most likely off on some ridiculous adventure in Vegas!"

No one had heard from Abel in five months and Rory was getting worried. Abel was a young regular at *Ethel's*. He and Rory bonded over being family disappointments and educational dropouts. It wasn't uncommon for Abel to disappear for a while, but five months had been the longest time yet and everyone feared; he had decided to leave *Ethel's* behind for good, though no one wanted to say it out loud.

Ethel's wasn't the same without him as if a brick supporting the foundations had been removed and everyone was walking on their tip toes waiting for the building to collapse. She forced her focus back to her muffin, the subject making her lose her appetite quickly.

Chapter Three
Keep the Change

Nia was pouring out another Guinness for Colonel when they came in. Dressed as if they were extras from a cheesy zombie prom movie. Four of them, taking the same cramped booth against the window wall. So that two could see the entire room and two could monitor the exit.

Each seemed as if they could split themselves into two parts; one part drank, chatted and joked around while the second part was alert, aware of everything and everyone in the building, always watching. Nia swore they would stare at her, even when they weren't looking in her direction, the feeling of someone monitoring her every move.

The young man with the spiked dark hair would order the most out of the four friends. He flashed Nia a cheeky smile, his brown hooded eyes sparkling joyfully. "Four beers, please," he fished for his wallet in the ruined suit jacket . "And a shot of expresso—haven't slept yet!"

"Twenty-three dollars and fourteen cents, please," Nia said, placing the drinks on the bar.

If this was another customer, she would have complimented him on the colourless dragon tattoo, bony wings curved around his biceps and the tail that snaked around his muscles on his right arm, a spiked ball ended the tail in the crook of his arm, the head hidden by his sleeve. Was it a homage to his Korean culture? She would have asked if the scales, so beautifully textured, hurt more than the simple rose that was camouflaged into his forearm around designs she couldn't make out in this lighting.

He handed her too much money with a bright smile on his diamonded shaped face, "Keep the change."

Nia smiled politely, "Thank you." She was always grateful for tips; bartenders lived off them, though every time he tipped her, a pang of guilt flooded her. She couldn't help but feel awful for the lack of customer service the team gave the four guys. She knew better than to get involved, no matter how polite they were or how well they always tipped; it didn't help to settle her guilty conscience as she shoved the change into the tip jar.

Isao Hino set the drinks in front of his friends. Earning a thank you from each of them. He slid into the booth, taking a seat next to Ash. Opposite him sat Link.

Link took a mouthful of his beer. "You know," he smacked his lips together and let out a sigh of approval at the fresh drink. "The change you let her keep could buy you another drink."

Hino looked over his shoulder and watched as the girl washed down the bar, laughing lightly at something the old man sat at the bar had said. "I know what it's like working in customer services: long hours, low pay." It might make us look less frightening if we're friendly, he meant.

Hino wasn't blind or stupid—despite Ash's claims—he knew the girl served them different to the rest of the customers, they all did and he couldn't blame them. His companions most likely preferred it that way, never having to engage in small talk at the bar while they waited for their pint to be pulled like every other customer did, but it didn't hurt to be friendly to the overworked staff.

Marius, who sat in the corner opposite Ash, rumbled a deep rich laugh, "You're just pissed because you won't get served, Link."

Link was the youngest in the group, having just turned 21. Marius, however, was the oldest and looked it. It wasn't his face that showed his age, the smallest amount of worry lines on his sculpted face. It was his eyes; spring green complimented his bronze skin. Those green eyes told stories of war. They were a century old and had seen unimaginable torture. So wise yet tired. The large teeth-bearing wolf tattooed on the left side of his neck had matching green eyes.

"They don't want to converse with us long enough to ID us," Link grumbled.

"Yeah, yeah," Marius waved his hand in a patronising manner.

Hino laughed and even Ash's usually tight lips tugged into a hint of a smirk. Ash was the uptight one in the group of four, shoulders back and held himself up proud and proper—well, as proud and proper someone in this business could be. Despite his lips being full, they were always set in a tight line, as if he had something to say and wanted you to know how displeased he was at holding it in.

Ash's rare show of joy was short-lived. "Davis's car is out front; he's definitely here."

“Ash, can we at least finish our drinks before we get to business?” Hino asked with a whine. “We’ve just sat down and I’m still tired from last night. We didn’t even get to change.”

The four were still in the expensive (blood-stained) outfits from the shootout from the night before.

“Boss said he wanted it dealt with,” Ash said, his constant narrowed blue eyes scanning the bar for his target but coming up empty. The bar was deserted, other than the old man and the bartender and themselves. The college students passed them as they were coming in, noses too stuck in their screens to notice someone had held the door open for them. Ash had made sure to empathise with his distaste at their lack of manners. “Drink your beer and let’s get it over with.”

Sighing, Hino mumbled into his beer, “You’re not even in charge.”

Marius choked on his beer, liquid dripping down his chin and Link hid his smile in his hands.

Davis was, in fact, at the bar. He was hiding in his hoarded office as he always did. For being the owner, Davis wasn’t involved with—well—anything. Taxes, stock checks and orders, schedules, anything that required thinking he’d pass down to Rory to take care of. He would say it was a learning exercise for the young woman, some life education that she wouldn’t learn at any fancy college or School. When in reality, Davis couldn’t be bothered to do it himself. Sometimes the team wondered why he kept the building after the original Ethel so harshly rejected his love proposal by running off with the money she had got for the place with one of the Brothel’s regulars.

Davis hugged a near-empty bourbon bottle he had swiped from the stock room, key in the lock—a chair under the handle for extra precaution—and a cigarette between his lips, flinching at every sound that came from outside the door. He had promised that he would have it all by Tuesday and he nearly had it all. It wouldn’t be enough; he knew it. Sooner or later, they’d come for payment and if he didn’t have all of it—

Back at the booth, Ash was starting to get impatient. His drink was hardly touched and had been left to go flat. He tapped his scarred fingers on the solid wood table that shook slightly with his leg bouncing under it. Ash hadn’t liked being assigned this job two months before. All of them silently protested against bringing their work to their haven. The place was a dump and as much as he hated the bar, it was their place. *Ethel’s* was the place they came to unwind—though always on their guard—after a fight or a mission, they would knock back drink after drink. It seemed the dive was the only establishment left where groups of colleagues and rivals hadn't already claimed—*'Ethel's* was theirs, and it was why they were on this job.

"Stop squirming; you're making me nervous," Hino hissed at him; he had a firm grasp on his empty bottle to keep it from knocking over on the shaking table.

Hino wasn't one to scare easily; he'd faced cage fighters double his weight, but the little freckled bartender, she had a temper and though she was aware of whom he and his friends were—he didn't want to risk being on the other side of the hostility.

Ash shot him a look. "You should be," he lowered his voice to a near whisper, "it's already been too long, the deadline was up a while back and we still don't have a cent."

Link sighed. Boss had been swimming in a success that made him forget about the smaller debts such as Davis'. And with the latest success and buzz calming down—Boss had remembered all the unpaid debts and assigned all of his employees to retrieve them. Boss trusted them to get his money back. Trusted him.

"We should have taken him out a month back," Link breathed.

Hino leaned closer into the circle, "So what now? We take him out? Send him a warning?"

He looked at his friends and then to his leader for answers and before Link could even take a breath to give out orders, Ash spoke the dreaded words.

"We brand him. Right here, right now."

All four faces drained of colour and their horror-filled eyes darted around as if searching for another option, but deep down, they all shared the same sickening feeling urging its way up their chests.

Marius swallowed the feeling down, "Without Boss's permission?"

"He told us to handle it, so we handle it, whether that be branding or a good beating," Ash said sternly and looked to Link, for they would only do this if Link ordered them to.

With a grave, tight nod of his head, Link gave the order.

Link mumbled all the way to his silver Jeep that the group had carpooled in. "Were they about to do this? Here? At the bar?" It wasn't like anyone would stop them. Could stop them.

The second he sat down at their booth; he scanned the room on instinct. The Spanish bartender was working. In minutes, the ginger bartender would come in with some kind of treat from the c neighbouring cafe.

Stood in front of the open trunk, Link pulled up the fake bottom; put a gun in Link's hand and he'll put a bullet between their eyes within a heartbeat. At least, the poor bastard would be dead. This was on another level. A level he had stepped to before if only to save the other boys from having to.

When you're a part of a gang, doing what you're ordered to do without question was always the number one rule. No matter what the task was, who the target was. No matter how horrifying or harrowing. Do it to them, so they don't do it to the ones you love. It's how you survive in a gang.

After having her chocolate fill and a catch-up with Charlotte, Rory was refreshed and ready for the last four hours of her shift. *Ethel's*, due to several incidents involving drunk customers, bartenders and a non-supportive boss, was understaffed. Herself, Nia and Nia's twin brother, Nicky, were the only staff left. With the twins in college and only available part-time, it meant that Rory's hours had increased. And the extra pay was great for her bills but doing four split shifts in a row was not ideal.

Rory was too tired after work to do anything. Getting out of bed at 6:45 AM to get herself and the bar ready to open at 8 AM. Finishing at 4 PM to walk her dog, Caspian, around the park and then napping until 7 PM for the second half of her shift. And finally passing out at 2 AM to do the same the next day. She didn't have a life outside the bar.

Sometimes she missed School, she had made a few friends there, but once she had dropped out, she lost those friends. And with the long hours, she had no time or energy to meet new people. Most of Rory's social energy was used at work for tips. *Ethel's* was in desperate need of more employees. The small team had convinced Davis to hold a recruitment day and it was partly their own fault that it fell through; they should have held the event on a Wednesday and not a Tuesday.

So desperate for a bigger team, the four men that came in every Tuesday had slipped their minds. And it was either horrible luck or the universe sending them a sign in the form of four gang members: black and blue, blood-stained shirts, bruised knuckles. Licking the blood from their split lips with wild grins.

The possible recruits cleared out quickly and applications were withdrawn. Some had the decency to make up some excuses: College hours and studying.

Some. Most. Withdrew their applications without saying a word and Rory, Nia and Nicky spent the rest of the day throwing peanuts into glasses. Nia may have accidentally missed the glasses and hit the table of the wounded.

Almost the whole of the Southside knew who they were. The black four-point crown outline inked on their left wrist gave it away. The unspoken rule of the Southside: don't mess with the 'Gods Among Kings'. If you weren't familiar with the gang, the power oozed off them in waves of danger and authority that forced your head down. As if they were royalty who would punish you if you dared look them in the eyes.

Suppose they were royal in some sense. 'Gods Among Kings' held authority over almost all Chicago gangs and mafias. On the south side, gang-related crimes were all over the news and front pages of every newspaper. Shoot-outs, robberies, murders, raids and vandalism.

Though the 'Gods Among Kings' were never named. Store owner attacked in his own store and his bank cleared out, four-point crown scratched into the counter—the news reported the authorities had no evidence to suggest who was responsible. Rory and her work friends had discussed the clear idea that they had men on the inside of the systems. Most officers would ignore the weapons strapped to their waists or turn around when some poor fool was getting beaten down in a back alley.

So, for that reason. The bartenders kept their mouths shut and carried on serving them. They could manage on their own—hopefully.

Rory made her short trip back to the bar, stopping at the paper sign that advertised help wanted.

Her eyes narrowed with resentment at the useless sign and she tore it off the door with a long, loud groan.

"Long day?" a honeyed voice startled her. It was thick and familiar. Link stood behind her on the sidewalk, watching with amusement as she picked the Sellotape off the door while she muttered incoherently.

She spun around with her eyes slightly wide with surprise and embarrassment. Her mouth pulled into a small smile as she said, "Long year."

She stared at the young man in front of her, who was flashing her an awkward crooked smile. She focused on his dimple on his left cheek to avoid his eyes. Dark curls tucked behind his ears and thick eyebrows just as dark. The slight shadow under the inner corner of his eyes reflected how exhausted Rory was feeling. Rory didn't know his name, but she knew him. Under the torn suit jacket hid a tattoo. Her gaze drifted down to his large hands, one grasping a thick black case so tight she could see the leather stress under his fingers.

He noticed her lingering attention on the case and clearly, he wasn't in the mood to share; his smile dropped into a tight thin line which aged him a few years and he looked between her and the door.

"You're in the way." Any amusement from before was now void. Irritation and tiredness allowed her to dare an eye-roll. She turned back around and pushed open the door mumbling something along the lines of 'Fucking gangs'. She had all intentions of letting the door smack him in the face, though her parents had spent Rory's youth teaching her manners, so she held it open for him.

"Thank you."

He couldn't help the small smile as she scowled and gritted out, "You're welcome."

Nia had sensed Rory's mood the moment she walked through the door. Mainly because Rory's hand was clenched around the pink box, crushing her treat. Nia cringed at Rory's thick brows that were sloped inwards.

Rory tossed the now-broken box on the counter. "Is it 4 o'clock yet?" she said through her teeth as if she couldn't control her words if her mouth was any wider.

"Want me to stay? I can say I'm sick?" Nia suggested, peeking into the box, her mouth-watering at the squished strawberry pie inside.

"No, go get your education; I'll be fine until Nicky gets here." She took a deep breath in, trying to shove her foul mood deep down.

"Then you'll go home and sleep?" Nia questioned, but it was more of an order. She slid out from the bar, grabbing her schoolbag that sat on the counter.

Rory laughed and slid behind the bar, taking Nia's place. "Yes! I promise! Now go before you're late!"

"Oh—" Nia said, throwing her backpack over her shoulder, "—I've cleaned the back room for you."

"Stop teasing; I'll fall in love with you," Rory joked.

Nia winked and opened the door, "Too late for that, Sweetheart."

Chapter Four
Mask

A verity of paperwork was spread on the bar surface, and Rory had to peal a sheet of paper listing the week stock list from the sticky wood. Sitting at the end of the bar, Rory wondered if Davis thought she was more experienced than she actually was. Form after form, from adjusting rota schedules to fit Nia and Nicky's college education, to the biannual health and safety check (although the fire extinguishers were 10 years expired, Rory marked everything as a pass), she forged Davis's signature effortlessly.

Skipping fourth grade, Rory graduated high school at 16. Mr Scott had kept a college fund for his daughter and along with the many scholarships Rory was granted due to her young age, dead parent and high intelligence, she had managed to pay tuition for three years of college and the first year of Law School—and then she dropped out.

On one of the rare occasions, the bald man had joined them down at the bar, he had overheard Rory telling a customer that he didn't stand a chance in court because he wasn't wearing the provided personal protective equipment he was required to wear. She said that if it was written in his contract, he couldn't claim the incident.

Davis was quick to take Rory on as his unofficial manager. She did everything for the same shitty wage.

Rory's foot tapped against the chair leg to the beat of the song playing on the jukebox as she chewed on the pen and read through some insurance documents.

A train of footsteps sounded and without averting her eyes from the papers, she asked, "Another round of drinks?"

A throat cleared, "Actually, we require something else."

This made Rory look up from her paperwork. Four gang members were standing above her.

"What can I help you with then?" she hesitated.

"We need to speak to your boss," Ash stated in a bored tone.

Rory looked up at him; his handsome face was hard. His nose and chin were sharp and angled up enough that he always appeared conceited: beautiful sharp features stuck in vain expressions.

An awkward cough broke her thoughts and she realised she was staring. '*This can't be good.*' She thought to herself. Rory knew that Davis wasn't a good man; it wasn't unknown for the man to make poor life choices.

Rory wouldn't put it past him to get involved with a gang, a bar owner on the Southside—it was inevitable, most gangs used bars as indecorous as *Ethel's* to meet up and do their business. Many would take insurance money from the gangs, but Rory wouldn't let Davis accept the cash the 'Gods Among Kings' had offered. Some owners went as far as to deal with the gangs. Loaned money with a promise to double the profits. Rory had also ensured Davis he wasn't to do that either.

"Can I ask why?" Getting uncomfortable with the four intimidating men towering over her, she slid out of her seat but it made no difference.

In the same bored tone, Ash said, "No. You can't."

Ash had forgotten the game plan. After the Davis job was handled, they still wanted to come back to the bar, so they agreed to be friendly, approachable. The bartenders already hated them.

"OK," Rory said slowly. Her arms crossed over her chest and back straightened in fake confidence. "Who should I say is asking?"

Hino smirked at her. "You've served us how many times? And you don't know our names?"

"Do you know mine?"

"You won this round."

"Davis isn't here." She turned her attention back to all four (her actively avoiding eye contact was a norm, she prayed they couldn't sense the lie). "Can I take a message?"

"His car is outside." Ash was sounding more frustrated as their conversation went on.

Rory let out a defeated sigh. "Well, he swiped a bottle of Bourbon this morning, so I can't promise he'll be functioning."

She turned to walk through the door that led to his office, but a large hand stopped her movements. She glanced down at the gripped hand on her elbow and up at the owner. Working at *Ethel's*, unwanted contact with customers was a situation she was familiar with and instinct told her to grab the glass of water on the bar top and throw it.

Ash's eyes dared her to act on whatever was going through her mind; "Don't warn him."

She glanced at his hand and then back up to his face.

"*Ethel's* is a gun-free zone," she told him, matching his serious tone.

His eyes slit, and the hand that wasn't bruising her skin twitched at his waist. Link was familiar with the action that followed the twitch, Ash's name left his lips in a single sharp note.

Ash removed his hand as quickly as he had grabbed her. "Just tell him some friends are here to see him."

Rory knocked twice on the brown door.

There was a slurred mumble through the door. "I'm not in."

"Yeah, tried that one, they saw your car," Rory tried the handle, but it wouldn't budge.

"Charlie, they've got guns."

Despite telling the visitors that they would have to wait downstairs in the bar, the four of them were strutting down the poorly lit corridor. Davis's office was located on the level above the bar. The layout of the four-level building was identical to the original Brothel layout—the bar (which acted as a cover for the Brothel back in the day), Dishwasher room and cellar were on the ground floor and 30+ bedrooms were left deserted on the other floors.

"Yeah, uh, you can't be up here," Rory stated but nonpaid her attention as they carried on towards her.

The men stopped in front of her and she took a step blocking them from the door.

"We've got it from here," Marius told her and the lock on the door clicked.

The girl turned the doorknob and opened the door slowly as if a tripwire would set off if the door opened too quickly. A strong smell of smoke hit her senses and nearly knocked her dizzy. Davis had just sat back down as she took a step into the room. The desk he was hunched over was littered with empty bottles of whiskey and cigarette dumps spilled out of the full ashtray. His yellow smoked stained fingers were shaking around a glass.

"Leave us," Ash ordered without looking at Rory. The four stepped into the doorway and all eyes narrowed on Davis, an insensitivity thicker than the smoke.

Davis's small brown eyes blinked at Rory, begging her not to leave him alone with them. As if she held any power over their actions.

"I think I'll stay," she declared, but the noticeable tremor in her voice betrayed her authority.

"Trust me," Hino said, his usual smirk and playful eyes were gone, replaced with a stone-cold mask or maybe the playfulness was the mask. "You don't want to see this and if you knew what was good for you, you wouldn't get involved."

She looked at the four men, all wearing the same face as Hino and were now not hiding their weapons. All their eyes were on Davis, whose eyes were on her. Rory dropped her own to the black case in Link's hand. Link stood still, his grip twisted on the handle and jaw set.

With an apologetic frown, Rory left Davis to the 'Gods Among Kings'.

Chapter Five
It's How You Survive in a Gang

Link set the case down heavily in the middle of the desk, knocking empty bottles to the side. Davis's eyes locked onto it. Tales of the black case and its contents were continuous whispers amongst Davis's weekly poker games with fellow bar owners on the Southside. Stories of gang members approaching customers, escorting them out—case in hand—only for the customers turning up days later with the scars and ghostly eyes.

"I've got three grand," he rushed out, stammering over his words. "I—I need more time to get the rest."

Ash stalked around the desk, stopping behind a sweating Davis. "Oh, Charlie, you owe him a lot more than three grand and he's given you plenty of time to gather the full amount." His usual lined lips were replaced with a wicked and cruel smile.

Davis helplessly scanned the room for a way out. Link was leaning his large hands on the desk, veins prominent and long fingers drumming. Marius was guarding the door with his giant arms folded. While Hino was flicking through some papers on top of the filing cabinet out of curiosity—or boredom.

"Where am I supposed to get that kind of money from?"

Hino snorted, "Should have thought about that before you got yourself into this mess."

It had been months and this moment was inevitable. Stupid, idiotic to think he could get away with betraying the 'Gods Among Kings' and come out untouched. When Davis heard about a great investment opportunity that would lead to real cash, he couldn't help himself. But like everything else in his life—it fell through. Leaving him destitute and in debt.

Lucky to have this long, Davis knew he couldn't conjure up the money he owed the gang. So, in desperation, Davis had sought out a way to buy himself time. Amongst his poker friends, customers, even the beat cops that patrolled.

"You won't kill me," Davis scoffed; calm took over his features but under it brewed panic and fear that he had been led astray by the beat cops.

Ash clicked his tongue and leaned over the back of the chair to say in his ear. "Careful, Davis, you're starting to sound confident."

"Maybe I should be."

Marius spoke from his position at the door, unfazed by Davis's sudden change of mood, his wide forearms readjusted in their crossed position, the muscles twitching. "And why is that?"

"Because I know something that could stir trouble—even for the likes of you."

Link spoke through his teeth, "And what information is that?"

Davis offered a dirty smirk, "Sawyer ran deliveries for me."

The four men concealed their glances at each other with quick blinks, "And I happen to have proof that he was out on a delivery that night."

He reached across the table to pick up his glass of whisky, hands only slightly trembling, "And while I'm no lawyer, I do have a friend who informed me that my little piece of paper can change the whole trial."

He took a sip of his whiskey to disguise the lip tremor that accompanied every lie; the paper was real; he did indeed consult his lawyer friend, but she never saw the paper; he only asked if proof someone was working could be an alibi.

With a firm tug, Ash pulled Davis's chair back onto two legs. Davis's glass dropped to the floor; the liquid didn't do visible damage to the already ruined carpet.

"What makes you think we have anything to do with the Sawyer kid?" Ash hissed.

"I s—saw—" he stuttered and took a gulp. "—what you did." His eyes pointed to Link.

"And this piece of evidence?" Hino's attention now entirely on the situation and not on the files. His curious child-like demeanour switched to demanding, harsh—his eyes wide in desperate insanity.

"I don't have it. I sent it away for safekeeping. I die and it gets sent to the kid's mother." If Hino had spotted Davis's upper lip twitching, he didn't comment—or calm his own paranoid twitching.

Link snapped open the case and Davis flinched, "Just because we can't kill you yet, doesn't mean we're letting you off." A metal rod was pulled out of the case, a blunt symbol at one end. A mini blow torch followed. "You still owe Boss money."

The old man's face lost all colour. His eyes frantically searched the room for help once more. The bar was on the level below. And even if someone could hear him scream, they wouldn't make it up the flight of stairs in time to prevent the horrors to come. Rory was no match for the four men, and Davis didn't know if anyone else was working right now.

The low buzz from the blow torch broke his hopeless thoughts.

"I can get the rest of the money!" he pleaded. "I swear I can get it with more time. If I just had more time!"

When he started to struggle in his seat, Ash's grip got tighter. Marius stepped away from the door and took the leather strap from the case, careful not to get in Link's way. The blow torch still heating up the iron rod.

"Bite," he ordered and shoved the leather strap in Davis's mouth and his teeth clenched down hard.

Link held the flame under the symbol while Marius and Ash struggled to hold the weeping man. Begging through the gag in his mouth for any mercy they could spare.

We warned him; it's for his own good. Link rationalised.

When the metal had held a blazing red for a minute, Link removed the flame from under the iron.

It's persuasion. Brand him. He will get the money and it's over with.

Link took slow steps around the desk and Ash and Marius, restraining Davis, turned his chair, so Link had access to his body.

It's how you survive in a gang.

Davis's feet were thrashing around, trying to kick Link away, but Marius's hands pinned his knees to the chair. Davis's shoulders tried to shake Ash's grip off with his legs now immobile, but Ash dug his hands into his skin and Davis's fighting was halted.

It's how you survive in a gang.

Ash tore back Davis's sweat-covered shirt. Link grasped his shoulder, hand over Ash's to steady himself and brought the iron rod down flat against his skin.

Blood-curdling screams tore from Davis, screams that even the leather gag couldn't muffle. His body thrashed and Davis threw his back against the wooden chair back and Ash held him against it. With every jerk of his upper body, the iron scalded even more. A constant relentless searing pain but he couldn't make his body lie still. Link pushed more weight behind the iron, his palm burning under the metal.

It's how you survive in a gang.

Link blocked out the sound of the flesh burning and sizzling: hair melting and skin blistering.

It's how you survive in a gang.

Link blocked out the smell of the burning flesh that permeated the room, taking over the previous stench of cigar smoke and stale alcohol.

It's how you survive in a gang.

When his friends poured alcohol over the fresh wound, Davis let out a soundless scream. Link emotionless packed up the torture device, taking extra care to place the pieces in their designated places and exited the office. The journey down to the bar seemed further than on the way up; the case felt heavier.

The young bartender's hands paused from cleaning down their booth when he emerged from the back room. Asute eyes seemed to shout, *I know what you did,* as they followed him to the door. And when he locked the case in the boot of his Jeep.

It's how you survive in a gang.

Chapter Six
Poor and Queer

Davis wouldn't let her call the police. He had told her unless she wanted a matching brand, she'd keep her mouth shut about the whole situation.

No matter how many times Rory showered or how much deodorant she applied, she couldn't rid the smell from her nose. Rory had to swallow down vomit several times while she disinfected Davis's wound. The office smelt of rotting meat, the body hair that had fried added a rotting egg stench and when she breathed through her mouth, she swore she could taste it. Three days on, she could still see the horrible four-point crown stamped into the old man's neck every time she closed her eyes, she supposed that was the purpose of the mark. Not only the motivation to repay the debt. It was the reminder, every time you looked in the mirror, every time someone saw your mark, every time the air got bitter. 'Gods Among Kings' would be repaid. And you wouldn't cross them again.

The early October wind was bitter cold, Rory's small nose was red and her green eyes watered as the wind hit her face. Rory would usually take her Dog, Caspian, to a larger park closer to her apartment. That park was her favourite, it was huge and each section was like a different world. There were the tree arches that gave her the urge to run in the Autumn leaves barefoot in long flowing skirts. The lake was the perfect spot to catch some sun and have a picnic on a rare sunny day.

Rory and Abel had spent many nights sitting on the playground swings, watching the sunset on the flowering trees. But on Tuesday, after the incident at *Ethel's*, when she couldn't have a nap after her shift without seeing the black case and crown, she took Caspian for a walk. Only to run into the lanky gang member—case not in sight, although that didn't stop Rory from turning around and leaving the park.

The new location had taken her an hour to find the exit. But she couldn't deny that it wasn't prettier. The Fall struck trees were full of orange leaves that matched her hair, those that had fallen already left a pumpkin colour blanket on the ground that made a satisfying crunch under her brown combat boots.

Rory pulled her jacket tight around her, sticking her hands in the warmth of the fake fur pockets. "I'm going to be honest, Casp," she spoke with defeat. "I have no clue how to get out of here."

"Me neither."

For a second, Rory had thought Caspian had answered her, though when Rory had dreamed of her best friend finding his voice, the thick Irish accent wasn't part of the fantasy. Looking down at the dog with her eyebrows high, a giggle reached her ears.

"Sorry—didn't mean to freak you!"

The owner of the accent stuck her arm out enthusiastically, her dark skin dotted with goosebumps—the tiny denim jacket not doing much to protect her from the windy city. "Chrissy."

"Rory."

Without realising, the two girls had begun to walk slowly, following the pathway a crowd of people were coming from—Rory was sure that was a sign of a way out.

"I'm new to the park," she told her new friend.

Chrissy tossed her head to either side, taking in the surroundings and looking for any sign to give their location. "Me too."

"New to the park or city?"

"Both," Chrissy laughed. "My grandparents were in need of a carer, I was sent across to look after them."

"I've been job hunting all morning and got lost."

"You're looking for a job? What kind?" Rory rushed out, stopping her steps; her hand reached to Chrissy's arm to stop her too.

"Anything. I dropped out of college and, now, I've gotta get a job."

"Any experience working at a bar?"

"Nope," she said perkily.

Rory gave the girl a smile that usually meant trouble, "A man is going to ask you that question again within the next hour," Rory's eyes landed on the large gates that signified their freedom and then turned back to Chrissy. "And you're going to say yes."

"Do you have any experience?" asked Davis.

They were standing in his office. Rory faintly smelt the horrors that happened three days ago, but Chrissy didn't appear to notice it. Maybe it was just in Rory's mind.

Chrissy looked behind her at Rory, who gave her a subtle thumbs up. "Yes, plenty. I'm Irish, alcohol is in our blood," she joked, trying to win him over.

Rory put her head in her hand and shook it. The girls had a chat on the way to the bar; no humour, smile and agree with him. Those were the three rules Rory had chanted. Davis looked up at her, not impressed at the joke. Rory took a step away from the wall.

"Come on, Davis, she has the experience and she can talk to customers." Rory said trying to dress up her new friend, "Besides, without Will, we've lost the eye candy!"

Davis sighed and looked Chrissy up and down; she had unbuttoned her jacket with the temperature change from the cold street to the stuffy office.

The girls stared at him, eyes wide, practically begging.

"Fine."

They squealed.

"You start tomorrow," he said, reaching for the whiskey glass on the desk, "you can leave now." He waved his hand, shooing them away.

Rory told Chrissy to go back down to the bar and she'd follow in a minute. Once Chrissy was out of earshot, Rory turned back into the room and closed the door. Davis didn't look up from his papers.

He was sporting a turtleneck today and Rory didn't miss the way he would pull on the fabric every few minutes. The jumper made it impossible to see the wound. "Is the fabric irritating the wound?" she asked quietly.

"You're irritating me,"

Rory huffed, "Did you at least get it checked out?"

Davis looked up at her, "And let the whole hospital know I'm in dept with a gang—that gang?"

"Well, aren't you?"

"I don't believe that's any of your business, Aurora," he hissed.

The use of her name had taken her back, in the same tone her mother would use to scald her. "Right. Remember that next time you need me to adjust the stock receipts," she added with as much venom as she could, "Al Capone," and slammed the door.

The fool must have been idiotic if he thought Rory didn't know what he had her do. She knew *Ethel's* didn't have the money to afford those types of alcohol and not in that quantity. There had to be at least seven grand worth of product: Vodka from Russia. Gin from Holland. Wine from Italy. And beer from every continent in the world.

Davis pulled Rory into his office two month ago and told her to change the receipts. Put the vodkas in a different order than the Gins. Back the dates up to weeks prior. After the other day, she knew it had something to do with the gang.

She cursed Davis when she got home that day. Condemned him for being stupid enough to borrow money, knowing he couldn't pay it back. Cursed him for bringing the bar into it. It didn't take a year of Law School to know the alcohol wasn't legal; they arrived during the closing shift, late at night in unmarked crates and not the usual delivery guy. Rory had cursed him for bringing her into it and if the gang found out?

She didn't want to think about that.

Wouldn't think about that.

Happy barks greeted Rory when she stepped onto the bar floor. "Hey, buddy," she said to Caspian as she bent down to greet him.

Rory hopped onto the seat next to Chrissy and dropped her head onto the cool wooden counter, but the sticky surface made her lift her head back up, feet dangling over the edge of the stool. "So, you've met Nicolas and Angel."

"It's Nicky," he corrected with a scowl, bending down to put some glasses away.

Rory mumbled an empty apology.

Angel was sipping on a colourful cocktail, "You can call me whatever you like, sweetie." She winked at Rory.

Angel had to be in her late 50s, but if you dare ask, she would claim she was in her early 40s living a tough life. She wore poorly made extensions and whatever hair she had left was dyed a fiery red, which clashed with the purple zebra print she was wearing today.

Rory flicked her short locks over her shoulder, "I've told you, Angel, it's not that kind of place anymore."

A rough voice spoke behind her, "Oh, that's a shame; I was hoping for a show."

Rory swung around in her chair and Nicky jumped up from his position behind the bar, his brown eyes widening. Rory leapt up and threw her arms around the man's neck, his arms wrapped around her waist, picking her up from the ground and twirling her around in his arms. When he placed her feet back on the ground, she had to steady herself. Nicky pushed past her and engulfed his friend.

"Who the hell decided to let you out looking like that, bro?" Nicky bellowed, taking a step back to assess him.

The stubble made Will look years older than he was. His dark roots had grown a length and the dyed dirty blonde locks reached his chin. Will's copper brown eyes seemed to have aged as well, though they still had that playful spark.

"I agree," Rory sucked in an exaggerated breath, "prison was not good for you, dude."

"I missed you guys too." He put a hand on his heart, mocking them.

Chrissy cut in, "Prison?" She inquired with slight amusement and shock.

Will turned to where she still sat at the bar, "And who is this beautiful lady?"

"Lady?" Chrissy exclaimed, "how old do you think I am?"

He flashed her a smile that usually had every girl swooning over him. "Oh, your beauty is timeless," he shamelessly flirted.

Chrissy snorted, "Pity your pick-up lines aren't."

"Oh, I like her." He smirked, eyes full of challenge, "The name's Will."

Chrissy took his hand and he brought it to his lips and placed a peck on the back of her hand, "Chrissy, the new bartender."

Rory, Nicky and Angel sat back and watched the two interact. This could either be amazing or terrifying. Before Will was hauled off to jail, he worked at the bar. His chiselled jaw and dark-tanned skin brought in many customers who would spend a ridiculous amount of money on water-downed drinks. Nothing sold alcohol more than his wolfish grin that had everyone weak at the knees.

Chrissy asked Will what he was in prison for as he shook his leather jacket off, his biceps had grown significantly since he was locked up. His white shirt straining around them, "Possession and GTA."

Chrissy's mouth dropped, "Of drugs?"

Nicky laughed loudly. "Will stole his father's car," his eyes crinkled, whereas his speaking voice was deep and smooth, his laugh was high and off pitched and Rory couldn't help comparing it to Nia's, his twin. "And his dad's medical bag was in the trunk."

Will shot Nicky an offended look but turned to Chrissy, "Wasn't happy I dropped out of school, took my car, that I paid for!" Will stressed and then he shrugged. "So, I stole his."

Chrissy took a sip from her drink and asked, "So is this the place for criminals and dropouts?"

"Uh-huh," Rory confirmed.

All it took was a one lined email and Rory's journey as a lawyer was over. Rory upgraded to full-time at *Ethel's* after she had dropped out of school and with the extra income, she moved from the college dorms to a one-bed apartment in a decent building.

When her mother cursed her for throwing her life away. Rory had quoted what her father had always told her, "Follow your gut. If the feeling leads to mistakes, own them, learn from them. If the feeling leads to success, own them, cherish them. There is no due date for the end of your journey."

"Safe haven for the poor and queer!" Nicky announced.

"All of you?"

"Well, sweetheart. Life would be boring if we weren't," Will answered and accepted the high five from Rory, "is Boss in?"

Rory rolled her eyes, "In a bad mood? Always." She dropped back down on the chair. "In his office."

Chapter Seven
Casanova

"Any witnesses?"

"No, Sir," Link stated. His voice was steady and robust as he had been trained.

He stood in the bright office, arms crossed behind his back, head high and shoulders back while he gave a report on the branding of Davis. Link had walked into the office and claimed that it was his idea to brand Davis without direct orders from the boss himself.

Link watched Erik Lenzo with careful eyes. The man sat on the desk chair like a king on a throne. Or rather, a God on a throne. Because that's what they were. Gods. Their gang had far more power and was feared far more than any other. Gangs were the kings of law, the kings of the city. They were the gang above gangs. They were the 'Gods Among Kings'.

Erik Lenzo settled back in the chair, his scarred hands crossed on his lap. "You are positive?" his voice was calm, bored almost but rich, nevertheless. "No customers?"

"Positive," Link confirmed, "only an old war vet who hasn't been sober since before he joined the war."

Lenzo hummed and Link forced his fingers to stop fidgeting behind his back. "No employees?"

"She's not a problem," Link rushed. It must have been too quickly as Lenzo's eyebrows raised, "She was made aware of the consequences."

Link couldn't get rid of the green eyes judging him as he had walked out of the bar that day. He could see her thoughts behind them, coming up with endless possibilities of what the black case contained. He wondered how long it took her to go and check on her useless boss once his friends had left.

Link had spotted her before she saw him; she was walking her dog through the park entrance; she was trying to get her ginger hair untangled from her scarf while her dog ran circles around her. When she looked up and saw him, she had practically run away.

Lenzo stood up, strutting up to the wall of windows that looked over the city. "You take full responsibility?"

Link swallowed. "Yes, my team were following my orders."

Lenzo let out a low chuckle and shook his head, "It's nice of you to take the blame." Link made to deny, but his boss just waved him off. "Branding? That's an Ash idea," he put his hands in the pockets of his tailored Italian suit. "No doubt he made you do it."

Link looked at himself. He looked out of place in the high-profile building in his worn light brown jacket and ripped jeans. To any outsider, he looked like a stray taking from the street as some sort of charity case—technically, he was.

Seven years ago, when Link was just fifteen, he had run away from a foster home. He stumbled into a deal at the docks seeking shelter for the night. Link fought off four of Lenzo's men but ultimately ended up getting his ass beat.

Lenzo was present and witnessed the young boy take on men twice his size with only his backpack as his defence. Apparently, he saw potential and took Link in and trained him—raised him. Link owed his life to Lenzo.

The older man walked up to his desk and leaned back on it with his large hands. Lenzo's sleeked-back hair had always been white as snow for as long as Link had known him; it was the same colour as his trimmed beard. The feature of his lived-in handsome face though was his crystal eyes, intimidating and cold.

"I'm not going to punish Ash," he spoke. "It was a smart move."

Link had forced his face to not show the relief that washed over him. Lenzo clicked his tongue and walked around back to his seat. "Visit the shithole tonight; give him three weeks for the full amount. The bar is more trouble than it's worth and I've grown bored," he ordered, shuffling through some papers on his desk.

"Yes, Sir."

When Link didn't move, Lenzo waved a hand to the door, "You're dismissed."

Link bowed his head and turned to exist. Lenzo spoke again, "Oh and, Lincoln," he said, eyes still on his papers, "if the bartenders get in your way, put them down."

"Yes, Sir."

The boys decided not to tell Lenzo about Davis's knowledge of Sawyer. There was a very high possibility that Davis was lying.

Was it the wrong decision?

Yes.

Would it bite them in the ass down the road?

Yes.

Did it change their minds?

No.

"That's an order, Lincoln," Lenzo hissed at him, "get it done tonight or it'll be you."

He had everything ready: the gun, the fingerprints. Take out the cameras. Wave the gun around and scare the cashier. Turn their backs long enough for him to phone the police. Get the hell outta there.

It was simple and straightforward—nothing they hadn't done a dozen times. The job was easy.

It was supposed to be easy.

Link shot up in his bed, sweat lined his forehead. He placed a hand on his racing chest and it took him a few minutes to catch his breath enough that he didn't risk hyperventilating. He swung his long legs over the side of his bed; his feet hit the cold floorboards sending a chill up his burning body. He stumbled his way to the window, his feet heavy and each step echoing in his head. He threw open the window and climbed onto the balcony. The bitter winds cooling down his bare chest.

Pull yourself together; you've seen people die before.

You've killed before.

Link leaned against the cool bars. He didn't know how many times he'd suffered from the nightmare. Sometimes it was the cashier's lifeless body on the store ground. Sometimes it was just the orders from Lenzo. Five months on and they would haunt Link at least twice a week. More if it had been a testing week, like the one he was having. When Link and his men received the order from Lenzo, they knew the job was off. They were ordered to ask no questions. Plant the evidence and let the officers in their back pocket handle the rest. Why were they framing him? Link didn't know why they hadn't just branded him or killed him.

His ringtone broke his thoughts. Link didn't need to read the caller id to know who was on the other end—only Marius rang him this late.

"Hello," Link answered with a breathless tone.

"What are you doing up?" Marius asked him due to the speed he had picked up the phone.

"You rang me." His breathing was still shaking and he struggled to level his tone.

"Oh," Marius said loudly. "Are you with a chick?"

"What? No."

"Whatever you say, Casanova."

Not wanting to have to explain the nightmares, Link let it go, "Why are you ringing me in the middle of the night?"

"You know that cafe next to *Ethel's*?"

"All American? Yes, they do nice pie."

"Well, the manager, she's friends with the bartenders."

"And your point?"

"You remember Isaac?"

Link racked his brain, "Oh, the new recruit—the goth, uh lip piercing and cursing the world."

"That's him," Marius said. " I got to talking to him in the elevator this afternoon. He was in All American a few weeks back and he said he overheard the owner say something about getting legal advice from *Ethel's*."

Link's eyes widened. "You think it's one of the bartenders?" he rushed out. "Aren't they all like—dropouts or something?"

"No names were mentioned, could be a customer? A regular is my bet." Marius lowered his voice.

While doing a stakeout a few month back on Davis, they learned he didn't really have much of a life. He went from the bar to his crappy one-bedroom apartment every day. If Davis had a legal friend, they had to be at the bar. And they had to find them.

"We've got orders to go tomorrow."
"Already got Hino doing research."
Link didn't get back to sleep that night; he didn't dare try.

Chapter Eight
Not a Long Time

Three turned to five.

Will had asked Davis if he could get his old job back as he needed work for parole. Davis hired him on the spot. Will had enjoyed teaching Chrissy the basics of the bar while Rory, Angel and Nicky watched them, testing the practice drinks.

Surprisingly, she picked it up pretty quickly. Her cocktails were on point, she nailed the spirits and after a few tries, she could pour the perfect pint. They also learned she had a pretty good aim. Nicky had commented about getting a step ladder for her so she could see over the bar. He never mentioned her small height again after she threw the cocktail shaker at him.

Chrissy and Rory were both in for the evening shift and had decided to grab something to eat beforehand. Chrissy chose a (rather big) cheese scone and then had another two. Currently, she was sitting with her round head in her hands, eyeing up the chocolate muffins in the display case.

Rory looked at Chrissy with her eyebrows drawn together, "How do you consume so much food in so little time?" she said, sounding impressed.

Chrissy smiled wide and said, "It's a talent."

"Still no sign of *A S Co*?" Charlotte asked; she took a seat on the customer side of the counter. An older couple had paid their bill and left, leaving just the three girls.

"Nope," Rory simply said, popping the *P*.

Chrissy took her attention off the treats. "*A S Co*? Sounds like a porn site."

"An acquisition company. They're buying the businesses in the neighbourhood," Charlotte explained.

While the two spoke about the company, Rory wasn't paying attention. After the incident, the four boys hadn't shown up at the bar—Rory prayed that they wouldn't show up tonight—though it was Saturday, she knew she was holding a wasted breath. Rory couldn't stop thinking of what she had done with recipes. She shouldn't have done it; she knew it was wrong. If 'Gods Among Kings' had found out, would they send the one with the black case after her? Would they just shoot her? What would happen to Caspian? What would happen to *Ethel's*? The bar wouldn't make it if she went down.

Charlotte cut her thoughts by clicking her fingers in her face, "I thought more employees meant you could sleep now," she said, half-joking, worry creeping through.

Rory played with the straw in her drink. "Yeah, no, I'm fine. Caspian had me up most of the night barking," she lied with a shake of her head.

"Sure," Charlotte said slowly, not believing her; being best friends for two years meant Charlotte could tell when Rory was lying; Rory would toy with her ears. Just like she was doing now.

Without thinking, Rory found herself asking Charlotte, "If anything were to happen to me? Would you take care of Caspian?"

Caught off guard, Charlotte spluttered.

"Well, he's already had a taste of the domestic life; he wouldn't make it out on the streets—and he's too small for a shelter, they'll bully him."

"Sure," Charlotte said even more slowly than before, putting Rory's weird question down to stress and lack of sleep.

Chrissy cursed, "We're late."

Chrissy came out of the changing room. It was previously used as a bedroom back when the building was a brothel, but Rory and Will had converted it into a changing room. The room was cut in half by a layer of lockers. Chrissy had been given free rein with her uniform (each employee had made the uniform their own, whatever they were most comfortable in). Black three-quarter sleeved shirt with 'Ethel's 1984' printed on her chest and jeans.

Rory whistled. "Wow, get a look at you, Irish!" she said playfully.

Chrissy spun on the spot. "Do I look like part of the team now?" she laughed; her hands smoothed her uniform down on her oval body.

"Welcome to the family," Rory said, swinging her arm around Chrissy as they headed down the stairs to the bar.

Saturdays were usually their busiest night. College girls and frat guys would come in for pre-drinks around 5:30 PM, regulars like Colonel and Angel were already there, but Angel would vanish for an hour or two through the night and come back with her clothes on backwards and a dirty smile. For an hour, between 8 and 10 PM, bar crawlers would flood the place and what was left of their regular biker customers would fan in and out all night.

When the girls walked into the bar, Angel and Colonel were already at the counter. Nicky and Nia were fighting about something undoubtedly pointless and Will was filling up the straw pot.

When his eyes met Chrissy, he let out a low whistle like Rory had, "Damn."

Davis walked through the front door. He went straight for the back door to the stairs and said to the team over his shoulder, "I'm not in."

Chrissy shot Rory a questioning look, but Rory just waved her off.

Before the night kicked off, the original team wanted to educate Chrissy on the people to expect tonight.

"JC," Nicky said, "white hair. Doesn't speak." The old man looked like Santa Clause if he had lost his job and turned to drinking. JC tipped his glass to Chrissy with a relaxed old smile.

Chrissy hummed, "What does JC stand for?"

"Jack and Coke, hold the coke." Will was leaning his elbows on the bar top; Chrissy and Rory were on the bar seats. "Unknown name, unknown age."

Nia came through from the stock room with various bottles, "Colonel. Also unsure on his name." She tilted her head in his direction, "Guinness. Sexist. Sometimes racist—let me know if he says anything."

Colonel nodded at her and Chrissy gave him a nervous smile.

"Now, the college groups," Will stated. "They're all underage, all annoying and bikers are always coming up to complain about them, but they all have trust funds, so don't ask for ID."

Chrissy gave him a weary look, "Isn't that illegal?"

"How old are you?"

"Twenty."

"Sweetheart, half the team are breaking the law being here," he told her. "Now for the gang," his voice dropped an octave. "Don't ask for their ID either."

Chrissy's eyes widened. "Gang?"

Will shot his head to Rory. "You didn't tell her?" he snapped.

"Why does it have to be me? I don't know them any better than you do," she said harshly. Will gave her a pointed look. "Fine," she wined. "*Ethel's* is like a hot spot for gangs, like GAK."

Chrissy interrupted, "GAK?"

"*Gods Among Kings*," Rory clarified. "There's four that come in and sit on that table—" she pointed to the table. "—If they ask for a beer," Rory leaned over to the taps, "it's this one. Don't ask for ID and don't ask them any questions. Though they do tip pretty generously, they're not to be messed with. Serve them and move on."

Chrissy nodded. "JC is jack and coke, Colonel is Guinness, don't ID college students and that beer for GAK?" she listed burning it into her memory.

"Don't let them hear you call them that," Nia shot over her shoulder with a laugh.

"We're about to get our first rush," Nicky pointed at the door.

The team could see five college girls through the blurry glass, all in a different neon colour skin-tight dresses, taking photos.

"Guess word got around that Will's back," he joked.

The group of bikers in the corner of the bar audibly groaned.

Will placed five shot glasses on the counter and filled them with tequila, handing a shot to each bartender. "Alright, guys. Here we go."

Everyone took their shot, dropping them back on the counter in unison.

Sliding off her seat, Chrissy grabbed a rag and spray bottle to wipe the tables down. When she passed the giggling girls, she gave them a sickly-sweet smile which they returned.

The jukebox died as soon as the girls walked in—the song now a high-pitched whine and everyone in the bar to cover their ears. Nia shouted Rory's name and Rory echoed Nicky's name.

He pulled out a Bluetooth speaker from behind the bar, "Don't worry, ladies," he announced as he raised it into the air, strutting across the bar's tiny dance floor, his black trainers sticking to the old wood (tonight they were fastened with neon green laces).

"Modern technology is here to save the day."

Nicky set the speaker on the shelf above the jukebox (giving the machine a quick punch to shut it up) and connected his phone to the speaker. Within seconds, Top 1000 Rock Songs, Nicky's homemade playlist, filled the bar.

On the way back, Nicky was pulled into a dance. Nia nudged Rory, "Should we help him?"

Rory snorted, "Yeah, because he looks uncomfortable."

Nicky looked the opposite, in fact. His face held no shame as he danced between a girl in a neon dress and a guy in orange chinos.

Nia rolled her eyes, "If our Madre could see him right now, she'd ship him back to Spain."

Rory laughed, "And then lecture the girl on how short her dress was."

You couldn't blame the students. Nicky was blessed with big cinnamon eyes, face and shoulders decorated with thick freckles and sun-kissed skin that had everyone swooning. His personality helped too. He was open, fun, soft. Here for a good time and not a long time was his catchphrase.

Colonel glanced at the dancing trio, "Back in my day if girls dressed like that—"

"I don't care how old you are—finish that sentence and I'll throw you out myself," Nia warned.

Chapter Nine
That'll Kill You

Marius lit a cigarette and stuck his free hand in his jeans pocket—hiding it from the wind as he and Ash waited outside the warehouse for Hino and Link, who were running late. Ash glared at Marius as the smoke from his cigarette blew in Ash's face.

"That'll kill you," he grumbled.

"So, will Lenzo if we don't return with any money," Marius said and put the cigarette back between his lips.

Since joining the gang and working together—the four had brought in more money, more deals and better results than any other team in 'Gods Among Kings'. Making them hated by their colleagues and loved by their boss. But after that night—five months ago—the four had been at an all-time low. Either set less important jobs or they were given jobs with an impossible positive outcome. Their job today was simple and they had done it hundreds of times. Their first chance in a long time to prove to Lenzo and their-selves, that they were useful. "Where the hell are they?"

As Marius had asked—Link's silver Jeep turned the corner and came into view. Link flawlessly parked behind Marius's Land-rover. Hino talking as they got out of the Jeep.

"All I'm saying is—It wouldn't kill you to let me drive for a change."

"Not after last time!"

"I said I was sorry!"

"Ready?" Marius tossed his cigarette on the ground and lead the way into the warehouse.

Rows of metal solid benches lined up and down the warehouse floor with workers sitting at every available space, working in undisturbed unison. Machines printing artwork, books and documents filled the 25,000 square foot warehouse and a strong scent of ink hit the boys. The four made their way through the warehouse—Hino stopped at a bench filled with books and picked one up, flicking through the pages.

"Didn't realise there was a high demand for kid stories in this business," Hino chuckled and dropped the book back on the bench.

The woman stocking the books into crates breathed out a laugh, "There's a high demand for everything in this business—You just have to put drugs in it."

Hino frowned and examined the books, confused as to where they had hidden drugs in the books. The woman picked the same book up as Hino had moments before and opened the front cover. She pulled back the paper glued to the hardback and revealed a thin pouch of white powder stuck to the cover. Hino smirked and clicked his tongue.

"Smart."

He allowed the woman to continue working and caught up to his team, waiting for him at the stairs that lead to the office. The four climbed the stairs and entered the office—it was a clean room; the four walls were made of glass that overlooked the entire warehouse. Two chairs sat at the desk, their target in the chair behind it.

Carter had borrowed a large amount of money from 'Gods Among Kings' to fund his business. Forging art pieces and documents, printing money and smuggling drugs into everyday objects—making transactions and travelling the drugs easier and without being detected. Carter had used his borrowed money to buy the warehouse and equipment. He had promised he'd make the money back within 18 months. So, Lenzo gave him 1 year. The boys were here to collect it. Ash and Link took the two seats; Marius stood office at the door, daring someone to interrupt them. Hino floated around the office—searching the filed documents and trinkets that artfully decorated the office.

Link's legs kicked up on the desk. "I must say, Carter, I'm impressed."

Carter was too frightened to reply. His fingers drumming on the armrest of his chair. A shaky smile filled his drawn face and hints of fear lit his twitching eyes.

"I wasn't expecting a visit today—" he stammered out—suddenly noticing the unkept stacks of papers on his desk. "—Can I get you all something? Water?—" Carter's eyes drifted to Hino pacing by the windows and watching the workers below. "—Another chair?"

Ash leaned back in his chair. "We're here for what you owe. It's collection day."

"I have Mr Lenzo's money—" He pushed back his chair and reached into his bottom drawer of his desk and pulled out a thick envelope, sliding it across the desk to Ash. "There's seventy-five per cent. The rest will be in check form if that is accepted."

"Money is money," Hino said from the windows.

Ash emptied the envelope on the desk and began counting the cash. In the meantime—Carter filled out the check—handing it to Link.

"If this doesn't clear—" Link threatened, his tongue teased with the pointed vampire tooth, an excited grin at the thought of what he could do if the check didn't clear. "—Well, you'll know what happens."

Carter's face drained of colour. "It will, I promise."

"Seventy-five per cent," Ash confirmed and pocked the cash inside his jacket. "It's been a pleasure, Carter," Ash knocked on the desk and stood up. Leading the three out of the office.

Marius was waiting for them at the bottom of the stairs. "Sorted?"

"Yes, that was refreshingly easy," Ash breathed out.

"Let's get out of here. I need a drink," Link sighed.

Almost out of the warehouse—Hino stopped at another bench filled with unbranded bags of flour. Like he had with the books, he picked a bag up and examined it.

"This will never pass for flour."

A young man sat at the bench frowned at Hino—"What makes you say that?"

He couldn't have been more than twenty. Wide eyes and carefully handling the products as if they would blow while his workmates were throwing them into boxes.

The three boys had noticed Hino wasn't following them and had backed up—watching the exchange just as confused as the workers who had stopped their task to listen to Hino.

"For one." Hino placed the bag back on the bench. "Who would steal flour?" Hino had confused the entire crowd. "I assume that's what you're doing."

The boy went red. "I don't—I haven't—"

"I'm not referring to you." Hino looked at the man who sat next to the young boy. An older man with a stern face like a bulldog. "That waste box under your chair looks pretty full."

The man's legs twitched, muscles warming up to run and Link and Marius caught the action, slowly moving around the bench to stand behind the worker.

"Bad batch, I guess."

Hino gave a crooked smile. "So, you wouldn't mind me checking? I used to do this, ya'know. Stocking drugs. A warehouse like this—less creative—" Hino was talking to the room and had attracted Carter out of his office to investigate. "We had less thievery too."

"Excuse me?" Carter dared.

Hino ignored him. "Let me see the box; if it's a bad batch, you've got nothing to worry about."

Carter took a step forward. "Show him the box, Sonny."

Sonny began to sweat. "I've worked for you for months. You know me."

"Then show me the box," Hino laughed, but there was no humour behind it. "Lincoln."

Link nodded to Hino and swiftly kicked a leg of Sonny's chair. Sending him sprawling on the floor. Marius stepped over the groaning man and reached for the box—sitting it on top of the bench. Hino sorted through the bags and inspected the contents. Turning to Carter.

"He's stealing products from you. Just like him—" Hino pointed to a worker across the room. "And her—And them two."

"You should use that wall of windows. It's amazing what you can see."

Chapter Ten
Sleep-Deprived, Possible Intoxication, Sugar Rush

Here for the cheap multi-coloured cocktails—a wave of students filled booths lined the bar and flooded the dance floor at the only bar that served the underaged. Fake identifications that wouldn't pass even the sketchiest establishments rested unseen in their purses as bartenders worked on their orders at the mixology station (a bar mat on the bar countertop).

Hitting *Ethel's* at peak of the night was a poor mistake on the gang member's behalf. They had slaved away the entire day for Lenzo—collecting debts, reviewing deals, Lenzo had even set them the task of cleaning out an unused warehouse that had taken up most of their evening and ran into their night.

"We're home."

Hino took a deep inhale through his nose. If Hino had to create a fragrance for a Saturday night at *Ethel's*, he'd say: cheap cigarettes, overapplied spiced aftershave, with hints of sick, sweat and hormones.

He fought his way to the bar while the other three made their way to their currently occupied booth. A bachelor party all in character costumes overfilled the booth. A Cupid, cowboy, the Queen of England, Gladiator and a priest.

Waving his half-empty glass, the man dressed as a Cupid slurred, "Can we help yuh?" His Chicago accent thicker than it would have been if he had been sober. His eyes glossed over and bloodshot suggested he had drunk one too many seven drinks ago.

"Move," Ash ordered.

"Nuh."

"I won't argue with a grown man in a dipper." Ash rolled his eyes, "Get up."

Minutes from starting a fight he couldn't win, Cupid's friend jumped in to save him. Unlike the rest of the group, the gladiator didn't trip over his words and he had clocked Ash's gun at his waist. He mustered a steady and convincing tone. "We better get a move on if we're going to finish this bar crawl."

Hino came back with four drinks a few minutes later and slid into the booth next to Marius, his back to the bar. "Does anyone miss when students were too afraid of the bikers to come in? Because I miss not having to wait in the queue."

"You don't have to wait in the queue."

Ash and Hino started to bicker about how polite it was to queue and how they couldn't wave their gang privilege for everything—which escalated into Hino demanding if his grandparents could immigrate to Chicago from Japan and build a life, a career, without privilege, he could happily wait in a queue. And then Ash had kindly reminded him that Hino was in the gang because he was paying off his grandparent's dept to the 'Gods Among Kings'.

Marius was stuck in the corner listening to the pair argue, letting both get their point across before he'd jump in to stop Hino from reaching over the booth to strangle the blonde.

Link was sat facing the bar—facing her. She hadn't noticed them yet. She was laughing with a customer while she pulled their drink. Her smile reached her eyes as she threw her head back. When she brought her head back down, her eyes met his and her smile dropped instantly and she pulled her eyes back to the customer.

He felt a sharp pain in his side. Ash said, "Where's your head at, bro?"

Link looked at his friends, who were staring at him in question. "Right, sorry," he apologised lazily. "What are we talking about?"

The boys gave him suspicious looks. He hadn't been himself for a few days, tuning in and out of conversations, circles under his eyes even bigger than usual from the lack of sleep.

"What were Boss' orders?" Hino asked him.

He breathed in deeply. "Three weeks," he said, eyes on his glass, "full amount."

"That all?" Ash asked, expecting more.

"Yeah, that's all."

He cursed himself for keeping information from them. Link had always been honest with them; they were always honest with him. All were loyal until the end.

The four had sworn that a few days after they had met. All set to the same task by Lenzo. They were assigned to check up on a minor gang—Lenzo extended a helping hand and pulled them out of trouble with the authorities. In return, 40% of their profits for an entire year went to God Among Kings.

Six months in, they had missed 2 payments, so the boys were sent to collect. Link almost immanently took the lead—though Ash and Marius had years in the gang on him—without much conflict. And led the new group into their first fight. As if they had been trained together for their whole lives. They fought in unison, taking down 30 men with only a gun each. Hino had run out of bullets and within an instant, Marius had thrown him a full clip. They saved each other's asses that night and laughed and complimented each other's skills over a few drinks at a run-down dive bar they had found on their way home.

They worked in harmony since. Taking bullets for each other in battles, taking responsibility for others' mistakes. Over the hundreds of missions, they had learned so much about each other, both good and bad. Link knew how far they would all go to obey Lenzo.

So, when Ash asked him if the only orders were to warn Davis, he couldn't bring himself to tell them about the permission to put down the innocent employees. Because he knew it wouldn't take much for them to pull a trigger.

Not all were innocent, he reminded himself. One of them could be the lawyer friend helping Davis and if it meant that his crew wouldn't face the consequences of the truth getting out about that night. Link shifted his focus back to the bartenders. William—Will was medicine, not law, though he had plenty of experience with it. The twins—the girl, she would often sit with classic literature and hundreds of notebooks at the bar, books Marius had on his bookshelf from the syllabus from his old college literature class. Her brother would turn up to his Tuesday afternoon shift covered in oil and rust—his shift after college. And Link had seen him fix his friend's cars outside the bar all the time.

New girl? She seemed friendly—already mixing in and chatting to the customers. She looked too young to be in the bar—not a surprise at *Ethel's*—it was a possibility she could be studying law at college. But this was the first time he had seen her—she hadn't been at *Ethel's* long enough to be considered.

And then there was her. The one who had served them hundreds of times without any contact and even attempted to stand against them the day they demanded to see Davis yet ran away from him in the park. Like the new girl, she was clearly underage. Unlike the new girl, she had been working at *Ethel's* long enough for Link to draw up a conclusion that she wasn't in education, not with the long hours she worked.

“What do we know about Angel?” Link asked, eyes on the older woman sitting at the bar chatting to customers in the line.

Hino frowned. “Not much, just that she worked at the original *Ethel’s* and works at the dry cleaners across the street.”

Hino had researched everyone he could think of last night and that morning. Coming up either empty or very dull.

“Coronal, the war vet, was sent home on honourable discharge three times but refused. Lives alone in an apartment a few blocks over. He doesn’t have any education higher than high school. The one who doesn’t talk—”

“—Doesn’t talk.” Marius, Link and Ash said at the same time.

“Right—” Hino carried on. “As for the rest of the bartenders, with no name and no legal trace of the bar having employees, I couldn’t find anything. William was arrested the night we—that night. And he’s just gotten out so he’s clean.”

“Do you think he knows?” Marius said.

“If he did, he would’ve said something by now.”

“So, it’s a possibility that Angel could be our law adviser?” Link asked.

“It’s possible,” Hino confirmed. “She could have picked up some legal advice from her—uh customers.”

Eyes stalked Rory’s every move, which made it very difficult to concentrate on her job. Distracted her enough to forget that she was pouring a drink—cold beer pooling around her hand. Luckily, the man she had been serving didn’t mention it as he flashed her a toothy grin and said thank you. The man sat on the empty seat at the bar next to Colonel. It was noticeably his first time in the bar. His blue tailored suit was crease free and probably still had the brand-new suit smell.

He loosened his suit jacket buttons when he’d reach the front of the line and scanned the area for a menu. With no luck, he asked Rory if they had one. He ended up going for whatever was most popular when she informed him the only menus they had were for the takeout down the street. He was polite and used manners, which took Rory aback and had Nicky gasping from his spot at his cash register, his words well-spoken.

He was perfect in every sense; even his short back and sides hair cut looked classy. Flashy suit and educated speech weren't what had turned people's heads; it was his eyes. A crystal blue.

Rory took advantage of the quiet queues as much as she could by fixing everything that had broken as quickly as possible. She started with the fridge light that had popped, tapped the kegs in the cellar, fixed the dishwasher again. She then joined Nia, restocking the bar.

The whole time she had felt his eyes on her and Rory didn't dare turn around and look at him again. Not even when it was his round to buy. Muttering the cost of his round and a small thank you when he slipped the change into the tip jar. Never making eye contact with him.

Not being the only one on edge—Rory had to nudge Will away from the cash register when the gang would get up to order. Will had been sending death glares to the boys since the moment they had sat down. If the tension between the bar staff and GAK members was any thicker, you would be able to see it.

Nicky and Nia caught onto Will's mood and replicated it without knowing, so the three were on edge. Will's mood was also the cause of Chrissy's. He'd become almost possessive throughout the night, constantly checking up on her or appearing out of nowhere whenever one of them came near her, making her frustrated. Rory didn't blame her—Will and Abel had acted the same way with Rory when the gang first showed up at *Ethel's*. The hovering and protectiveness was suffocating and annoying and an inconvenience.

Being the only one that knew about the 'Davis incident', Rory was closer to the edge than everyone else. The memory of the scene, Davis's green face, his hollow eyes, the awful, mauled skin, played in the back of her mind and the eyes burning holes in the back of her head was not a good mix.

Her mind was going round and round, lack of sleep making her vision blurry or maybe it was the tension blinding her. It could have been the alcohol she and Will had been throwing back all night. Either way, she didn't see Nia rounding the corner. The tray of glasses Rory was holding fell to the floor earning a round of applause from the small crowd. The loud noise startled the four gang members, their hands going down to their guns but relaxing and getting back to their conversations once they deemed the situation wasn't a threat.

Curses flew from Rory's mouth as she apologised to Nia and then another set of bad words followed when she cut her hand on the glass. Red liquid spilling from her palm.

Nia gulped at the blood. "Why don't you get that cleaned and I'll sort the mess out?" Her tone was calm and sweet.

Rory stood up and grabbed the rag off the counter and pressed it to her cut. She hissed loudly. Cleaning products on the rag stung her wound.

Nicky turned to the scene, "Rory, why don't you go and get some air." Rory didn't listen and picked up a clean rag from under the bar, knocking a box off the shelf, spilling cocktail sticks all over. "Aurora," he said firmly, "take five."

Huffing, she threw the rag down on the bar and stormed out the back door, hard enough for it to bounce off the brick wall, slamming closed, scaring the cats that gathered around the bins.

Their hands flew to their guns tucked in at their waists at the shattering chaos. College students had cleared the bar half an hour before, leaving a mess that the bar staff had hurried to clean up. With the room less packed, *Ethel's* team's cold glances were less avoidable.

Link watched the shattering scene at the bar and excused himself from the pointless conversation the boys were having and followed the girl out the back door. It was easy to sneak through the 'EMPLOYEE ONLY' sign as the rest of the staff were occupied with cleaning up the smashed glass.

Link didn't know why he had followed the raging woman any more than why he hadn't taken his eyes off her all night. He had watched the way she would interact with the different customers. Watering down drunk girls' drinks, faking a laugh at jokes to get a tip from the frat boys. Sliding a drink to the regulars just before their glasses were empty.

He was hit by the door and blinked, steadying himself.

The alley reeked badly. A lamppost at the opening poorly lit up the narrow alley; rows of overfilled garbage dumpsters lined the brick walls. He could faintly hear heavy breathing through the music from inside and sirens and cars in the distance. Following the breaths around the side of a rather repulsive garbage dumpsters, he found her.

She was hunched over the side of it, hands on her bare knees. Link wondered if she could smell the dumpsters that she was supported on; he supposed she was used to it by now—working here. Orange hair curtained her face. He debated whether to speak to the girl or leave her out here, alone, in the dark alley that leads into a building filled with drunk, hormonal humans.

"It's not safe out here." He internally cringed at his choice of words.

Rory's head whipped up and she stood up against the dumpsters, the cold metal cooling her burning shoulders. She hadn't seen him follow behind her.

"And it's safer in there?" Rory's voice was tremulous despite the sarcastic words, "With all the guns and the gangs?"

Link moved forward, coming into the little light and Rory forced herself to stay in her spot. Her small eyes were wide and full of panic as she watched him stalk towards her. Unsure of his motives. She cast her gaze to the steel door, the bins covering most of it so that she could only see the flickering neon pink sign that read *Ethel's*.

His narrowed eyes raked her body. A predator stalking his prey, noticing every move, her quick glances for a way out, the twitch in her muscles as they fought the urge to move.

"Your knee is bleeding." His steps stopped and he stared at her knee, covered in blood.

"You cut it on the glass?"

She snorted, "Wow, great observation skills, Marple." When he tilted his head, she continued, "I haven't read Sherlock."

That earned a deadpan look.

She held up her stained palm. "Good try, though."

He clicked his tongue, "You always this smart?"

"I try to be."

He hummed and ran his hand over his mouth, "You didn't seem that smart when you dropped those glasses back there."

She clenched her jaw and hissed out, "I was distracted."

"By?"

"Sleep-deprived, possible intoxication, sugar rush."

"That it?" he asked her, eyebrow raised.

She was suddenly all too aware of the gun at his hip and the lack of cameras around.

"Yep."

She closed her eyes the second the word squeezed out.

Link smirked at her. "You're a terrible liar."

She huffed out. Rory made her way past him to go inside, but he grabbed her upper arm. Holding her in place.

"What did Davis tell you?" his voice was low.

Rory swallowed, "I know he owes you money. That's it."

Link had guided her backwards, her back hitting the bin behind her. His lean frame towered over her and she had to crane her neck to look up at him. His blue eyes were cold and narrow and sent threats and warnings that suggested he wasn't playing. "If you're really that smart, then I suggest you learn to keep out of our way."

"Too bad I'm a dropout then." She was testing her luck, but the alcohol had overridden her common sense.

With no hint of a lie—Link was relieved. Rory had confirmed what he had already figured out. She wasn't in education, none of the bartenders was the lawyer informant. They didn't have to kill their alcohol source.

The steel door hitting the brick wall distracted Link enough for Rory to snake out of his grip and duck under his arm. Chrissy was dragging a trash bag half the size of her to the closest garbage dumpsters. Rory caught up to Chrissy to help. The two struggled to lift the bag up high enough to dump onto the mountain of trash bags that piled onto the dumpsters lid.

"What the hell is in here?" Rory grunted. "Did you kill Will?"

Chrissy let out a breath passing for a laugh, "Not yet." She dug her heels into the ground for grip, "On the count of three."

"One—" Rory started.

"Two—" Chrissy said.

"Three." The weight of the bag left their shoulders and landed on the pile. "You're welcome." Link smirked down at them.

Chapter Eleven
What Happened to Sawyer?

Ethel's was calm; only the regulars and the booth of gang members remained. Will had been staring at the well-dressed man at the end of the bar long enough for it to be weird. There was something about the man that was familiar to Will and he's been trying to rack his brain for a conclusion, but he couldn't put his finger on it.

"Hey man," Will called Nicky back as he passed him. "Do we know that guy?"

Nicky and Will angled their heads and stared. "No," he dragged. "But he does look familiar."

When the familiar stranger rose from his seat and moved in their direction, Will quickly averted his eyes and smacked Nicky on the chest, muttering orders to look away.

Will tried to act oblivious as he turned to the man. This close, he could see his features more clearly. His eyes were such a light blue. The stranger stuck his hand out to Will and Will took it.

"Hey man, saw you looking at me," he spoke calmly with a smile. "Came to see if I could help you with anything?"

Will looked to Nicky and then back to the man. "Oh, I wasn't looking at you," he stuttered. "I was, uh—"

"It's no trouble, man," he laughed. "I'm Emmett."

"Will and this is Nicky." Nicky gave him a small wave. "I'm sorry—it's just that—you look really familiar," Will confessed.

Emmett smiled, "I've been visiting the cafe next door recently?" he suggested.

"Nah, man, I haven't been in there for ages; I've been in prison." Will gasped loudly. "That's it! That's where I know you from!" He slammed his hand on the bar.

Emmett's eyebrows knotted together. "From Prison?"

"Nah! You look so like our friend, Sawyer. He's got duller eyes and longer hair-"

Chrissy and Rory had come back to the bar just as Link and his pals approached Will, a fresh bandage on Rory's hand thanks to Chrissy's first aid. Sensing trouble—the girls rushed over. Nia had emerged from the backroom as well—Rory's screwdriver in hand.

"What do you want?" Will's attitude was bitter.

Chrissy, new to the city was unaware of the dangers the four gang members truly held, spoke up. "Is there a problem?"

All eyes went to her and Rory subtly took a step in front of her. "Davis isn't in."

Link looked at her, his jaw set. "I thought we've already established you're a terrible liar?"

"Do you see his car outside?"

The tension that had built over the night was dangerously coming to its tether. Everyone could feel it. Angel had gathered her money and stuck it in her bra and was quietly making her way to the door, pulling JC with her. Colonel didn't make it so subtle as he took off with his glass of Guineas.

"This has nothing to do with the lot of you," Marius said, his voice level. "You don't need to be involved."

"Like you had nothing to do with Sawyer?" Will snapped in a temper. Instant regret flooded his face as everyone turned to him. Knowing he had said something he shouldn't have.

Marius snapped his head to Will and, in a dangerously slow voice, said, "I have no idea what you're talking about."

"What do you know about Sawyer?" It was Emmitt who had questioned them.

Ash in his usual bored tone said, "What happened to Sawyer was his own fault."

"Who's Sawyer?" Chrissy asked.

"Abel Sawyer," Rory went behind the bar to the small group of hung photos of the team. She lifted a photo frame from the wall and placed it on the bar top.

"Abel is a regular, a friend. He'd come here almost every night, but he hasn't shown up in almost half a year. No one's heard from him." Her voice was sorrowful as if she was grieving.

The picture was of the bar team and Abel. They all held drinks in their hands and had a smile from ear to ear. Abel's arm was slung around Rory's shoulders and pulling her tight to his side.

"So, what the hell happened to Sawyer?" she demanded, finger-pointing to the photo.

Emmett picked the picture up and examined it—examined the similarities Will had spotted moments before. They had the same square jaw and dark olive skin. Abel's hair was shorter in the picture and his face clean-shaven. The arm-hugging Rory was a clean canvas compared to the tattoos he had collected the past five months.

Gods Among King members looked as confused as *Ethel's* bar staff, but Ash turned his nose up at Emmitt. "How do you know him?"

"Abel is my brother."

One hundred questions flew at him all at once. The bar team were interested in the secret brother that their best friend had failed to mention. Whereas the gang's questions were more of an interrogation, "When was the last time you spoke to him? Did he tell you anything about his incarceration? How close are the two of you?"

"Incarceration?" Nia screeched, causing everyone to stop dead. Nia had ears like a hawk and had heard the word through the chaos.

One time, Nia had spent all day setting up a Surprise party for Nicky. She had put up party banners and pansexual flags, blowing up balloons—the whole lot. She had given Rory and Will one order, just one. Not to touch the table filled with candy. But like the children they were—they didn't listen and the second she left the room, they were straight at it. Stopping dead when they heard her call from the other room ordering them to step away.

Nia's hand tightened on the screwdriver, ready to jab it into their necks. "What do you mean, incarcerated?" Her voice was tight as her eyes narrowed in on her targets.

Marius made the mistake of opening his mouth. "Calm down, kid."

"Calmada?" she hissed.

"Nia—" Nicky warned.

"Incarcerated?" Nia asked again, voice steady and less aggressive after her brother's warnings.

Nicky gave his sister a nudge to back down and Nia heaved a sigh of frustration. The four men ignored her as they stared at Emmitt. And Emmitt returned their stares—no fear behind his eyes as they sized him up and attempted to figure him out.

It was just luck that Emmitt had crossed paths with the four gang members at the bar. Abel had spoken about the bar multiple times and now it was his last hope. Emmitt would refuse to leave the bar tonight without any answers.

"Are you going to answer her?" Chrissy broke the silence and received a selection of responses: Nia agreed. Nicky and Rory cringed. Will fumed. And Link, Marius, Ash and Hino took offence. Chrissy stood in defence—not understanding the grave she had just dug.

"Excuse me?" Ash almost laughed at her audacity to question them.

"Don't talk to her like that," Will ordered and attention went from Chrissy to Will as he rose from his seat. The moment the gang arrived, Will had been itching for a reason to throw a punch. Aware he'd be overpowered, but the resentment on behalf of Abel Sawyer made the risk worth it.

Ash—who had shared Will's urge of violence—clicked his tongue and took a large step forward as Will planted his feet firmly on the floor, distributing his weight in the likely case that Ash threw a punch first. The room went still.

"Will," Nicky warned as he did with Nia, but Will didn't pay any attention. Nicky was the level-headed member of the team in conflict. Always de-escalating situations, often enough—just saying their names would call order. "William."

The second time a charm—Will begrudgingly stood down, turning his back on Ash—who saw this as winning round one. Ash snickered and before anyone could register what was happening, Ash was on the floor, clutching his bleeding nose. Marius took hold of Will's right wrist that was still balled up and backed Will's steps up away from Ash, struggling to get up.

"NIA," Rory and Nicky shouted after her when she slipped past the two and advanced for the first GAK member she could reach.

Hino dodged her swings with no effort needed and appeared almost bored of the whole situation. Nia blurted insults and phrases that Hino couldn't make out or translate as she used the screwdriver to attack his arms.

"You get Nia—" Nicky instructed Rory, "—I've got Will."

Will and Marius were engaged in a fistfight, each taking turns to get the upper hand, but knuckles were already bloodied and eyes were starting to bruise. Will grunted, one hand attached to Marius's shirt and the other clenched into a fist that collided with Marius's chin with enough force to leave his ears ringing and eyes watering. Marius stumbled, Will's grip on his shirt kept him upright so he could get another hit in the same spot. Marius's teeth sang and he dropped to the side.

Swinging his leg out, Marius hooked his leg around Will's and brought him to the ground with him and swiftly climbed on top, knees on either side of him, squeezing his sides. Will's eyes widened as Marius's giant fist came down on his nose; he could taste the blood on his lips and lifted his arm to jab Marius in the ribs and took position on top.

The screwdriver scratched Hino's forearms, drawing up blood and leaving thin lines of broken flesh. Nia hadn't slowed down and didn't seem to be running out of energy any time soon and Hino wasn't prepared to use offence any time soon. He called on Link for help, but Rory had looped her arms around Nia's waist pulling her away before Link could advance.

Pulling Will from Marius wasn't as easy of a job for Nicky. Will and Marius were rolling around the floor, neither staying on top long enough for Nicky to separate them from each other. Nicky tagged Rory in—Rory leaving Nia in Emmitt's firm grasp on the struggling girl, still in the mood for a fight.

Like Nia—Ash hadn't had enough and advanced on Will and Marius —revenge for his swollen nose the only thing on his mind. Ash reached the fight, grabbed Rory's upper arm and threw her out of the way and into a hard body. Link's hands steadied Rory and brought one of her arms around her back. Telling her to stay out their way, but Rory's mind remained on helping Nicky save their dumb-ass friend. Rory brought her head back and head-butted Link's nose. Link dropped his grip on her.

"Stop," Link growled at Rory throwing her fists at him. She favoured her right hand, her punches weak. He grabbed her fist as it came close to his throbbing, bleeding nose but didn't expect the left hand to punch him in the jaw. Hard. It was through blurred vision and singing teeth that he had remembered seeing her write with her left-hand days before. Sneaky and impressive is what he would have thought if he wasn't blinded by the pain shooting up his jaw.

With Link now focused on his throbbing face—Rory made to help Will—Nicky nowhere to be seen. She pried at Ash and Marius, attempting to get them off Will. Marius and Ash had overpowered Will and he lay on the floor with his arms up—protecting his face from the relentless punches from the more skilled.

"Link?" Rory guessed. "Get them to stand down!" Rory screamed over her shoulder. "They'll kill him."

Link didn't get a chance to give any orders. A piercing screech echoed in the room. Everyone stopped and covered their ears, wincing at the loud noise. Nicky was blowing a silver whistle, holding one of the bar's first aid boxes. He pulled it from his mouth and took a second to regain his breath.

"EVERYBODY STAND DOWN NOW!"

Ash and Marius backed away from Will and Will rolled onto his side and pushed himself up—Rory and Chrissy taking an arm each and walking him to the closest seat. Will dropped onto the chair with a groan. His left eye was already swollen and bruises decorated his both cheeks and chin. Chrissy used her thumb to wipe away the blood from his split lip and he hissed and reeled back. Nicky threw an ice pack to Rory and she shoved the icepack into Will's hand and stormed away to check on Nia.

She was unharmed but still clutching the screwdriver, Rory slowly slipped it away from her fingers and placed it out of arms reach in case Nia had the urge to use it again.

Marius was in a similar state to Will, bruised face and bleeding nose—hugging his sore ribs. Blood from his nose and busted lip covered his chin and left dark patches on his dark shirt. His cheek was swollen and his mouth was filled with blood. Nicky had passed an ice pack and a clean rag to Marius and Marius thanked him. Hino was also handed a rag to clean his arms up—wincing when the cloth touched his scratches.

Rory took the last ice pack and pressed it firmly on her knuckles. Link picked up a rag and carefully cleaned the blood still pooling out his dislocated nose. He covered his nose with the red-stained fabric and with a quick motion, he snapped the nose into place. Under his blue eyes, red bruises were forming that ran down his nose that was now slightly bent to the right.

Link rubbed his aching jaw and raised his eyebrows at Rory. "Where'd you learn to punch like that?"

She flexed her fingers and closed her fist. "Middle school."

Link looked to Emmitt, “We didn’t have anything to do with your brother.” Link placed the rag on the bar top and turned his attention to the rest of the room. “You’re lucky we like drinking here. Otherwise, that stunt would have ended a lot sooner.”

“I have life insurance, not health insurance—” Nia bit. “—Better make sure you’re a good shot.”

With a nod, Link told his boys to leave. None of the guys argued as they sat up and followed their leader out of the bar.

“We didn’t warn Davis,” Ash said as he climbed into Link’s jeep.

Link opened the car door and didn’t look at Ash when he said, “I’ve handled it.”

Rory placed the melted ice pack on the bar top and wiped her damp hands on the back of her shorts but stopped when she felt something in her pocket. She pulled out a small piece of paper and unfolded it. On the paper was four words, “He’s got three weeks.”

Chapter Twelve
You're Rich, Right?

"That's an order, Lincoln," Lenzo hissed at him. "Get it done tonight or it'll be you."

He had everything ready: the gun, the fingerprints. Take out the cameras. Wave the gun around and scare the cashier. Turn their backs long enough for him to phone the police. Get the hell outta there.

It was simple and straightforward—nothing they hadn't done a dozen times. The job was easy.

It was supposed to be easy.

Everything was going to plan. The cashier was held in his spot with a gun pointed at him. Link was in the office, trashing it to make the robbery more believable.

He wasn't there to witness the cashier fight back.

He wasn't there to stop his friend from attacking the cashier.

He wasn't there to drag his friend from the mangled body.

Link awoke for the second time that week in a cold sweat. That night couldn't have gone any worse. They weren't any closer to finding Sawyer's alibi; William was back and starting fights; they were in a petty bar fight that Lenzo was going to love. The bartender's Link had promised wouldn't be a problem—had become a big problem.

Times like this, when the horrors that Link had witnessed—what he had done—had invaded his dreams, causing him to wake up shaking and sweating. They made him wish he had chosen the other path seven years ago. Lenzo had promised he made the right decision in choosing to learn and train and serve. Link was a survivor from birth. Losing his parents, through all the foster families, he had survived. He was promised revenge on the families who had mistreated him. He was promised to become a man that no one dared to cross. No one could touch him.

Times like these, he still felt like that scared, hungry, weak boy standing in Lenzo's office.

And he hated it.

The bar team agreed to go home and sleep on the revaluations of the night and regroup early the following day. Though sleeping wasn't popular that night and it was obvious as they all sat in a booth at 'All American'. Charlotte didn't ask any questions when she arrived at 7:30 AM to open the cafe and found five zombies at the door. They ordered a coffee each with an order to keep the refills coming. The rain pelting on the window filled the silence and their moods matched the miserable weather.

Ethel's was closed for the day. The night before, Rory had gone to deliver the note Link had slipped into her pocket to Davis. She didn't know if he had planted it when he had her pinned against the dumpsters or when he restrained her in the fight. Either way, Rory was pissed she didn't notice. She asked or rather, told Davis that the bar would be shut tomorrow and he mumbled a fine while holding a lighter to the note. She didn't stay long enough to watch the flames burn the message.

Tired eyes lazily drifted to the door at the sound of the bell. Emmitt, dressed in a suit, shook off the rain from his umbrella and carefully shut the door. Emmitt looked to the counter where Charlotte was cleaning. "Coffee, please."

Charlotte smiled and grabbed a cup.

He made his way to the group and slid into the booth next to Will. The circle booth just managed to fit them all in.

Next to Will sat Nia, Nicky, Chrissy and then Rory. No one had the energy to start the conversation. Rory's thoughts had kept her up all night. For the last five months, she had joked around with everyone, coming up with wild theories on the whereabouts of her friend.

Putting bets on how long it would be before Abel Sawyer would show up at *Ethel's* with an impressive story and a scar to prove it. Maybe he had booked a last-minute flight to some tropical island. No. He was in prison. The endless possibilities of what happened—what he did—had Rory out at dawn with Caspian at the park, hoping the fresh air and long walk would ease her mind. It didn't. Instead, she ended up lost in the maze of the park, crying on a bench.

Charlotte came to the booth with fresh steaming coffee. Blonde tight pony bouncing behind her. "I see you're finally getting around to *Ethel's,"* she said as she filled up everyone's drink, her optimistic aura making Nicky wince and shrink in his seat. It happens that Nicky's way of dealing with bad news was in a bottle of Tequila—and Rory would be lying if she said she didn't finish her own bottle the night before too.

Emmitt gave Charlotte a small smile. "I have yet to, actually."

He brought the cup to his mouth and blew lightly, everyone eyeing him as he took a small sip, waiting on him to elaborate. Emmitt reached into his suit jacket and pulled out a small card and handed it to Will. "*Ethel's* was next on my list."

The card was simple, white with a blue border and read:

Emmitt Sawyer
Acquisition Manager
A S Co
(219)-219-17070

Will tutted, "Not only does Sawyer have a secret brother—" he tossed the card onto the table and sat back in the seat, arms crossed and his lips formed a tight line. "—He's rich."

Nicky reached for the card. "You work for *A S Co*? Amelia Sawyer is your mother?"

Emmitt nodded.

Charlotte set the coffee pot on the table. "Abel Sawyer is a Sawyer? Huh, didn't make that connection." Charlotte took a seat. "And why does Will look like that?" she cringed at his bruised and swollen face.

"Will started a bar fight," Nicky told her.

To say Will felt betrayed was an understatement. Sawyer was the one who Will would go to for advice for his relationships, finances and fashion. They swapped song recommendations, stole items of clothing. Will was the first call Abe had made when Abel's first boyfriend had broken his heart.

They told each other everything.

Scoffing, Will said, "If Abel's hiding a secret brother, who knows what else he's hiding—or lying about."

Rory breathed out quietly, "Jesus Christ."

She stared at her untouched coffee. Abel was their friend. *Ethel's* was a place where you could forget about the outside world. It didn't matter if you were a school dropout or criminal or secretly wealthy. Your family background didn't matter. Because in *Ethel's*, you were yourself without judgement. Rory was upset Abel didn't trust her enough to share his family with her. But he didn't deserve what Will was saying. Not until they knew the whole story.

"Oh, give it a rest, Rory," Will snapped. "He's not here; you don't need to defend him."

Narrowed eyes shot daggers across the table. "What's that supposed to mean?" Rory asked through gritted teeth.

He matched her sour expression. "Every time," he leaned his arms on the table, "you always protect him, every time." Will spat out, "He's in prison, Aurora; how are you going to defend him now."

Rory's knuckles turned white with the tightening grip on her mug. "Which you failed to mention." Her breathing got heavy with anger at the boy sat opposite her as he dared to question her, "I heard what you said, 'Like you had nothing to do with Sawyer?'" His eyes twitched and she saw him swallow, but she continued, "How did you know about Abel? William."

There was truth in what he was claiming about defending Abel. Rory knew there was. The memory of her first day at *Ethel's* forced itself into Rory vision. Two years ago, a barely 17-year-old Rory lied to a very scary looking Davis about experience and age and was shoved headfirst into a Saturday night alone. Of course, Colonel, Angel and JC were there. JC's jack and coke was easy and it only took four tries to get Colonel's guineas perfect. But she panicked when Angel asked for some fancy cocktail Rory had never heard of.

To her luck, the young guy at the end of the bar, dressed in black leather and eyeliner, started to list ingredients and when Rory had collected them, he gave her instructions to make it. He had cheered when Angel approved of the drink and gave Rory a high-five. For the rest of the night, the stranger whispered steps and instructions to the girl. And from that moment on. Aurora James Scott was wrapped around Abel Sawyer's finger.

"The day I was booked," Will's voice was full of shame, enough for Rory to soften her eyes and relax the grip on her mug. "It was the same night I crashed the car; Abel was at the station, cuffed to a bench," he swallowed, not meeting anyone's eyes. "I didn't get to talk to him for long, but all he said was that he was going away for a long time." Will looked up at Rory. "He told me not to tell you."

Why wouldn't Abel want Rory to know? If anyone had any chance of getting him out of whatever mess this was, it was Rory. Sure, she never finished Law school, but Rory had aced her 'Criminal Law Classes' and Abel knew as such. So, if Abel was facing jail, Rory should have been his first call. She felt sick. And it wasn't because she hadn't eaten anything since last night and the only thing on her stomach was Tequila. Had he been so ashamed that he couldn't face her? Did he fear that she would be disappointed in him? Did he not trust her?
Nia asked the question on everyone's mind; she was the only one with the guts to ask. "What did he do?"

"Nothing." Emmitt was quick to reply, "He was set up; that's the only explanation." He gripped his mug like Rory had. "He didn't do it."

Chrissy spoke quietly; her accent softened, seemed to smooth everyone's nerves. "If he didn't do it, then why was he charged?"

"Someone set him up—and they did a great job at it," Emmitt's voice was quiet even though the cafe was empty, the rain scaring customers away, "According to the report, they found fingerprints on a weapon."

"Just fingerprints aren't enough to build a case, not with the right lawyer at least," said Rory absent-mindedly.

Hope crept on Nia's face. "You're rich right, you have a high-profile company?" she asked Emmitt, "Surely you have a family lawyer?"

Emmitt shook his head, "He refused one," he sighed, "and my mother is rich; it's her lawyer and my mother and Abel, they don't get on."

"So, she's just going to let him rot in jail for something he didn't do?" Charlotte nearly shook with anger and turned to Rory, "You have to do something." She looked back at Emmitt again, "Rory's good at this legal stuff; she was going to be a defence lawyer!"

Rory looked around the booth and everyone's eye was on her, pleading for something, anything.

"You guys remember I'm a dropout, right? I can't actually do anything."

The group didn't change their expression. Rory felt herself shrink in her seat under pressure.

“I can look at the case—but I can’t do anything. Don’t get your hopes up.”
Rory had a feeling it was already too late.

Chapter Thirteen
You Don't Work on Sundays

Emmitt agreed to meet with Rory through the week. She had given him Davis's number before they left the cafe and wished him luck. Help Abel. Buy the bar. Two birds, one stone. He didn't know which would be harder, judging by Rory's unconvincing smile.

But he was step closer to helping Abe. Abe would follow Emmitt around all day when they were kids, looking up at him with his big blue eyes—not the light blue like Emmitt's, a shade darker—his curls that were always un-kept bounced around as Abel tried to keep up with his big brother and his friends. With an innocent voice, he'd ask, "Can I plwy in duh twee house too, Emmy?" And when Emmitt had laughed and told him he was too small and childish.

Little Abe wouldn't tell their mother of his older brother's mean claims. Instead, he'd sit at the tree trunk and wait for them to come down. Most days, Abel would wait hours. And if Emmitt was feeling extra kind, he and his friends would climb down the other side of the tree and leave Abel waiting all night.

It had been so long since Emmitt had seen that smile. The smile Abel had worn so beautifully on the photo at *Ethel's*. So painfully beautiful. Emmitt thought back to all the times he had visited his little brother in prison and tried to recall a moment when he had worn that smile, but he drew a blank. A ghost of the smile when he had first gone to see him maybe, but nothing that bright. Emmitt couldn't help but think that the cause of that smile was the fire-haired bartender.

Abel and Rory weren't smiling at the camera; they were smiling at each other. His arm was over her shoulder as he hugged her tight to his side while Rory gazed at him like he was the world. Abel didn't talk much about the relationships in his life. He would bring some girls to family dinners—back when he was invited—they were decent girls. Always dressed nice, not too revealing but short enough skirts for the Sawyer's mother to turn her nose at and not bother to remember their names.

He had brought a guy once. A lanky punk with spiked boots, though their mother referred to him as Abel's friend the entire night. Emmitt assumed his mother thought Abel had brought the mohawk rocker to vex her. But he never looked at them the way he looked at Rory in that picture. Emmitt didn't miss the hurt in Rory's eyes, the death grip on the mug, the flinch when Will insinuated Rory was always defending Abel. Rory had said she didn't want to give Emmitt hope. But maybe it was herself she was saving.

Ice eyes reflected off the floor-length window of his home office. Watching as the rain flooded the city. One hand in his suit pocket and in the other, he held a small glass of whiskey. The room was massive, one of the biggest in his loft apartment—the open kitchen and living room taking the top spot. Oak brown furniture decorated the office, a large dark oak desk stood at the top of the room.

Behind it was a wall full of books, papers and files, trinkets from his travels (little things he had bought at markets that didn't hold much value) and photos ranging from his childhood with Abe and himself and his partner, Khenan.

"I thought we agreed the office would be locked on the weekends?" the groggy voice asked from the double oak doors. Bare feet padded on the wooden floor and Emmitt welcomed the strong dark bronze arms that wrapped around his waist.

Khenan leaned his head into the crook between Emmitt's shoulder and neck and kissed it softly. Emmitt hummed, "I was just going over a few things for work."

"It's Sunday," he mumbled in his neck. "You don't work on Sundays."

The couple had made a deal that weekends were for them only. The pair both worked long hours on weekdays which made it challenging to spend time together. Getting home late, eating whatever one of them brought home and then passing out on the couch watching trashy TV. So, they made a deal, on the weekends they would wake up late and spend the day doing whatever they wanted, devoting hours to prepare a special meal, going into town for some shopping, trip to the zoo. The only condition was: it had to be together and just the two of them.

Khenan pouted. "And you weren't in bed when I woke," he lifted his head up so his words weren't muffled, "you know I hate waking up alone."

Emmitt turned in Khenan's arms to face him; the hand that wasn't holding the drinking glass lay on his bare chest; despite Khenan's lack of clothes, heat ran through Emmitt's hand. "I met up with some of Abel's friends; they might be able to help."

Emmitt felt the groan under his palm rise up Khenan's chest before he heard it. His arms fell from Emmitt's waist and he took a step back. "We've talked about this, Emm," Khenan ran his hand over his face and he fell back on the couch with a grunt, "you can't help Abel if Abel doesn't help himself."

This wasn't an unfamiliar conversation for the couple. Everyone was innocent until proven guilty, and it had been proved that Abel was guilty. Khenan didn't buy the prosecutor's claims during the extremely short and cursory trial. And whether Abel had chosen the public defender specifically because the nervous and inadequate defender hadn't any experience in a criminal court had been a constant thought in Khenan's mind whenever the case was brought up.

Abel was facing life. No matter how many numbers they put in front of it, or however many appeals, Abel wasn't getting released to see any liveable years on the outside. If only he would say anything—something. The entire inquest, the trial, he hadn't spoken a word in his defence.

Sighing, Emmitt took a seat on the coffee table opposite Khenan. He placed the glass next to him and turned to his fiancé. "One of his friends," he said softly, "she might be able to help." Khenan didn't say anything, so he carried on, "She said she'll look at the case to see if she can find anything we missed."

"What makes this girl different from the others who could help," Khenan asked.

While chasing leads, Emmitt met with a few people with whom Abel had crossed paths, all promising they could help. Which turned out to be fake alibis and legal crap they heard on a TV show.

"Rory," Emmitt said, "she has a real legal background, not anything fancy but," he sighed and shook his head. "It's weird," Emmitt stated. "Of all the wild stories Abel would tell, of the interesting characters he would meet. He never mentioned the ones at the bar."

"The bar?"

Again, Emmitt shook his head, freeing them from the lingering thoughts of the secret life his brother seemed to have led. Emmitt knew Abel would frequent at the dive bar, he had mentioned it a few times in passing. But this was more than a regular hang out for his brother. Abel had a new family there, a patchwork group of dropouts and family rejects.

"I think she meant something to him, different from the rest."

"Did she tell you that?"

"It's more of a feeling."

"It took you three years to figure out you had feelings for me," Khenan snorted.

"It took me twenty years to figure out I had feelings for men, so don't take it personally."

Khenan sat forward and took his partner's hands, rubbing smooth circles, "If she can help your bother, that's fantastic." He stood up and pulled Emmitt up with him. "But today is Sunday and you don't work on Sunday." Khenan kissed both Emmitt's cheeks, heating them up, "And I want pancakes."

Emmitt laughed. "OK," he leaned in and kissed him softly. "Let go have some pancakes."

Chapter Fourteen
How Far Would You Go?

"It's not much—" Rory announced; opening the frail door, she stood aside to let Emmitt in. He walked in and took a quick look around the apartment. The open kitchen and living room making the small space appear slightly larger. A simple round table was in the centre of the kitchen. Two dark blue armchairs sat on either side of a small two-seater of the same colour and a wood coffee table in the middle of them, the legs covered in scratches from a dog. Simple. Humble.

The sound of the door shutting lightly drew his attention back to the homeowner. She shook off her jacket and threw it on the coat rack. "—But it's home."

Rory wasn't used to guests at her home. Nia had spent the night only a few times, but Nia's place with her twin was larger and closer to *Ethel's,* so everyone would go to the twin's for gatherings.

Even Rory's mother had only been once. Rory had made the mistake of believing her mother would be proud of the tiny home she had made for herself. The rent wasn't too high. Part-time wages at *Ethel's* just covered it, but going full time gave her some change to play with. She used some of her inheritance to buy new furniture, like her bed, sofa, chairs and fridge-freezer. The rest were second-hand bargains she had picked up with the help of Abel.

Marian Scott couldn't look past the second-hand furniture or the small fire exit windows that were a fire hazard themselves or the homeless man camping outside the building. Rory's proud smile dropped and all the hope left her green eyes when her mother—dressed in a cream swede coat—turned her nose up at the apartment. Her brown heeled boots clicking on the old floorboards as she surveyed the room, running a gloved hand over the windowsill and tutting when red paint flaked off.

Marian stayed for a quick coffee and left Rory with a sinking feeling that she had let herself, her mother and her father down. Her mother had never been back to the apartment and Rory would consider herself fortunate if she never returned.

Rory took her hair out of the braid and ran her fingers through the strands to smooth it down. She kicked off her boots and dumped them under the coat rack, leaving specks of dirt and mud on the floor from the rain outside.

"Do you want something to drink? Water? Coke? Tea?" she asked Emmitt, who was standing in the middle of the room; she made a gesture with her hand inviting him to sit.

Emmitt placed his swede briefcase on the coffee table and pulled out two thin files. He placed them on the table and put the briefcase on the floor. She stared down at the files, neither of them making any effort to pick them up.

Stamped in red ink marked 'Clarified' and she raised one eyebrow at Emmitt, "This is illegal, you know?"

He shrugged and asked, "How far would you go for him?"

She took a deep breath and opened the file. She knew whatever was in the it wasn't true; Abel was a bit rough around the edges, but he wasn't a criminal, or rather a murderous criminal. *Ethel's* attracted a lousy crowd; it wasn't uncommon for a drunk customer to get too handsy with the bar staff—if Abel was there, be damned sure the night would end up with Nicky mopping blood off the floor and Rory fixing Abel up in Davis's office or the locker room.

She clung to the memory of cleaning up Abel's face while he wore that stupid yet all so charming smile he would use to pull her out of her bad mood and looked down at the pages. It was the most basic case she had ever read. The practice cases she studied in law school had more detail. No witness reports, no police notes signifying investigation. She read through the evidence and forensics report. A gun was found at the scene with prints that were a definite match to one Abel Patrick Sawyer. Thread fibres with a 56% match with a jumper owned by Abel Patrick Sawyer.

Rory kept going through the file, truly confused at the lack of detail and evidence. She turned to Emmitt, watching her intensely as her mouth kept opening and closing in shock and confusion.

"Is this it?" was the only thing she managed to get out. Emmitt just silently handed over the second file with a grim face and when she saw the contents. Her stomach dropped.

Photos. Lots of them. Of the crime scene, Rory guessed, but they resembled a scene from a slasher horror film. From what she could make out with all the blood, it was a store. The floor and counter were stained red. Two drag marks left a trail of red going towards the door and multiple red footprints were scattered all over the scene in a chaotic mess.

The next lot of photos had her lunch raising to her throat, but she swallowed down the bile and forced herself to look at them, *Do it for Abel.* She pushed the vomit down again when she saw the victim. His face was swollen and lumpy and bruised. The nose was at an odd angle. One eye was twice the size as the other. So swollen you couldn't make out eye colour. His face was busted. Beaten to death.

Abel wouldn't do this
Abel couldn't do this

Rory had seen him fight multiple times. Always provoked. Never anyone smaller than him. He knew the limits; he wouldn't do this. Abel was kind. And funny. And damaged. Whoever did this was a monster with no control, someone had snapped and couldn't hold back. Abel wasn't a monster. He wouldn't do this. Not Abel. Not her Abe.

"Rory?" Emmitt calling her name pulled her back. His eyes were soft like he knew exactly what she was thinking. She could see in his eyes that he had felt the same when he saw this. Now they were screaming for help.

Clearing her throat to clear her mind, she read through the autopsy report. "Defence wounds, the skin under the nail, no match—" she mumbled as she read and pulled the skin at lips. "Blunt force trauma, right ribs broken and bruised." She stopped and reread it, this time louder, "Right side—" she flipped back to the photos of the victim and winced as she studied it, "—The right eye is worse than the left," she said to herself.

Emmitt could see her brain working in her eyes. She had zoned out again. He noticed the way her eyes had dulled when they saw the photos and he watched her throat swallow. Emmitt stared at the girl, started to wonder if showing her this was a mistake. He knew her and his brother were friends (maybe more), but he didn't know how she would take all this. He couldn't help himself to think she doubted Abe.

He watched as she continued to mumble away to herself. Emmitt had read the files so many times he could recite them line by line. He hoped she'd see something he didn't and when she stopped playing with her ears and her mumbles got more audible, he knew she had.

"What is it?" he rushed too aggressively; he was scared he had scared her.

"Could be nothing," she started, but her drawn eyebrows said otherwise. "Most of the damage was to the right side and Abel's left-handed," she said, still going through the file, flicking back and forth between the pages.

"The Cause of Death was blunt force trauma as a result of excessive beating, but they found a gun with his prints on—If Abel had a gun, why would he waste time and risk leaving evidence by beating the victim? Fibres from a jumper is trace evidence, it cannot be used on its own, not without the DNA match from under the victim's . Nothing is linking him to this. See this—" She pointed to the drag marks on the photo. "—The footprints either side—someone pulled—the attacker—away. Why wouldn't they look for an accomplice?"

"Why is he locked up then? Surely, the judge should have seen this?" Emmitt questioned. He leaned back into the sofa and unbuttoned his suit jacket.

"He didn't have an alibi, didn't ask for a lawyer, pleaded guilty," Rory listed, "as long as they can close a case."

"Or someone powerful was whispering in the judge's ear—Like a gang."

"That could explain why there was nothing on the news about it and the multiple footprints."

Emmitt lifted his eyes to hers, looking for any sign of hope that she could give him. Rory could see the desperation. He had been searching for hope for five months and coming up short. No lawyer would touch the case with the defendant not willing to try and anytime he tried to get a retrial, someone (mostly Abel) would shut it down.

"Rory," he almost whispered, his voice tired and strained, "I can't go back there to see him with nothing." His voice broke, "I need to get him out."

Just like his voice, Rory's heart broke. It was his face—Abel's. Darker hair, lighter eyes, but the same boyish face and pink stained lips pouted with sadness. For a second, it was Abel sitting back on her couch, begging for help.

"If he had an alibi, maybe," Rory stressed the word 'maybe'.

"Was he at *Ethel's*?" Emmitt perked up a small amount with hope.

"I don't know, but we wouldn't count as a solid alibi," she told him and he urged her on. "We're all underage; we'd just get ourselves arrested. The only one of age was off wrecking his dad's car."

"No cameras?"

"No cameras and he always paid in cash."

Emmitt sighed and rubbed his hands over his face, then through his hair, messing the perfect strands up.

"He has to tell us where he was." He looked past the girl to her bookshelf that was fixed on the wall closest to the door. The shelves were filled with old textbooks and novels and pictures. Most photos of her and Abel.

"What was the relationship between you and my brother?" His voice was quiet and soft, as if he spoke too loud or quick, he'd break her.

A light laugh passed her lips. *What were her and Abel?* They were close—really close. There were times when he'd walk her home and he'd throw an arm around her shoulder, pulling her tight and not letting go. Rory's lingering lips on Abel's cheeks after a peck. His fingers danced along her legs when they would curl up and watch a movie. She had feelings for him: a stupid schoolgirl crush on the older dangerous cheeky boy.

Rory was too antagonistic and stubborn and impended to her own feelings and Abel was too maverick and tameless. Rory knew they could never be more than the dodging around their feelings—pining forever. So, she simply said, "We're friends."

The quirk in Emmitt's eyebrow let Rory know he didn't believe the lie. "Nothing more?"

"Nothing more."

The older Sawyer nodded. He sat up and checked the time on his watch, "I'm going to visit Abel tomorrow morning—" He packed the files into his briefcase along with the unopened can she had given him, "—Shall I pick you up on the way?"

Rory couldn't bring herself to speak and nodded in agreement. Her finger and thumb rubbing her earlobe—a nervous habit.

Emmitt rubbed Caspian's head on the way to the door and gave Rory a sincere thank you.

"I would do it," Emmitt could just hear her voice, quiet but steady and sure. "I would lie for him." Emmitt's features relaxed as he understood.

"That's how far I'd go."

And she closed the door.
And she ran to the bathroom.
And she threw up.

Chapter Fifteen
What Happened to You?

The buzz every time the metal doors opened triggered Rory's fight or flight. Unable to stop her legs from twitching as she forced them to stiffen to stop the urge to flee from the building with every entry granted and the sound grew louder and more haunting as they moved further up the line.

Queues for visitors stretched across the entire room. In front of herself and Emmitt, a woman (not much older than Rory) quietly told her twin boys some rules: 'Don't reach across the table to Daddy', 'Don't raise your voice too loud'.

Rory made a note of the rules and repeated them like a mantra in her head. She tried to make herself appear less nervous and skittish to the guards that patrolled up and down the line. Not wanting to give them a reason to use the batons in their hands or the taser at their hips.

Two heavily tattooed buff men wearing leather vests stood two places behind them. One bald with a face filled with piercings and the second had a thin white mullet. The bald one greeted one of the guards and the guards discarded them with their nose's turned up, like the bikers were something they had stepped in. Mullet placed a stubby hand on his friend's arm to prevent him from biting back.

But it wasn't the six-foot bikers that scared her the most (she was sure she had seen them at *Ethel's* before anyways); it was the young woman behind her, with a little girl who looked too comfortable and too young to be in the building. The woman didn't need to explain the rules before going in. She didn't need to keep a tight grasp around her small hand to ensure she didn't run off or step out of line. Because the look on the small child's face as she gave one of the guards a friendly smile told her that this wasn't her first visit.

Rory wondered how many visits it would take before she would stop twitching at the third light on the left that flickered every 48 seconds.

Emmitt nudged Rory lightly on the arm and her head snapped to her right to face him. She cleared her throat when he motioned to the woman behind the plastic screen. Colourless hair was pulled back into a low pony, sideburns greying. Rory tried not to focus on the wort on her left cheek or how the hair poking out of it moved when she spoke.

The woman's dead eyes lacked any emotion but annoyance. "Inmate name and number."

Emmitt gave her the information and she asked about their relationship with the inmate.

"Brother."

Knowing that she had to be family to visit Abel, Rory squeaked out, "Fiancé."

The woman looked her up and down, drew her lips into a judging smirk and scribbled down on the form. "ID."

Emmitt and Rory handed over their IDs and she scribbled down on the paper again.

A set of rules were droned out that Rory didn't take in. There was a ringing in her ears that made her mind go foggy. She couldn't hear what the woman was saying, but she could see Emmitt empty his pockets into the pale bucket. She followed his lead and emptied her own into the second bucket: the keys to her house and *Ethel's*, her phone, half a pack of chewing gum and a penny she found outside.

She was handed a visitors' badge and followed Emmitt to the metal door. A tall guard stared her down; in his scarred meaty hand, he held a long metal detector. She faced Emmitt, who mouthed, "It's alright."

Rory stuck her arms out to the side as the man scanned her front. She tried to peak through the window when the guard bent down to check her legs, the room was almost empty and she wondered why the queue took so long.

Rory thought back to her first year of law school and tried to recall the prison fieldtrip she went on while the guard scanned her back. The banging on bars and chants when the group of students walked into the Cell Block was enough to make anyone sick. And the prisoners she had spoken to—she had seen how being incarcerated could change someone. Some went in and came out better. Some went in and came off worse and she couldn't think out how Abel would come out—if he came out. '*He would come out.*'

The pair sat at a table in the middle of the room, away from the guards that lined the three pastels blue bricked wall. Emmitt let his eyes wander around the room. He remembered most of the faces from his previous visits from the past 5 months.

Abel Sawyer wasn't supposed to have visitors, but Emmitt pulled the Sawyer card and Abel was allowed 30-minute visits with restricted company. The time limit wasn't long enough; by the time Emmitt had caught Abel up on his personal life—which Abel always demanded to know and Abel always had plenty of questions to stall—time would be up and he would have accomplished nothing.

Emmitt had seen his little brother change over the five months. The orange jumpsuit got baggier over his time behind bars; the fabric hung off his shoulders and exposed his dirty white vest. His face had hollowed out with fatigue and a sickly hue had taken over his usual dark tan skin. Emmitt had watched his brother deteriorate right before him and that broke his heart.

So, when Rory took in a very audible sharp breath. He knew her heart had just shattered too.

His hair was never tame in the time they had been friends; she could count on both hands how many times she had forced him to go get a haircut. But this was the longest and worst state she had ever seen it. The dyed gold curls had lost their shine (growing out as their dark roots) and bounce and hung off his head in a tatty mess.

Abel was the first to come through the gate and Rory watched as the guard lined them up against the back wall and unlocked the chains that connected the inmates by the feet. Abel made a joke Rory couldn't make out and the smaller guy next to him laughed lightly. At least, he hadn't lost his humour.

Rory held her breath when they turned back round and his eyes scanned the room for his brother. The smile left his face as his eyes landed on her. Within a matter of seconds, Abel's face shifted emotions too many times for Rory to keep up. She didn't, however, miss the fury.

A rather intimidating looking guard walked Abel to their table with a firm hand around his shaking arm. In fact, his whole body was shaking, from anger or malnourishment she couldn't tell. Rory sat on her hands to stop them from reaching over to grab his as he was cuffed to the table, the guard telling him to behave before returning to the gate. She wanted to hold his hands; she wanted to brush the hair from his face. She wanted to patch up his bruised knuckles and his split lips.

Abel ignored her pity filled eyes and directed rage to his brother, "What the hell is she doing here?" His voice was low, so no one on the surrounding tables could hear them.

Her own eyes narrowed and pity was washed out by blinding rage.

"Me?" she whispered aggressively. "What am *I* doing here?" she repeated. And when Abel didn't look at her, the rage increased.

Emmitt ignored her too. "Rory can help; she's reviewed the case."

"She's a law school drop-out working part-time at an ex-brothel."

Even though Rory knew the insult was just to drive her away—it didn't stop Abel's words from stinging. He had said it loud enough for the tables surrounding them to hear and she cringed at the disgusting smirk a large inmate gave her. The chains that held Abel to the table clinked under his grasp as he strained to contain his anger—catching the prisoner's perverted stares.

She shook the unconformable feeling from her body and said, "One: please stop talking like I'm not sitting right here. Two: I work full time now and Three: you are in no position to demand any explanation for why I am here, Abel Sawyer." Her sharp tone forced Abel to meet her eyes. Abel's lips pouted like a child getting in trouble; his eyes looked smaller and lifeless without the black smudge eyeliner she was so used to seeing him wear.

"What the hell have you gotten yourself into, Abel?"

His face hardened, "You read the case, right?"

Abel put up a front, playful, cocky, played everything off as a joke and brushed all serious things away with a sarcastic remark. Rory was the first person in a long time to see through the barrier and the first person in an even longer time to be granted access behind it. A lot of late-night park walks, midnight chats on the fire escape and early morning coffee. And now she was watching him build it back up, brick by brick.

"Don't bullshit me, Abe," she said sternly. "I know you didn't," Rory hesitated, "—Do that."

Abel's dull sapphire eyes dropped to his hands that were fidgeting with the metal loop the chains were thread through.

"Why didn't you come to us, Abe. Come to me?" her voice was less harsh as she pleaded for answers.

"I didn't want you involved." His head was low and she lowered her head to try to see his face, but his hair curtained his face, hiding behind the ruined curls.

“Don’t want you involved,” he corrected. The chains on his wrists were long enough for him to reach his hand up and drag his hair back from his face. “Take Rory home,” he ordered Emmitt, who was looking rather awkward.

“Talk to us, Abel,” Emmitt pleaded with his brother. “Please, just,” he let out a long breath, “talk to us.”

Abel sighed and shifted in his seat, “This is above you,” his eyes flicked between the two people who he cared for the most, his brother and his Rory. The hurt evident in both their eyes and he hated himself for causing it. “Take her home, Emmitt. Now,” he said firmly.

Rory placed her hands on the table palms down and very slowly inched them towards Abel’s bruised and scarred ones. She was aware of the guard looking over at the movement, but it didn’t stop her from sliding her little finger against his. Abel looped his finger around hers, savouring the little contact the guards were allowing them (another benefit of being a Sawyer—paying off guards to look the other way from time to time).

He thought back to all the times at *Ethel’s* where she’d pass him a drink and his hand would touch hers. All the times they found their hands slipping into a hold on their park walks and all the time her hand grasped tightly in his as he struggled to pull her through his window whenever his front door wouldn’t open and he needed her to fix it. He craved those touches, her hands. But as long as she was safe, he’d go a thousand years without touching them again.

“It’s not too late. You spend plenty nights at mine watching movies,” she started, prepared to swear in front of God, a judge and jury and lie her ass off.

“Rory,” he groaned, but she continued.

“And we walk Caspian most nights—”

“Rory,” he pleaded again, he wasn’t going to let her do this. He’d known first-hand what prison could do to a person. Abel thought of himself as a tough guy, strong-willed, but his time so far locked up had tested him in ways he never wished upon his greatest enemies.

The lack of sleep from paranoia—waiting for an attack, flinching at every noise—was enough to break a person. The only way Abel was still alive was because he got landed in soldiery confinement for almost half of his sentence.

He couldn’t begin to think about the effects prison would have on her, on his friends. The thought alone was enough to break him. So, he couldn’t put them at risk, from a false alibi or from the dangers outside the gates.

“I’d tell them you’re lying,” he told her and watched as she struggled to keep her frustration in.

It wasn’t just frustration she was trying to contain; it was the tears threatening to spill. She removed her hands from the table and Abel missed the warmth instantly and she ran them up and down her face. She dug her palms into her eyes.

“Jesus Christ,” she mumbled. The three sat in silence for a few moments, all of them too scared to say anything in case their emotions overloaded.

And when Abel slouched in his chair, exposing the left side of his neck and shoulder. Rory’s leash on her emotions nearly snapped completely.

“Tell me this is a joke,” she hissed out through her teeth. Too scared that if her mouth opened any wider, burning rage would come shooting out like fire.

“Please, Abe. Tell me you didn’t get involved with—” Rory took in a sharp breath through her nose, “Them.”

Abel panicked, “How did you know?” He quickly scanned the room, making sure no one was paying attention to them and lowered his voice.

“I’m not stupid Abel, everyone in Chicago knows that mark.” Rory was seething. He had the nerve to question her when he was the one branded. It had scared already and Rory had wondered how she had hadn’t noticed it before now.

“Did Link do it?” she whispered out. Not entirely sure she wanted to know the answer or what she would do if she found out. “Does Will know? Is that why he asked if they had anything to do with—this?”

“Stay away from Link, Rory; you hear me?” Abel’s voice turned dangerous, nothing like she had heard before. It was a new tone that she didn’t like. This wasn’t Abel—They didn’t tell each other what to do; he never ordered her around. Commanding. Threatening. “Aurora?”

She narrowed her eyes and shot him a dangerous look, “If you won’t tell me anything.” Trouble sparked her sleep-deprived eyes as she rested her elbows on the cold table, “Maybe Link will.”

Abel’s nostrils flared and Rory knew she had crossed a line. She wished she could hop back over it, take the threat back. Abel didn’t miss the regret wash over her, but it didn’t stop him from scalding her like she had to him minutes ago.

“Aurora, this is not the time for your rebel antics; you can’t get involved, they’re dangerous and they won’t tolerate your smart-ass remarks and harmless threats.”

Rory huffed and mumbled, "Harmless threats."

Abel almost missed it. "Hmm?"

Rory looked between the two brothers. Emmitt sat back in his chair, hand covering his forehead, rubbing soothing circles to ease his headache growing due to the bickering. And Abel had his elbows on the table, entwined fingers resting on his chin, waiting for her to speak.

Sighing, Rory explained to Abel, "There was a fight at *Ethel's*," his hands dropped from his chin and she sensed the lecture coming, so she rushed out, "Will was defending Chrissy's honour or something and you know what Nia is like and they wouldn't listen to Nicky."

"Who the fuck is Chrissy?" Abel exclaimed.

It wasn't the bar's finest moments. And Rory instantly regretted the whole night once she had slept the alcohol off.

Rory didn't know why the fight had gone on for so long, why one of the 'Gods Among Kings' didn't end them. Link had stood there—he didn't engage it, nor did he stop it. Maybe that was why she and her friends were still alive—Link was their leader, that was clear. Perhaps they wouldn't kill them until Link wanted them to.

Emmitt gave into Rory's eyes, begging for back up and said, "She did do some nasty work to that Link's face."

Rory closed her eyes and prayed to the Gods and Goddess and whoever in between to take her away before Abel put her in an early grave himself.

"Don't tell me you punched him," Abel all but begged, but he knew the answer just by looking at her left hand. Fading bruises coloured her knuckles.

She didn't dare look at him. He groaned and mumbled something she didn't catch but felt the need to defend herself. "He twisted my arm, literally!"

Her long-sleeve shirt covered faint handprint bruises from Link restraining her.

Abel's eyes shifted from fed up with what Rory could only describe as possessive rage, "He touched you? Did he hurt you?"

"Oh," Rory spoke, her turn to rest a hand on her chin, "you get to demand answers from me, but you won't tell us anything?" The line was long gone now. That faint blur all the way back there, yep, she's never getting back over it.

He sat back in his chair, his hands resting on the edge of the table. If he wasn't chained to the metal, his arms would be crossed. He just shrugged his shoulders, giving Rory nothing but a smirk that screamed, *Ask all you want, but I'm not saying anything.*

Rory clenched her jaw in frustration. "That's how it's going to be?"

She didn't like this one bit. Abel and Rory enjoyed the usual back and forth bickering and quips, but the visit had left her exhausted and unsettled. She was struggling to keep the tears in and Abel shrugged again. With a broken voice, she quietly agonised out, "What happened to you?"

His blue eyes flickered with remorse for the pain he was causing her and grief for the boy he once was and wished back with every second he stared into her green eyes.

"Go home, Aurora," he turned to the warden and flicked his head to the table. The guard stalked forward, slinging his keys in his hand. "And stay away from them."

Rory wanted to reach out and grab his hands as he was pulled away from the table. Abel nodded his head to his brother, who copied the action. Emmitt stood up, walked behind Rory's chair and placed a soft hand on her shoulder to pull her away, but she shrugged him off, waiting for Abel to turn around.

He didn't.

Rory pushed her chair back, Emmitt just moving in time to dodge it as it flew back and she stormed towards the exit.

She sat in Emmitt's car while Emmitt drove away from the prison. Only when it was out of sight, she let the tears fall silently.

Chapter Sixteen
You Want to Talk About It, Sweetie?

Strangely, tonight was quiet at 'All American'.

Charlotte sat on one of the high stools on the customer side of the counter. Everything to be done to close the café had been completed an hour ago. Her blue eyes shifting from the magazine to the clock, counting down the minutes until she could get out of there.

She was due at her parent's house for a late dinner in one hour. Her siblings and herself would all meet at their parent's home for dinner to go over how their respective cafes were doing in sales and profit. They would go through reviews and come up with solutions to solve whatever was going wrong. Which was rarely ever.

As soon as the clock struck 8 PM, the lights were off and the door was locked. Charlotte lived in a bohemian apartment filled with plants and amateur artwork that was a twenty-minute drive from 'All American' and a half-hour drive from her parent's home.

With only an hour to change out of her pinafore into a pencil dress that her mother would approve of, Charlotte headed next door. Besides, she needed to speak to the bar staff. As always, the bar was full of underage hormonal college students, unfaithful spouses and rocker disappointments.

She pushed her way through the crowd, hugging her bag close to her chest. She walked into a girl with short hot pink hair; Charlotte couldn't take her eyes from the girl's face: lip, nose and eyebrow pierced and stunning grey eyes that seemed to sparkle with the glittery smoky eye makeup. She placed a hand on Charlotte's forearm and apologised with a bright smile. Charlotte blushed and waved the accident off, but the words didn't come out in the correct order and she fled the scene.

Ethel's changing room was the largest room on the first floor. Busted up lockers split the room down the middle. Charlotte turned left and stopped at the fourth locker that had 'Lousy' written on a piece of tape.

Once dressed in a baby pink business pencil dress that stopped just before the knee, Charlotte threw on the nude heels and reviewed herself in the mirror. Her blonde hair was out of its high pony and fell pin straight down her back. She had retouched her mascara and her lips were painted a nude pink. Happy with her appearance, she closed her locker and heading down back to the bar.

Will and Nicky were behind the bar, no queues to serve, but the bar was still flooded with customers. Charlotte made her way through the crowd to the bar, trying to ignore the stares and whistling from men. Despite the sticky and uneven floor, she walked with ease in her heels—years of practice paying off.

Nicky had a glass of white wine ready for Charlotte on the bar top and she drank the whole glass in one before she had even sat on the stool.

The boys shared an amused look and Nicky said, "You want to talk about it, sweetie?"

"Another please," she asked and used a napkin to clean her smudged lipstick. While Nicky got her a refill, she said, "Family dinner night."

Will and Nicky said, "Ah."

The family dinner wasn't what made Charlotte down the second glass of wine like she had with the first. It was what had to come after the dinner. Both her older brothers were married and her mother was under the impression that at 24 years old—Charlotte should be looking for a partner to settle down with. So, to keep her mother off her back, she would use dating apps to find suitable men to take to family gatherings.

She would date a guy for a few weeks, attend a dinner or party to show her new man off to her parents and then call them the morning after to tell them it wasn't working out. No matter how polite they were to her parents or how much her parents approved of them. Charlotte always found something to justify breaking up. One would interrupt her whenever she was talking. One would smack his lips every time he drank. The last guy didn't put the shopping cart back in the cart bay.

Tonight's victim, she hadn't found anything yet. He was the perfect gentleman and she could hear her mother's approval already. But she'd find something by tomorrow. He was due to arrive anytime now so they could head to her parents together. But first, she had to tell the guys what she had wanted to say to them all day.

"Third?" Nicky laughed, pointing to her empty glass. "Or do you just want the bottle?"

"I better not," she shook her head. "But I've got to tell you guys something. Is Rory back?"

Will sighed, his eyebrows frowned. "Rory said she'd try to get in, but I doubt she'd be up for it."

"Understandable," Rory told Charlotte about going to visit Abel Sawyer in prison with his brother, she begged Charlotte to come for support, but they both knew it was best if Rory and Emmitt went alone. Charlotte had worried about her friend all day. Rory was strong with a fragile heart. Everyone had limits. Seeing Abel behind bars could be Rory's.

"Anyway," Charlotte shook the shivers away. "Some guy came into 'All American' around lunchtime; he was asking a lot of questions about Abel and all you."

Will, who was leaning with his arms folded on the bar top, stood up straight. "What type of questions?"

"He asked opening times, which was weird because I've seen him in here before. He asked if the staff—you guys—were friendly. Someone had told him he could get legal advice from one of you. He asked how you guys deal with police because he had also heard about Davis—" she lowered her voice and leaned in despite Nicky's playlist pounded through the Bluetooth speakers, "—Hiring underage staff."

"Then it got weird; he mentioned an old college friend coming here often."

"How's that weird?" Nicky asked. "Plenty college students come here." He motioned to the crowd of college students dancing and rubbing up against each other and Charlotte cringed.

"Because his friend was called Abel Patrick Sawyer. Said he hasn't seen him in a while and asked if anyone had heard from him. And considering recent news, someone asking for Abel is suspicious."

"Abel's middle name is Patrick?" Nicky scrunched his nose up.

That earned a slap across the back of the head by Will. "Missing the point, Bro!" he scolded; he turned to Charlotte, who looked like she needed that third glass of wine. "You said you've seen the guy here? What did he look like?"

" Korean, dark hair, short and spikey—" Her hands motioned the spikes on her head. "—Brown eyes, tattoos: a dragon up his arm—A crown."

Will ran his hands over his face. "That's all he asked? Doesn't sound like he was being subtle, which means they want us to know they're asking questions."

Charlotte nodded, "If he had anything to do with Abel being set up, then it means Abel was involved with them—Does Rory know?"

"Let's hope not." Charlotte jumped in her seat and turned to find Nia standing behind her.

Nia wore one of Nicky's colour block stripe button-ups with black jeans rolled up at the bottom of her short legs. Charlotte couldn't see Nia's freckles in the dark bar, but she could picture them.

"Charlotte, you look—" Nia started.

"Beautiful," a fruity voice came from their right and cut off Nia. A man, mid 20s stood to the side. His mousse brown hair sat perfectly away from his forehead. His eyes looked deep brown and adoration full for the blonde angel in front of him. Nia didn't blame him, as she often wore the same expression.

The man took a few steps forward, cutting in between Nia and Charlotte. Nia stepped around them and said in a flat tone, "I was going to say uncomfortable."

Charlotte's back was pin straight even though the stool had no back. '*Probably to stop her dress from creasing,'* Nia thought. Her long legs were folded and one heel rested on the footrest on the stool. The other foot was bouncing. A habit Nia had noticed Charlotte doing multiple times in certain situations. When her father had visited the café to assess Charlotte's work. When her two brothers came to *Ethel's* for some drinks and met Nia and the bartenders.

The man picked Charlotte's hand up to his lips and kissed the back. Charlotte gave him a closed-lip smile, the kind you give when you receive a present you don't like but don't want to hurt their feelings.

Nia rolled her eyes at the gesture and mimicked it to Nicky, who gave her a stern look.

Charlotte faced the others, Nia now behind the bar. "This is Gavin. Gavin, this is Will, Nia—" Charlotte's head tilted, "—You aren't in uniform."

'Nia never came in on her night off, but she was behind the bar in her regular clothes, smart clothes,' Charlotte thought. Smart enough to wear on a date.

"I'm just picking a book up I left here yesterday." She disappeared under the bar but popped up within a few seconds, holding a thick textbook, "Studying."

"On a Friday?" Charlotte quizzed.

"You sound so shocked, Char," Nia laughed.

"Study date?" Will asked; he was pouring Coronal a Guinness.

"Oh yeah, the chick with the lip ring," she told him with a cheeky smile and he sent her an impressive nod.

"I'm Nicky," Nicky introduced himself to her forgotten date.

Charlotte carried on forgetting about Mr Perfect. "Do you have an exam coming up?"

"Next Tuesday, on a chosen novel."

"What novel did you chose?"

"*To Kill a Mockingbird, Harper Lee*," Nia told her.

"*There's too much risk in loving,*" Charlotte quoted.

"*No, There's too much risk in not.*"

Charlotte swallowed, not breaking the intensity between them—a force drawing Charlotte in. One thousand things filled Charlotte's head, moments and conversations and unimportant things that didn't matter. The urge to tell Nia them all was almost too consuming. Because Nia would listen, Nia would always listen to Charlotte's rambling and Nia would somehow make them feel important. Charlotte's pink lips pulled into a growing smile, but her date snapped her back to the bar.

"You ready to go, babe?" Gavin asked her; he swung an arm around her shoulder and she cringed at the nickname. She tore her eyes from Nia and the tight smile returned. Nia's eyes stayed on Charlotte, however.

Charlotte stood up and smoothed her dress down, her clutch bag hung over her shoulder and she waved goodbye.

Chapter Seventeen
They Never Left

Four black hoods took shelter from the vicious rain pelting down on Chicago Port between shipment containers. The wall of red, green and orange metal boxes shielding them just enough that they could communicate without shouting over the monstrous wind and clanking of metal containers banging off each other.

All four as miserable as the Fall weather. They cursed their boss for sending them on a job that was so amateur. Shipment security was one of the first jobs that a member was set, the basic mission that didn't take much skill. It was used to test loyalty. The four hadn't done a shipment security shift in almost four years. No one wanted to state the obvious reason why they were spending their Friday night doing a rookie job.

Lenzo didn't react how they all thought he would when four of his best men turned up covered in bruises, bandages and blood. The rest voted Ash to tell their boss what had gone down, seeing as he was the one who provoked the bartenders into the fight. There was a long pause, Lenzo stalking down the line. While he took in all the black eyes, crooked noses, bandaged arms. All held their breath waiting for punishment for stepping out of line and getting involved in a brawl.

But Lenzo just laughed. Loudly. Obnoxiously. "Who did that?" he had asked, pointing to Hino's bandaged arms and Lenzo roared out a laugh when he informed him a bar girl had done the damage. He had kept them for almost half an hour, laughing and taunting them—bartenders, untrained and drunk, wiping the floor with his best boys.

He held Link back after dismissing the boys, "She's not a problem?" All amusement and mockery had vanished, "You've never disobeyed an order, Lincoln. Don't start it now."

So, there they were, stood in the freezing cold rain, overseeing a trade. Link had ordered Hino and Ash to do sweeps of the docks for any sign of trouble.

Hino kept complaining about the rain soaking into his trousers and he couldn't keep still for longer than five minutes, shuffling and moving around to keep warm. And as for Ash, Link could still feel his rage boiling after his actions at the bar.

Marius leaned against the orange container, watching his friend with careful eyes from under his hood. The bruise under his right eye was a dark yellow and matched the one on his jaw. He hated Will with every bone in his body, but he had to admit, the boy had a mean punch. Marius remembered back to the night of the fight, the crew had prepared for some kind of resistance, the way *Ethel's* employees had stared them down with hateful looks and the poor customer service skills let them know that they weren't welcome in the bar. But he wasn't expecting a full brawl. He learned 3 things that night:

1. The bar team can—and will—hold their own
2. Abel Sawyer had a brother.
3. And something was up with Lincoln.

A difference in his brother's mood had been noticeable since that night five months ago. Marius could still picture Link's face when he came crashing into the store front, his eyes frantically searching the room, trying to piece together what had gone down within the three minutes he had left the room. The only time he had seen his friend look scared.

Not scared, terrified. Horror washed over Lincoln. It stayed for a moment and then his features hardened, his eyebrows drew together and his lips were tight as he gave orders to the other three. Commanding them with such authority, he dared them to challenge him. None of them did. The Link that walked into the store that awful night, hadn't walked out.

Darker bags dulled Link's down-turned eyes, now more grey than blue. Link's lack of rest made him more irritable, his patience was wearing thin and he snapped out at everything. Poor Hino didn't know how to react when Link growled at him to stand still.

"I think you're taking 'watch my back' a bit too literally," Link mused with a slightly raised voice so Marius could hear him over the rain.

Lifting his head to see through his hood, Marius took in Link's postures; his tone was light, but his shoulders were tensed and squared back, his fingers were drumming on his legs.

"Maybe I should."

"If you've got something to say, Marius. " Link turned around, but the dark hood of his coat hid his face, "Say it."

He straightened up from the container; Marius swore the metal ridges were now tattooed into his back, "Are you OK?" Before Link could give his routine, "I'm fine, " Marius pointed his finger at him, "no bullshit either."

No answer came from Link. Marius clicked his tongue. "If you won't answer that," he started; he walked close to Link, rain sinking into his trainers from the flooded ground, "then tell me what order you disobeyed."

Eyes widened slightly. "I've got no idea what you're talking about." Link wiped the shock from his face. Marius was last out of Lenzo's office before Link and hid behind the door—listening in.

He raised a single eyebrow at Link, almost to say, *Don't bother lying*. Link looked over his shoulder to make sure they were alone before he said as quietly as he could without the rain drowning it out.

"Lenzo gave the order to put the employees down if they get in the way." He should have told them—it was an order, for crying out loud, but they were innocent and didn't know what they were getting in the way of. And for a few members of the group, that didn't matter.

"That's the order?" Marius asked, confused and underwhelmed by the simple order his friend had withheld. And a tiny part of him was disappointed; if he knew that they had permission to get rid of them, there would have been a Will sized grave in the ground. He said as much to Link.

"We don't murder innocents," Link exclaimed, his voice raised. "Not again." The words were heavy as they left his mouth.

"William isn't innocent," Marius said. "Or have you forgotten about Sawyer? They all know him and you heard what Will said, whether Sawyer told William about what he saw or not, he knows something and we can't trust him to keep his mouth shut."

"Just William. The others had no idea. You saw their reaction."

"If they didn't then, they sure as hell know now. This is what we do. We eliminate threats and if they know about Sawyer that makes them a threat. You saw how the girls reacted to the news—we don't know how stupid they'll be—"

"No one touches the girls," Link's voice was dangerous.

He made to turn but went still when Marius said, "You mean no one touches the girl."

He forced all expressions from his face again as Marius carried on, "That is where you disappeared off to that night, right?" Marius questioned, but he already knew the answer. "Followed her out the back? What did you do, Lincoln? Did you warn the girl, threaten her?"

Marius 's intention wasn't to mock or tease; it was to make him angry enough to get the truth out of him. The girl saw what they had done to Davis. She had stared them down as Marius, Hino and Ash left the bar—not waiting for them to go before she had scurried up to see Davis. The dread, fear, accusations in her eyes.

"Or maybe it was a different kind of chat," Marius suggested.

Anger control was something Lincoln had struggled with in his teens, but Lenzo taught him how to contain and control the anger and taught Link multiple ways to keep his head calm and temper tethered. None of which were working right now.

Marius was treading on fragile ice and he knew it, but it was the only way he was going to get Link to talk. Usually, Marius knew Link's limits, but recently, the limits were unknown.

"You got close enough to her to be covered in her blood though." When Link returned to the booth, his white shirt had spots of red on the sleeve. "Did she give you any information?"

"She doesn't know anything." He balled his fists up so tight his knuckles turned white, "And nothing happened."

"Maybe we should let Ash talk to her; see if he—"

Rain and rage blurred Link's vision as he lunged for Marius. Marius knew he had gone too far when his back hit the metal container behind him. He shifted to the left just in time to dodge the fist hauling towards his face. Link's fist hit the metal with a sickening crack.

Marius spun behind Link and pushed him up against the container, one hand holding his unharmed hand behind his back and the other across the top of his back, keeping his face flushed against the cool metal.

"Calm down," his voice was stern while the rain and Link's struggling made it hard to keep his grasp. Marius kept repeating the words over and over.

After a few more attempts to get out of the hold and failing, Link gave up. Marius slowly let go when he could no longer feel Link fighting him and Link pushed off the container, his split knuckles throbbing, but he made no move to attack. His chest was rising and falling rapidly; he closed his eyes, taking in deep breaths, letting the sea air soothe his temper.

"I don't know what's happening, man," Link said still with his eyes closed. The voice was broken. Lying to Lenzo, the soft spot for the bartenders, the nightmares. All of it getting too much. Slowly chipping away the wall that protected his sanity. "She won't be a repeat of that night. She can't—I can't—"

"The nightmares are back again, aren't they?" Marius questioned; his voice softer.

"They never left," Link whispered it so quietly Marius missed it.

"You have to stop blaming yourself, Link," he sighed. "You couldn't have stopped it; none of us could."

Link finally opened his eyes and looked at his friend, Marius's face held no pity, which Link was thankful for; he was their leader and he didn't want to appear weak to them, but he was also their brother; they were sworn to protect each other, from guns and nightmares. Before they could carry on, Hino and Ash came around the corner.

"They're here," Ash told them; he noticed the tension between Marius and Link.

Links fists were balled up, but the weather made it impossible to see the damaged knuckles still causing blinding pain. "What's going on?" he asked.

The pair gave each other a look, silently agreeing not to say anything.

"Nothing," Marius lied easily. "Don't want to keep them waiting, do we."

Wooden crates slid off the ramp onto the wet concrete, splashing dirty rainwater up the sides, staining the light wood dark. There were four crates, all stamped fragile and stood waist height to the boys.

A Cockney British accent that Link had grown to hate over his time in the gang shouted at the men who were carelessly handling the crates, "Can you lot read over 'ere!" the voice went through Link and he didn't hide his groan when the dark-haired man came into their view.

"Ha!" the man shouted as he reached the top of the ramp and saw who was there to greet him, "Wot 'ave you done to piss off Lenzo to be put on shipment security?"

His obnoxious laugh had the boys seething and Link blocked it out by imagining his pinched face as a dart board.

"You know Boss—" Hino shouted across the crates, "—always up for charity work." The boys sniggered and got a deadpan glare from the man.

His dark hair stuck flat on his forehead, making it look even more oily than it was. The sour expression remained on his thin face as he failed to light his cigarette, the rain preventing the lighter from sparking. He tossed the soaked cigarette on the ground with a grumble and gave Hino a once over; not finding his comment worth his time, he turned to Link. Link's lips were pulled up in a light smirk—not because of the comment his friend had made but because he just got a bullseye.

He stomped off the ramp, the wood groaning under his boots. "Let's get this ova with," he said as he reached the bottom and hugged his small jacket around himself, poorly shielding him from the rain.

Link gave him a fake sad smile and turned to Hino, "Com'on Hino, that's not fair," he placed a hand on Hino's shoulder, rain from Hino's coat soaked his hand, "you know Boss only helps charities that have a chance of making a difference."

"Ah!" the man sighed, not taking offensive to the insults; he smirked, "you were always my favourite, Link."

The smirk dropped when Link replied with, "Yeah? I'm your sister's favourite too."

Ash grumbled behind them, clearly not impressed with the back and forth. His legs were sore from scouting the area, his socks were soaking and the winter coat he was wearing, wasn't suitable for the winter.

"We haven't got all night, Tommy."

Tommy, also done with the back and forth, tore his eyes from Link to Ash.

"Right," he said and stuck his hand out. One of his men, who the four 'Gods Among Kings' members noted was considerably taller than everyone else on the port, handed him a metal crowbar.

The large man stepped up to the crate in front of Link and used the crowbar to crack open the lid. The wooden top dropped to the ground with a thundering bang. Link stepped up to the crate and peered into the container.

"Like promised," Tommy confirmed.

The crate contained everything, from standard handguns, sharp throwing knives, gold knuckle dusters.

Tommy Ascot had been Lenzo's weapons supplier just as long as Link had been in the gang. Link was present at their first meeting; in the same spot they now were stood. The pair of hotheads clashed from the moment they met. Lenzo thought that with the two being similar ages and both new to the business, they'd relate and the deal would run smoothly. Tommy insisted that Link was a charity case in way over his head and Link thought that Tommy was an obnoxious bastard.

"They're all full," Tommy motioned to the other three crates and then tucked both hands under his armpits for warmth.

"You know the drill, Ascot," Marius spoke.

Tommy sighed and gave the order. Three of his men, each with their own crowbar, opened the remainder boxes and the crates were filled with similar weapons. But one. Ash went forward to inspect the black briefcase that lay on top of a rather exciting and large gun. He threw Tommy a confused look and pointed to the object, "What's this?"

Lenzo didn't mention anything about a briefcase. It was thick and it was just plain leather. Nothing stood out about the case, just its presence amongst the guns.

"Ya Boss asked for it to be sent over," Tommy said. "Thought it would be safer to ship it over with this. It was supposed to be shipped months ago—but seeing as you lot messed up." He let out a laugh, "'Av been dying to know—which one of yuh did it? Who killed the poor sod?"

Their faces dropped. Whatever was in that briefcase was the reason, they were sent to that store. Lenzo had a nerve questioning Link's loyalty; when he had told Tommy what was in the case—Lenzo told Tommy why they set Abel Sawyer up. Even they didn't know why they set Abel Sawyer up.

No questions asked was a norm for the boys—no prior information on who they were setting up was not. They had assumed it was a money issue—it was why Link had branded him before they got the order to frame him. After the night went south, Link had burst into Lenzo's office—covered in blood and face brewing storms.

Bodies of security guards lay on the floor with broken noses from trying to prevent Link from entering a meeting between his Boss and some lesser gangs—demanding answers. And as if Link hadn't dragged blood onto his freshly cleaned carpet and interrupted his meeting—Lenzo had told Link he had failed and the job wasn't theirs anymore.

His rage rose for the second time that night and he clenched his fists, his knuckles stung, still bleeding. Marius sensed the anger radiating off his friend and knew that he had to step in before Link put them down. He cast a glance at

Link, his hands so close to the gun strapped at his hip. Knowing Link wouldn't need much of a reason to end Tommy where he stood.

"The rain is going to ruin the goods. You got our payment?" Marius asked Tommy.

Tommy turned to one of his men; they took their phone out of their pocket and, after a few moments, gave Tommy a thumbs up.

He clapped his hands together and said cheerily, "As always, 'av' hated it." A few men in high vis jackets stepped up to the crates and hauled the lids back on. "Till next time. Try not to kill anyone."

Chapter Eighteen
Baby Tooth

If there was one thing Erik Lenzo hated, it was begging. Begging for mercy was wasteful. He didn't care that they had a family to feed. He didn't care if they swore they'll have the money with a little more time. Mercy wasn't in his vocabulary.

Since birth, Erik was set to take over 'Gods Among Kings' once his father retired or died. Being the latter, Erik took his place on the throne and set the record of the youngest leader to be appointed. 19 years old Erik had everything. A throne fit for a God. Fared by everyone so much, no one dared to touch him—power over his city. 'Gods Among Kings' had thrived under his reign. A hand in every single gang, major or minor. Trading favours for profit.

All that power and control could get boring after 37 years. Lenzo hadn't been out on a job in a long while. Age wasn't enough to slow a man like Lenzo down. Every now and then, he would get his men to report any issues or disputes and pick the one that sounded the most fun and take it on himself.

A lower gang that Lenzo had never heard of had betrayed them in a panic. A few of their men were picked up by the police a week back; saving their own skins, they made a deal. Information for less jail time. They had reported everything they knew—which wasn't much—to the two officers interrogating them. Unlucky for them, the officers were on Lenzo's payroll and had sent Lenzo the interrogation transcripts.

White sleeves were rolled up to his elbows. Bloodstained hands and busted knuckles effortlessly pulled the tie off his neck and it was folded neatly on the tray of sharp objects. Hands danced along the weapons, a large butcher's knife, knuckle dusters that were stained, pliers.

"I don't consider myself to be indecisive," Lenzo started; his voice was casual like he was deciding what sandwich to choose for lunch. "I'm just spoiled for choice." He tapped his chin with his index finger and turned to his left.

No windows let light in; 2 out of the 4 industrial lights in the basement in one of the gang's many warehouses cast a deep yellow glow, putting tonight's unfortunate subject under a haunting spotlight. Red liquid dripped onto the floor, covering the old stains of bodily fluids. The young man, barely 23, wept pathetically but had stopped struggling after the third time gaining conscientiousness.

Tears were lost in his swollen face, not that it mattered; he had learned the hard way that Lenzo didn't care much for mercy seekers. Nor did he care that he wasn't one of the men who ratted him out.

"Have you had your wisdom teeth removed yet?" Lenzo inquired and tutted at the boy's whine. "I'm going to take that as a no."

He snatched up the pliers and examined them under the light; happy with his choice.

Lenzo advanced the boy slowly, taunting him to emphasise how helpless he really was. Bound to the chair with ropes so tight they cut through the skin. Even if he was able to free himself. The extent of the beatings rendered him almost immobile. His left knee was capped by a bullet. Every finger on his right hand was bent at an odd angle and his fingernails scattered the floor. Each time screaming: he didn't know where his boss was.

Lenzo tested the pliers out in his hand and looked at the victim he hadn't bothered to learn the name of. "This can all be over, my boy, all you have to do is give his location up."

"I don't know," the boy said on the exhale of his breath. The same answer he had been swearing for the past four hours.

Lenzo closed the distance; with one hand on the back of the matted hair, he yanked the boy's head backwards, so he faced the ceiling. Lenzo forced the pliers into the clenched mouth with difficultly but managed to grab onto a back tooth.

The boy struggled against Lenzo's firm twisting and tugging on a random tooth. He gagged and spat saliva mixed with blood out at the man, but Lenzo wouldn't give up. Agonising pain worse than the leg shattering and finger breaking shot through his mouth, gums and jaw. He thrashed relentlessly as he let out blood-curdling screams. Blood splattered across Lenzo's aged face and if the man wasn't ripping the teeth from his mouth, the boy would have told him the red brought out his eyes.

Iced eyes twinkled with relived youth and the most wicked smile exposed his own perfect teeth as he twisted and pulled one last time with a snap and crack. Lenzo examined the tooth like an archaeologist would with their exciting finds. Long roots attached to a small tooth was covered in blood and gum tissue.

Like winning an unexpected prize, Lenzo gasped and grinned ear to ear. "A baby tooth!"

The boy's head was still facing the ceiling, tipped back resting on the back of his neck. His mouth hung loose and blood poured down his chin while he moaned and mumbled out, *I don't know,* repeatedly through sobs.

The tooth hit the metal tray with a ping and Lenzo moved to remove another tooth but was interrupted by three loud bangs on the steel door.

Pliers still in hand, Lenzo made his way to the entrance, unlocking and pulled it open. Ash stood on the other side.

His blonde hair kinked due to the rain, winter coat discarded in his car, leaving him in a plain grey sweater. Lenzo took a step to the side and invited him in. Ash cast a passing glance at the broken boy who lay limp in the chair, but his hard face showed no sympathy or remorse.

"You ordered this to be brought straight to you?" Ash lifted the black case that he retrieved from the crates Tommy sent over.

Lenzo made room for the case on the metal tray and patted the spot to urge Ash to place it there. "Let us have a look then." When Ash flicked his eyes to the third person in the room, Lenzo waved him off, "Oh, you can kill him; he's no use."

A shot echoed off the concrete walls that left ringing in their ears for a few moments. The whimpering had stopped and the boy's lifeless body slumped in the chair, a pooling hole now in between his eyes.

Pocketing his gun at his hip, Ash stalked to the tray and flicked open the case. Inside lay metal templates. There were four sets. His boss removed them one by one and lay them flat on the table away from the bloody tray.

Lenzo held one up and examined it like he did with the tooth under the industrial lights. Blood still on his face as he marvelled at the metal. Ash looked at the ones on the table.

Two $50 and one $100 bill templates that would print flawless money.

"Why hide this from the guys?" Ash asked, confused.

Moments after Tommy had left and the boys departed to their own vehicles, Ash received a text from Lenzo, instructing him to bring the black case to this location and strict orders to not include the other three.

The first time he had ever hidden anything like this from his boys, Ash was fighting his instincts to shoot a message in the group chat to confess. He may be cold, shallow and a pain in the ass. But they were the only people on this shitty Earth that Ash could say he cared for. He would never forget all the times they had jumped in front of a gun for him or backed him up in a fight. Ash didn't show it. But deep, deep, deep down inside of him lay a tiny red beating heart.

"How pissed was Lincoln when he found out Ascot knew more than him?" Lenzo asked Ash.

"Worse than when Hino crashed his Jeep." Ash smiled faintly at the memory of Link gaping for words as Hino pulled up in Link's silver Jeep, hood caved in and lights shattered. Hino scrambling out of the wrecked Jeep to hide behind Ash while Link promised him a painfully slow death.

"That's why."

Ash spun around on his heel to face his boss. "I'm lying to my team for revenge?" Ash dared to question.

"You're lying to your team because I ordered you too," Lenzo stated with authority. "Lincoln may be the leader of your club." He approached the table and started to stack the templates back in the case, "But I'm the God of this fucking Empire."

"You're lucky the four of yours still have your heads after the stunts you've pulled the past few months. Fucking up with the Sawyer case, getting into bar fights. I'm starting to think I need to find a replacement." *A replacement for Link.*

Ash set his eyes on the wall behind Lenzo as he lectured him like a teacher would his students. Sympathy for Link settled in him as he wondered if this was what he felt whenever Link covered up for one of their mistakes.

"Link covers for us all," Ash vouched for him.

Ash was still bitter that Link was the leader of their group and not himself. But he knew that Link was the best person for it. Ash didn't believe he could do what Link had done for all of them, taking the heat—the punishments. Always on the receiving end of Lenzo's temper. Ash had seen how the job had plagued Lincoln and he wished that if it came down to it—he would take on some of the burdens to lessen Link's responsibility—he hoped he could step up.

"I'm aware of what Lincoln does." Lenzo dipped his hands into a bowl filled with water.

"Counterfeiting and Laundering," Lenzo tapped the case, "pays for all my fancy suits."

"Not that you deserve to know," Lenzo's voice was now calm and collected and Ash struggled to keep up with Lenzo's mood. "Five months ago, Kennedy's group were tasked to bring in some recruits."

'Kennedy was a rotten man,' Ash thought. He oversaw two guys who were just as dis-likeable. They weren't as high rank as Ash and the boys and Kennedy despised them for it. Ash hadn't heard from Kennedy or his group for a while now, almost five months.

Lenzo dried his now blood-free hands with a cloth and sat down on a wooden chair. Ash remained standing.

"They had strict orders to keep it under hush and not to attract anyone who would likely cause trouble. Simple enough task."

Ash was starting to figure out why no one had heard from Kennedy in a while.

"The Sawyer kid overheard Kennedy and his men talking at that dive bar you and your merry men love so much."

Ash couldn't remember seeing Kennedy at *Ethel's,* but he didn't doubt for a second that if one of the staff or regulars overheard recruitment conservations, they'd put a stop to it. William made a point that gang activity was banned there.

"Kennedy flagged down a few young men who had potential and Sawyer, drunkenly, followed them to the warehouse by the docks to put a stop to it. A group were meeting at the warehouse to discuss a deal to acquire them," Lenzo pointed to the case. "Sawyer must have overheard the plan to sell counterfeit cash to failing businesses."

Ash just nodded; he had wanted to know this information since the night they set Sawyer up and he wasn't going to risk not finding out the rest of the story by opening his mouth.

"He stirred up some trouble—ran his mouth with threats that weren't empty. Lincoln suggested branding rather than my alternative when I gave the first order, however that didn't shut him up, so I had your team set him up. I wasn't sure if he had said anything to William, but he got himself locked up anyways!"

Without thinking, Ash spoke, "But William is out now and Sawyer's brother is asking questions."

"Brother?"

Ash fought the urge to facepalm himself. The boys agreed to keep it quiet until they knew more themselves. Clearly, they weren't given much information because Lenzo hadn't carried any research out himself. The plates must have been good if they had Lenzo giving out orders without any background knowledge—Sawyers were a big deal, not only on the Southside but the whole city. A family ran Equity Firm that owned half of the companies in Chicago. Filled with high-class lawyers—respectful employees that Lenzo didn't control.

"You're sure they're related? Older or younger?" Lenzo pushed, sounding stunned. The first time Ash had seen Lenzo look unsure and not the person who knew the most in the room.

"Emmitt looks older—not by much. But they're related. He had no clue who we were and no one at the bar showed any signs of knowing we had anything to do with Sawyer either."

Lenzo was too distracted in his own thoughts to sense the lies that Ash effortlessly spewed.

"Keep an eye on him—them," Lenzo corrected. "Don't make any moves," he ordered.

Lenzo stared at his computer screen. The HQ building was empty at the early hours of 4 AM. Sat in the dark, curtains drawn to lock out the sleeping city—the only light came from the screen. Once Erik had heard a Sawyer was becoming a distraction—Lenzo only went as far as to search his date of birth. 4 years too young.

Lenzo read the first article he saw when he searched for Emmitt Sawyer's name. An article about the young and the rich.

Emmitt Julian Sawyer. Acquisition Manager. 25 years old.

Lenzo stared at the picture attached to the top of the page. A young man—Emmitt—chocolate brown hair styled back, not a hair out of place, crystal blue eyes, almost identical to Lenzo's own. He was smirking at the camera with one hand in his tailored suit and the other around a woman.

He enlarged the photo to get a clearer picture of the woman. Blonde hair pinned into an elegant side bun, deep blue eyes that sparkled at the camera. Full lips pulled into a proud smile on her slight lined doll face. Generous curves were beautifully complemented in a navy-blue envelope dress.

Lenzo took a sharp breath.

"Amelia."

Chapter Nineteen
Sleepless

Aurora James Scott couldn't sleep no matter how many times she tossed and turned—half a bottle of tequila in her system seemed to buzz. Everything reminded her of Abel. The bed she was sleeping in, where they shared a special night. The set of old oak drawers in the corner he helped her carry up the four flights of stairs. The doormat at the entrance of her bedroom that he stole from Ms Nealson one drunken night. Everything reminded her of Abel and she hated it. So, she changed Into her jeans, threw her boots and jacket on, grabbed Caspian's leader and headed out of the Abel tainted apartment.

Link paced around his dark room, unable to wind down from the meeting a few hours before. The unknown contents of the case haunting his every thought. The four exposed bricks walls seemed smaller than they usually were and the opened window let no air through. The brown wooden floorboards were worn down enough; if he kept with the constant back and forth, he'd end up in the apartment underneath. He grabbed his jacket off his bed and left the shrinking walls behind.

Chapter Twenty
Fire at Will

Too busy kicking stones and ranting to her dog about her worries (who was more focused on the stones skimming down the pavement) Rory didn't realise she had entered the old park she used to go to. Caspian must have missed it as Rory had to tighten her grip on the leader to stop the pup from running off into the raked Fall leaves.

Caspian turned left like second nature. The trees provided shelter from the bitter wind. Rory wished for sunshine so she could wittiness the flames of the Fall archway that would not too long turn into a skeleton arch in the cruel winter.

Most would find being in a deserted park at two in the morning, the only light source coming from a dull lamppost—which was long overdue a bulb change—at the end of the tunnel of trees, scary. But Rory took bliss in the silence (besides her boots crunching in the leaves and puddles and Caspian bouncing around). Her troubles and anger washed away with the wind that blew leaves and dust around her feet.

Some kind of flying insect flew past the beagle's face and Caspian started to chase it. Snapping into the dark air, had Rory in a fit of giggles. She snorted when Caspian got himself tangled around his leader and tripped up. Once she had composed herself, Rory got down on one knee, a dirt patch staining her light jeans. She had to dodge his tongue that was trying to lick her face as she de-tangled the leader. Rory scratched Caspian behind the ear while she praised him for being a good boy.

The pup's tail that was rapidly wagging went stiff and his ears perked up. His head snapped to the end of the trees. Rory looked over in the direction his low growls were aimed.

A dark silhouette stood at the base of the arch. Rory slowly reached to her back pocket for her phone. Just as slowly, she stood up on her feet and brought the shaking phone up, torch shinning in the dark. Her eyes strained to focus on the stranger looming ahead. But it wasn't a stranger. And the anger that the wind had washed away moments ago came flooding back.

Laughter. Laughter his ears were slightly familiar with disturbed his wallowing in self-pity. Two o'clock visits to the park weren't uncommon for Link. The lake at the end of the tree arches was his happy place. He would skim stones through the water, watching his troubles and anger ripple away with each bounce on the moon reflected surface. The usual drunk or junkie would pass by, but the subtle weapon fastened to his hip made them change their minds quick.

Genuine laughter was a change of intrusion. Link couldn't help but seek out the source of the sound. The pile of stones in his hand dropped and he followed the sound to the tree arches. All the vigorous training Lenzo subjected Link to seven years ago had helped him more times than he cared to count. The months of centring his balance and focusing his weight, practising in simulations where Lenzo set him up against some of his best members—*Toe then ball. Toe then ball.* A skill he was calling upon now as he sneaked up silently to the arches.

The lamppost let Link Identify Aurora before she could identify him. He watched as she slowly stood, using her torch to see. He expected her to turn and run. During the fight at the bar, he had slipped the warning note for Davis into her pocket, half intention to frighten her. Apparently, it didn't work.

Rory let her anger dominate her better judgement. Her phone and Caspian's lead dropped to the floor. Her fists clenched at her sides as she stormed her way to the end of the arches towards Link. Link stood still as she advanced in on him. It wasn't until Rory was out of the arches that he saw the determined hatred on her face. Rory charged at him with as much power as she could muster and slammed her hands on his chest, knocking him backwards.

She pushed him back with enough force he stumbled. "Was it you?" she demanded. "Was it fucking you?" she spat the words like venom from her tongue as she continued to shove him with all her strength. "Did you brand him?"

She threw herself at him; Link planted his heels into the ground to stop himself from losing his balance. Her pushes turned to unorganised punches at his chest when she realised, he wasn't budging.

"Answer me, dammit!" Rory screamed. But he stood still, taking her beaten until she tired herself.

Rory's chest was heaving as she dropped her sore hands from his chest. Link ignored the pain in his chest and stared at her with a pointed look. The only sign of her attack was his ruffled shirt under his jacket.

His eyebrows raised as if talking to a child, "You quite finished?"

Her left fist rose and collided with his cheek. Hard. Link's balance was knocked with the impact. All her anger concentrated on her fist. Link stumbled and braced himself on the sticky lamppost. Rory clutched her fist in her other hand and she swore at the shooting pain.

"Yeah, that's going to bruise," Link said breathlessly.

"Good," she spat back, massaging her fist.

"I was talking about your hand but thank you for the concern, Link straightened himself up but jumped back instantly as her dog began snapping at his feet. He looked helplessly at Rory and for a split second, the idea of setting her pup on him satisfied her rage."

"Casp, down." The dog complied but sent low growls at him. "Don't mock me, Link. Not tonight." Her voice was full of hate and something Link thought was pain. "Was it you?"

"You're going to have to be more specific, sweetheart. I've done a lot of things."

"You know exactly what I'm referring to. Did you brand him."

Link took a threatening step closer to her and tilted his head, "What if I was the one? The one who branded Abel Sawyer. What would you do, Hmm?"

He took another step towards her and Rory forced her body to stay put.

"What would you do if I told you that we followed Sawyer one night from *Ethel's*. Followed him escorting the ginger bartender home. Blue curtains? Four stories up?"

Rory's heart missed a beat. He knew where she lived. Her home, haven. The place away from gang activity and poor music and rude customers. She could hear her mother's voice in her head like it was her stalking around her in a circle. '*I told you the apartment was the wrong decision. I told you it wasn't safe to live here. Come back home, go back to school.*'

Link, now standing behind her, leaned down, his hot breath fanned over her ear. "Very chivalrous of him. Do you invite him up?" his plummy tone moved to her left ear as he implied, "give him a treat to say thank you?"

His accusation hit a nerve and she took a step away from him and spun around, "Mine and Abe's friendship is just that," she clarified. "And whatever happened has nothing to do with you."

Link smirked at the girl, "But you wanted something to happen?" It was written all over her face. In the photo at the bar, the passion that she fought for him with. A slight tremor in her voice at the word 'friendship'.

"But not that night, no." He took slow steps towards her and this time, her body gave into the urge and she backed away with each of his steps. "That night, he kissed you on the cheek, waited until you waved down from your window and then he went home. Three blocks up from you, apartment Three C. Lovely brown armchair."

Rory was with Abel when he got the chair. Brown leather already pealing when he bought it from a junk sale. Abel loved it, said the creases made it look vintage. Rory disagreed, but after spending nights curled up while watching a movie while Abel spread out on the matching brown sofa, she grew to love it.

"What would you do if I told you that Ash held him down on the chair while I took a red-hot poker to *Abe's* neck?"

Her back hit the lamppost and she sucked in a breath. Pain flashed her green eyes as he continued with the horror story.

"What would you do if I told you that Marius had to hold his legs down as he fought back. What would do, Aurora?"

Rory squeezed her eyes shut as if it could stop her from hearing the taunting. Caspian still sat on guard, low growls growing louder with Link's proximity.

"Did you enjoy it?" she seethed, the tequila still buzzing and taking over her nerves. "Did you like listening to the screams when you mauled an innocent? Like Davis?"

Her eyes slowly opened to find him gawking at her. The wind teased his hair and covered the tips of his eyelids, to taken aback by her lack of fear or stupidity.

"Davis isn't innocent," he said in a matter-of-fact tone.

"Abel Sawyer is."

Link laughed bitterly, "You'd be surprised, Sawyer got what he deserves."

Rory's voice was quiet, "No one deserves that."

Link nearly took a step back at how broken her voice sounded—like she had been crying for hours. Maybe she had. But he didn't know what to say, so he said, "Stay out of it, Aurora, you won't be warned again."

She rolled her eyes, tired of being told to stay out of things that were affecting her. She was losing her best friend in jail; her boss had a countdown on his life. She wanted—needed—someone—anyone—to tell her what was going on.

"Was it your idea?" She was grabbing at things now to insult him, to try to get answers out of him. Make him angry enough to slip up. "Or were you just following orders like a lap dog?" Rory took a stab in the dark.

She must have hit a nerve as Link brought his hands to grip the top of her arms. Link's nostrils flared and his chest started to rise and fall with anger and Rory hissed in pain as her back was pushed further into the metal post. Caspian growled louder than he had been and waited anxiously for Rory's signal to attack.

"I'd be cautious of what you say next, Aurora." Link's tone was calm and for a moment, Rory felt the fear creep up in her again. Just for a moment.

"When you and your buddies dragged through *Ethel's* for the first time, I thought, fine, you'll drink your beers and you'll be gone." Anger at its peak, Rory couldn't stop the words from coming out. "Then you showed up the next night and then the next and then the next. And the team agreed that we'd keep our mouths shut and serve you—"

"For someone keeping their mouth shut, you sure talk a lot."

Link's arms still held her against the post and she had to crane her neck up to meet his eyes. Rory ignored his interruption.

"No matter how bruised and bloodied up you were or how many guns were strapped at your waist. We'd serve you."

"The gun is still there." Again, she ignored his comment.

"When you guys asked for Davis, when you branded him, a floor above me, in his own office. I was pissed, but I kept quiet. Do you know how I've spent my day? Visiting Abel Sawyer in prison. And when I saw what you had done—"

"For almost two years, I've put up with you dragging gang crap into my bar. You've given Davis a deadline that he cannot meet and yes, maybe Davis isn't innocent and yes, maybe it's too late for us to help him. You saw a fraction of what *Ethel's* is capable of the other night. Be damned sure that if you go after Abel Sawyer again, you'll have the fight of your life."

Link knew that the bar team would put up a hell of a fight. They fearlessly loved Abel Sawyer and that kind of love was the most dangerous. Link also knew that 'Gods Among Kings' would come out on top. That was what worried him the most. They would only be doing what he would do for Marius, Hino and Ash. Protecting the ones they loved.

"You should be scared of us." That was the only thing he could bring himself to say.

Rory took one look at the gun at his hip and then back up to Link's face and said so calmly his iron grasp fell from her arms as if she had burned him:

"I'm a Law school dropout, living off shared tips and black coffee with student loans higher than my anxiety level. You've threatened the life of the guy who pays me and the life of the people I most care for in this word. We should fear you? We're not the ones with something to lose. Fire at will."

Chapter Twenty-One
An Example

Link, Hino, Ash and Marius sat outside Lenzo's office on metal chairs like schoolboys waiting to be seen by their principal after misbehaving. Which—technically—they had.

Hino sat on his hands, legs bouncing and flinching at every sound. Marius was slouched, his muscled built too big for the tiny chair. Ash sat up straight, head forward, no expression on his face. But his fingers twitched, hidden under his folded arms. He contacted the others as he left the warehouse the night before to give them a heads up that there was a high chance that they'd be pulled in by the boss in the morning. He also filled them in on his conversation with Lenzo.

Once the redhead had left him dumbfounded to his spot at the park last night, the last thing Link wanted was a phone call from one of his brothers informing him that their boss now knew they are keeping secrets. There was a high possibility that he'd end up with a bullet between his sleep troubled eyes by the end of the next hour.

Link berried his eyes in his palms, elbows resting on his knees and he swore if Hino didn't stop shaking his legs, he'd shoot himself and save Lenzo the trouble. Ash told them that Lenzo just knew about the second Sawyer and nothing about Abel's alibi and Link was in two minds of just coming clean about everything. To everyone.

Lenzo wasn't the only one Link was keeping secrets from. He hadn't told the boys about last night's confrontation with Rory.

Link spent the rest of the night—or early morning—going over what she had said. The speech laced with sureness . He had tried to scare her off but scaring her was a long-gone option. And now he knew that she had a law background.

The possibilities ran through his head. She may be Davis's lawyer informant, but if she had proof to get Abel Sawyer out, wouldn't she use it? She didn't know he was in prison until the fight—maybe she didn't know it was Abel's alibi? Questions and possibilities flooded his head too quickly to process logic. He really didn't want to kill this girl. Something told him she'd like it too much.

Her phone vibrated in his leather jacket; Charlotte had been ringing all morning and Link was regretting picking it up from the park ground.

"You going to get that?" Marius gruffed, hangover worsening by the second.

"No."

"Then turn it off," Marius demanded and Link pulled the mobile from his pocket, pressed ignore and watched as the caller ID switched to the lock screen, Marius glanced over and frowned. "When did you get a dog? And why haven't I met her?" he sounded genuinely hurt and Link rolled his eyes.

"Him," he corrected, "and I didn't."

Marius leaned in in a hashed tone, so the others didn't hear him, "Did you get any sleep?"

"Not a wink."

"He's ready to see you now," a bittersweet voice cut their conversation. All four boys turned their heads to see Elide, Lenzo's assistant, standing outside his door. Dark shiny hair always pulled into a high pony and she always matched her heels with whatever dress she was wearing. Elide hated the four of them. She disliked everyone—always acting like they had asked her to do the most impossible thing, no matter how small the question or task really was.

But she hated the four boys mostly. Link and Hino and Ash all thought the reason was Marius.

"You're looking beautiful today, Elide." Marius's hang-over vanished as he stood up, his rough voice now smooth. "Is that a new dress?"

"No." He made her way to her desk—hiding the small smile at Marius's compliment. Marius made to follow with a challenging smile, but Link grabbed the collar of his brown jacket and pulled him after them to Lenzo's office.

"She wants me," Marius swore.

"Obviously," Ash said without turning to face him. "The sight of her walking away speaks loudly of her love."

Lenzo leaned back in his chair behind his desk, hands together as if preying. He stared at the four boys in front of his desk. Trying to decide where to start—who to begin with.

Hino looked like a kicked puppy, eyes shifting all over the floor, trying to focus on one thing, but his nerves wouldn't allow him to. His bottom lip pouted slightly.

Towering over him a good few inches, Marius had lost his flirty smile and his hang-over was slowly creeping back up. Dark circles shadowed forest green eyes and his lips, usually full, were chapped and drawn into a line.

Link and Ash, two ends of the perfect soldier coin. Link hadn't bothered with his hair that morning and it kinked around the ears, desperate for a trim, deep blue eyes focused on the painting behind Lenzo. It was an abstract painting and Link couldn't make out any shapes or hidden meaning through the block colours—the only colour in the office.

Ash's blonde hair was in his signature perfect quiff. Lighter blue eyes focused on the same painting. He could spot the colourful birds hidden in spirals of red and blue and green and yellow and purple.

Lenzo took in one deep breath and drew his hands to rest on the arms. "Who would like to explain to me—" His voice was soft as if trying to get kids to confess, "—Why you four held information regarding Abel Sawyer's secret brother?" His finger went to his chin as he waited for one of them to speak.

Link took a single step forward, "I believed Emmitt wasn't a threat to the situation."

"Hmm," Lenzo narrowed his eyes at Link. He remembered the first time Link stood in front of his desk and took the blame for one of his men. He couldn't care for the reason now, but Lenzo knew he wasn't to blame but punished Link for it anyways. And Link carried on taking the heat for his team. Link's flaw, Lenzo had always thought since that day, his loyalty.

Lenzo believed Link this time though, if he thought the man wasn't a threat, he'd try his best to keep him out of the gang's knowledge. Out of Lenzo's knowledge. The photo from the article flashed in his mind; identical ice eyes stared back at him. A tiny part of him, a part untainted by 'Gods Among Kings', thanked and understood Link's intentions for keeping it a secret. Lenzo was haunted by the photo of Amelia and Emmitt Sawyer. For the first time in his life, he didn't know what to do.

He pushed it all back to the tiny spot deep down. "While I'm deciding what your punishment will be—" It wasn't Link who had flinched. It was his three friends who all couldn't keep the guilt from their faces. "—I'm getting bored of

Davis. Finish him off." The words flew off the tongue like giving a death order was normal for a Saturday morning itinerary.

"How?" Ash asked, seemly un-bothered.

"I'm thinking." Their boss tapped his chin, a wicked flint in his eyes, "Order 131." He smiled at himself, satisfied with his decision. "Yes, it's been a while since we've used that one."

They nodded and took their leave. But Link remained glued to his spot by Lenzo's eyes. He could see the cruelty in his eyes and he knew he had decided on the punishment.

Ash hovered at the door, reluctant to leave Link alone, but Lenzo waved his hand and Ash shut the door and left his brother to their boss' mercy.

"So ungrateful, we take you in, feed you, put clothes on your back and this is how you say thank you!" The man bellowed at 13-year-old Lincoln. "Ungrateful delinquent!"

Lincoln gritted his teeth as the belt came down across his back; bright pink welts marked his skin and trickles of blood dripped from the cuts where the metal broke the skin. He tried not to scream, not to cry or show that it affected him. For that would only end up with another 10 hits.

This time, he was being disciplined for bad grades, Math, English and Geography. Failed them all. The school contacted Mr and Mrs Sutton that morning to share her concerns regarding Lincoln and his inability to stay focused. The teacher didn't know what awaited Lincoln when he returned to the Sutton's after school. But Lincoln was aware.

Lincoln had stood in the driveway of the property—gathering the courage to face his foster family—almost an hour he had stood and stared at the front door.

He had tried, tried so hard in his lessons, but he couldn't get it like the rest of the class could. He could never understand as easily and it made him angry, so he lashed out, papers flying across the table and loud shouts of protest and frustration.

"This is what happens when you step out of line, Son."

"I'm not your son," Lincoln gritted out; his voice so young yet filled with so much resentment.

"What did you say to me, boy?" Mr Sutton's beefy face turned beetroot red and the leather under his grip groaned.

"I said." He stood up from his place on the kitchen tiled floor, his knees ached and he stopped the cry of pain as he turned to face Mr Sutton, "I am. Not. Your. Son."

His thin arm came over his face. The skin burned where the belt connected with his arm instead of his cheeks.

Lincoln couldn't remember what happened afterwards; he just remembered waking up in a hospital bed, no sign of the Sutton's but a woman with a welcoming smile sat by his bed. She brought him back to the orphanage despite his kicking and screaming.

The memory was one among many that plagued his dreams over and over and over. And was one of the very few he told Lenzo about. At the age of 15, Link, brand new to 'Gods Among Kings', had no idea what mistakes he made by telling his new mentor some of his awful experiences with foster families. Experiences full of torture and pain. The run-away had no idea that the stories Lenzo seemed so sympathetic about would be his go-to whenever Link needed disciplined or punished.

His third foster family, a hunched woman with pointed features and scabby pores all over her face had punished Lincoln within 3 days of joining the grim family. Taking the blame for a missing wallet he knew one of the young kids had stolen.

Link had forgotten he told Lenzo the form of punishment the family had used. Until he messed up. 16-year-old Link was still fighting for control over his anger. He got into multiple fights with some of Lenzo's men, so Lenzo took him down to one of the warehouse basements, tied him with his arms wide and hosed him down with freezing water. The pressure burned his skin and left bruises that lasted for weeks.

It wasn't always that Lenzo used one of the past tortures to punish Link. Though when Link saw Lenzo's wicked smile, he knew that this time was one of them occasions. Link was escorted down to sub-level two of a warehouse by two of Lenzo's men, Jeffords, who was the tallest out of the two. His hard, uneven face never shifted expression, nor did he ever talk. Ever. He would grunt or nod instead—Ash had told Link he had bit his own tongue off during a police interrogation.

Tenner, the second man, had the most punchable face Link had ever seen. His slimy smile, his yellow eyes, sharp tongue. Link guessed Tenner was enjoying escorting him down to whatever punishment met him.

The elevator pinged, sounding their arrival and the three men stepped out. They all took a minute for their eyes to adjust to their dark, damp soundings and Tenner and Jeffords grabbed Link by his arms and forced him forwards. Link bit his tongue and decided not to let them know he was more than capable of walking independently.

They walked down the poorly lit corridor, the row of doors getting longer and longer the further Link was escorted. He wrecked his memory for all the stories he had told Lenzo 7 years ago, but he couldn't remember which foster families he had mentioned. Being hosed down was a punishment used when his temper got the best of him. Mr Hardgrove's punishment (being locked in the cage he kept in the cellar, not enough room to stretch his limbs), he had outgrown that—literally.

He stopped in front of a door, Link swallowed as Tenner turned the metal knob and pushed the door open. He knew the moment his eyes spotted the two posts in the middle of the room. Immediately recalling and regretting telling Lenzo the memory of Mr Sutton. He had cried. The only time he had cried in Lenzo's presence, he couldn't help the waterfall of tears that flooded from his eyes as he told Lenzo about the night, showing him the scars. Not once had he spoken about the night to anyone other than Lenzo, not even the boys. And not once had Lenzo been cruel enough to use it against him.

Link knew better than to fight the two men as they stripped him from his jacket and shirt, chaining him to the posts. Cuffs on each wrist and they forced him to his knees. One light hung from the ceiling above Link's head and swung back and forth. Link was too focused on his breathing to realise his boss had entered the room. Lenzo's suit jacket was discarded on the back of the door hook and one hand went into his pants pocket and the other held a length of black leather braided into a thick rope. Link and Lenzo both took a single deep breath.

"I am sorry to do this, Lincoln, but I've got to make an example." Link wanted to believe Lenzo, but the way he swung the whip at his sides suggested he was eager to use it. "And you've messed up so much recently."

Lenzo took slow steps towards Link; he had seen Lenzo do this several times to scare his prey, keeping them on edge.

“First the Sawyer set-up went sideways, then branding Davis without my permission—with witness’ might I add—the fight with the bartenders, the lying about secret brothers. The list just keeps getting longer and longer.”

Lenzo knelt in front of Link, so they were eye level. His ice eyes dominated Link’s dark eyes and Link lowered his eyes to the floor.

“You’re at the centre of it all, Lincoln, you’re the one stepping forward and owning up to everything,” Lenzo spoke soft but patronising. “Until one of the others steps up or until you give one of them up.” Lenzo grabbed Link’s chin and forced his head up, “I’m going to have to keep punishing you.”

Link, without a second thought, said, “It was all my idea. My men were acting on my orders.”

Lenzo hummed as if he expected that exact answer, “OK, how many would Mr Sutton issue?”

“Ten.” Link didn’t dare lie. He knew Lenzo would remember a detail like this.

“Ten, right.” He now stood behind Link, leather whip sweeping against the floor and Link tried not to flinch, “Why don’t we do—” he paused to think, “—Twenty? And I want to hear counting.”

“Yes, sir.” His voice was tight.

Link sucked in a breath, anticipating the hit. He was launched forward at the impact of the first hit. His skin tingled under the leather as it turned bright red.

“One,” he breathed out. He made his voice steady.

The second hit came with even more power than the first and he launched forward again, “Two,” Link gritted out.

Another—the third hit had stuck his side and cut along a rib. The skin too sensitive and Link let out a scream. “Three.”

After the 15th hit, Link couldn’t keep himself up, but the tight rubber bound his arms to posts on either side of him prevented him from flopping to the floor. He could feel the wet trail of blood and sweat running down his back and soaked the waist of his jeans. Blood had poured down the front of his body and the liquid seemed to follow the rigids of his abs—dropping to a puddle on the ground. Some hits were replications of his scars and the raised skin broke easier.

“I don’t hear counting,” Lenzo’s voice sounded behind him, too lively. “Do we need to start again?”

“Sixteen!” Link shouted. “Sixteen,” he breathed out again, more desperate. Almost pleading for the last 4 hits to end this.

Link couldn't breathe; the muscles in his body hurt too much as his lungs contracted, trying to fill up. "Tw—twenty." His body sagged.

His back ached and stung and cried. Lenzo moving swiftly in front of him had Link hissing at the breeze on his bare back.

Lenzo tutted and lowered his head to get a look at Link's face that was pale and coated in sweat, "Your problem, Lincoln." His voice was just a whisper, "You try to preserve the innocence of everyone like someone should have preserved yours."

Link found some strength to meet Lenzo's eyes, his eyelids too heavy to stay open for long.

"But what you don't understand, Lincoln, innocence is meant to be broken; it's meant to be tainted. No one can stop that." The next part came out in a harsh whisper, "No one can stop me."

Lenzo got to his feet; his white shirt spotted with blood. The door opened and Tenner and Jeffords took a step into the room.

"Clean him up and send him home," Lenzo ordered to the two and turned back to Link. "The last thing we want is a family like the Sawyers after us; Emmitt Sawyer doesn't get touched, don't approach him, don't look at him, don't think about him."

Link nodded his head as best as he could.

"If Davis is still breathing within three days," Lenzo started as he walked to the door, whip still in hand, now covered in Links blood. Tenner and Jeffords unchained Link from the posts and his arms dropped in front of him to keep him from colliding with the floor. "The whole bar team gets a bullet in their head. And you'll be the one to put it there."

Chapter Twenty-Two
Hypothetical

Link's 3 friends looked sorrowful as they sat hunched over their beers. Ash still flicking the phone in his hands. None of them seemed to be in the bar, not noticing Link's presence at the top of their booth.

Hino spotted him first. "What?—Are you?—" he stuttered, trying to find the right way to ask. Link never spoke about his punishments with the boys, just brushed them off and promised he was fine.

Link put a mask on and smiled cockily. "I'm alright, Hino."

Hino shifted to make room for him and Link slid in the booth, getting the other two's attention, "Nothing I can't take."

His tone was light, but the boys knew the heaviness he was hiding. They didn't doubt he couldn't handle whatever Lenzo threw at him; they'd seen him take a bullet and still manage to kick some asses.

Marius acted just as Hino did and showered him with guilt, pity and concern. Which Link brushed off with jokes of them repaying him by buying his next few rounds. Link met Ash's eyes and they gave each other a nod.

"So, 131?" Marius let of a sigh, "It's been a while." He let out a half-hearted laugh.

The boys hummed in agreement and Ash slid the phone over the table to Link and he stopped it with the palm of his hand. His fingers hovered over the contact.

Link looked up and they all sat with the same anticipating stare as if they were watching a horror film and knew something would be popping up to scare them.

"Another drink and then Order 131?" Link asked in the most casual tone he could muster. Everyone agreed and Hino volunteered to go to the bar.

The queue parted for Hino as he walked up the bar. Hino stepped up to the bar and smiled at Rory, his smile slightly brighter now that Link was with them and in one piece. He glanced at her new name badge and asked, "Can I get a bottle of Bourbon, please? I'll take the first one you get your hands on, Rory."

"Yellow Label? Four Roses?" she asked, already making a move to collect it from the shelf. It was the one Link or Ash usually asked for. Marius and Hino always asked for the first one in reach to make their job easier.

"Yellow Label is perfect. Thank you, Rory." Hino's extensive use of her name he had just learned made her chuckle.

"Now you know my name." She placed the bottle on the bar top and reached down to grab 4 old fashioned glasses. "Can I get yours?"

"Hino, Isao Hino." Hino retrieved a bundle of bills and handed them to Rory.

"And your friends', Isao Hino?" Rory had caught names from Link the night before in the park and she needed to put a face to them.

Isao Hino hesitated for a moment and debated whether to tell her, "Big guy in the blue—" he pointed. "—That's Marius. "

Rory mouthed the name and Hino pointed to the blonde who had pushed Rory during the fight. "Next to Marius —Ash, he's the rude and uptight one."

Rory let out a small snort, "Link isn't the rude one?"

"Obviously, you know our Lincoln." He turned back to her, but her eyes stayed burning holes through Link's back. Uncertainty in her eyes as if she was trying to determine what type of character he was.

"He's not a bad guy, well, if you look past the whole gang member thing." Rory kept her eyes on him and Hino could see her mind ticking away behind her eyes. "Link has a good heart. He will threaten, fight and kill. Like all of us, better than us. But he has saved us all, more than we—and him—would admit. Out on the field and behind closed doors. He has a code and a heart and a stubborn loyalty that protects everyone but himself."

"I don't know what you think you know about Abel Sawyer, but whatever it is, it isn't on Link. What happened to Sawyer—he was let off easy thanks to Link."

Rory turned to Hino with a plastered smile. "Would you like a bucket of Ice for your drink, Isao Hino?"

"I would not but thank you, Rory." He grabbed all 4 glasses and the bottle and made to turn around but stopped and said, "Keep the change!"

Rory went to put the money away, but he came jogging back to the counter, his order still in his hands. "You know all that Sawyer situation was hypothetical, right, because we had nothing to do with his imprisonment?"

His friend must not have told him about their ‘conversation’ last night. So, she just gave him a deadpan look and watched him back away. Her activities the night before had played a huge role in her sleepless night. Drunk and angry, the perfect mix for a regretful result, especially in Rory’s case. Had she really threatened a gang? Not just a gang, but ‘Gods Among Kings’? Yes she had. And though in the moment it had felt good, powerful. Sobar Rory felt completely different: stupid, foolish, maybe a tiny bit scared, and a whole lot of awkward.

Link stood on the sidewalk; the loud music and drunken chaos shut behind the door and sounded worlds away. The only contact on the burner phone was highlighted, waiting for Link to press the call button. Davis wasn’t innocent; he stole from them, failed in paying them back, held an alibi hostage that could save someone important to the bar. Link had witnessed how he treat his staff. Saw several bartenders’ walkout mid-shift due to harassment.

He had no problem putting a hit out on his life. But order 131 was unpredictable. Sometimes they would answer and take the job, sometimes they wouldn’t. This meant not only would Link have to follow through with the hit himself, but he’d also stood outside in the freezing cold wind for no reason.

His jacket was lying over his seat inside, leaving him in a t-shirt and his dark jeans. His fresh wounds were cooled as the wind rippled through his shirt. Slightly stinging the cuts but eased the burning.

Numb fingers pressed the call button and Link placed the phone to his ear. It rang for a long while and just when Link was sure no one was going to pick up— The line clicked and a disembodied voice spoke.

“Yes.”

“Order 131 GAK,” Link spoke down the line. It was the code he had used every time they were giving an order 131.

“Name. Deadline. Requests?”

Link couldn’t tell if the voice was edited or if the person on the other end actually had such a raspy voice, “Charles Davis. Three days. If you see an employee logbook—remove May twentieth of this year.”

“Sixteen Thousand. Fifty now, Fifty on confirmation.”

"Deal." Link knew the drill. He would fire out a text and the money would be transferred and he'd keep the phone on him till confirmation.

The other side of the line went dead and Link rolled his eyes. "So dramatic," he said to himself.

"But isn't that your speciality?" An amused voice came from behind him.

"Oh, you know me so well," he mocked, not having to turn around to identify his favourite redhead.

Rory sat down on the bench that leaned up against the bars frosted windows, bending over to rub her bare legs that were already covered in goosebumps. "How is it so hot in there but so cold out here? There's no happy medium."

"It could have something to do with the sweaty drunks and thick walls?" Link now faced her. Rory had come out for air before she would get changed and have a drink with Charlotte.

Link had joined her on the bench, the phone still in his hands; he sat on the opposite end of the seat, keeping a comfortable distance. The sun had nearly set and covered them in a dusty light.

"It was rhetorical but thank you." She peered at him with a sarcastic smile.

Unlike his smooth deep spoken voice, Link's laugh was a few octaves higher and inconsistent in pitch. With his head pulled back and eyes crinkled with the sincere smile, Rory forgot that he was a member of the 'Gods Among Kings'. She forgot he was dangerous. This Link wasn't connected to Abel Sawyer or Charles Davis. He was a young guy, sitting outside a bar, making jokes with the young bartender.

But without his jacket, her eyes caught his crown tattoo. The fight in the bar, the night before, and Hino's words all played over in her head. She should hate him completely; he had branded Abel and Davis; he played a role in Abel's imprisonment. But the Link at the end of the bench, he was a Link she wasn't familiar with. He didn't even bear a gun at his hip. The only threat about this boy was the tattoo and the loose curls tickling his eyelashes.

Rory's eyes wandered down, lost in her thoughts; they landed on the phone in his hands and chuckled. "Is that seriously a burner phone? What are you doing? Hiring a hitman?" she mocked.

Link looked at her with his famous 'don't ask' look and her mockery dropped.

"Oh, for fuck—" Rory's curse got stuck when Link twisted to place the phone in his jeans pocket. Red blotches covered the back of his white shirt.

Without thinking, Rory reached out to his shoulder and pushed him away so she could see his back. “What the hell have you done to your back? Is that blood?” She scrunched her nose up in visible disgust.

Link’s mood instantly shifted back; he shrugged her hand off.

“You should get that checked out.”

She pulled her hands in towards herself, forcing help wouldn’t get her anywhere with him, but his back needed to be checked out and the smell of cheap antiseptic liquid suggested it hadn’t been cleaned properly yet.

“Look, you can either let me clean it up for you and put you in a clean shirt or you can go back inside, continue to drink alcohol while you drip blood everywhere, do you know how hard it is to remove blood from leather? Ethel’s can’t afford new furniture or a lawsuit when you catch an infection from the bar. Besides, If I can see the blood, your buddies can too. And who would you rather deal with?”

He didn’t speak or appear like he was listening, so she stood up and made her way inside, but Link’s hesitant voice stopped her.

“Fine.”

Chapter Twenty-Three
Mr S

Link stood in the doorway, hesitant to enter the locker room and in two minds to turn and join his friends back downstairs. She was correct; his back did need to be looked at. Link wasn't warm to the idea of Rory or his friends helping him. Lenzo ordered Tenner and Jeffords to clean him up. Jeffords silently cleaned his wounds with old medical supplies while Link lay on his front, trying to ignore Tenner's taunts.

Jeffords had used an old off-brand antiseptic which stunk of hand sanitiser and crusted at the lid. There were no dressings to cover them, so they opened and bled freely. Link could feel the shirt sticking to his back. Rory had offered to help and he couldn't stand the guilty looks he'd get once the boys saw his wounds, so she was the latter evil. She was darting around the room, searching lockers and cupboards. She noticed Link still hadn't entered the room, standing in the doorway, arms tensed at his sides.

"You're going to have to come in," she said lightly and pointed to the wooden bench. "Take a seat there."

She didn't leave room for an argument as she disappeared through a door; the sound of running water told him it was a bathroom. Link slowly entered and looked around the room. Lockers were labelled with tape—he didn't recognise any of the names.

"Rory Burke?" he guessed; he raised his voice so Rory could hear him through the door.

"Try again," she laughed, but it was muffled through the door.

"Rory Scott?"

"That's the one, Aurora James Scott," she said proudly.

"James?" he questioned; he was staring at her locker as if he could see through it and see the contents like they would give him some secret peek into her life.

"After my father," she shouted just as proud as before.

"He's not a teacher, is he?" he asked.

"He was," Rory's head came into view with a quizzing look; the rest of her body hid behind the door. "How did you know?"

"He taught at Sinister South? History?"

Rory nodded. Her mother resented her father when he got the job at a deprived high school the locals called Sinister South. The school was filled with fosters and expelled students and students that had run-ins with the law. But James Scott loved it. He loved the students and teaching them. He thought of it as giving them a second chance to prove that they were more than bad grades and a few poor life choices.

"Mr S was everyone's favourite. History was the only lesson I showed up to. Didn't treat us like the delinquents we were, always knew how to help." Link remembered fondly.

Rory didn't have a hard time believing that Link had attended the school and she believed everything he said regarding her father. He was the purest man she had ever known. She missed the times she would sit in his office (the spare room until they moved into her mother's parents' house), her lying on his old worn couch with a glass of milk while her father sat in his desk chair with a beer and listened thoroughly to her venting about whatever annoyed her that day—mostly her mother. He would have the greatest advice or speech that fixed everything.

"Yeah," she said quietly but not unhappily. "He was always good like that."

"Was?"

Rory met his eyes; he could only see half her body, still hiding behind the door.

"I thought I told you to sit," she demanded and disappeared behind the door again. Rory loved talking about her father—but talking about that night was something she couldn't talk about, ever.

Link mocked her childishly but sat where she instructed. He sat at the end of the bench facing the full mirror hung on the wall. His hair was—as always—a mess. Jet black and curled around his ears. Circles under his eyes were as dark as ever. He considered trying the spoon in the freezer trick that Hino suggested; it was easier than Marius 's idea of sleeping. His eyes filled with almost disgust at his appearance and Link tried to think back to a time when he didn't look like this—sad—pale—alone—dead.

Rory had returned into the room carrying a small bowl of water, a rag and a first aid box. She placed them down by his feet and straddled the bench behind him. She lightly gripped the bottom of his shirt and glanced at him through the mirror, asking for permission.

"No questions asked," he ordered, but his tone didn't hold the sharp edge it always did when he told her what to do.

"No questions asked," she confirmed and slowly pulled his shirt up, blood stuck the cotton to the skin and she cringed, pulling harder and making him wince.

Link watched her face drop through the mirror. Shock, concern and utter disbelief at what she was seeing. Lashes covered his skin, red-raw and broken skin from repeated whips leaked fresh blood that joined the dark sticky ichor that coated the side of the wounds. The skin was painted with similar scars years older.

She stopped her fingers from running along the raised skin and cleared her throat.

"I'm—I'm going to need a bigger rag," she trailed off, removing herself from the bench and heading back into the bathroom again.

Rory had patched up the guys and Nia multiple times, cuts, scrapes, bruises. But nothing this bad. Nothing this complex or dark. She pulled a larger rag from the mirror cupboard. The bathroom was small, a shower small enough for one, a toilet and a sink with a cabinet under and above. She closed the cupboard and checked her reflection in the dirty mirror. Hair half out of the tie and stands framed her flustered face.

She braced two hands on the sink and said to herself, "No questions asked."

Link was leaning his elbows on his knees as Rory slowly cleaned his back with warm water. Removing blood so she could get a better look and determine how to treat him, but the more blood she wiped, the more they bled. She should have asked Will to help; he had more knowledge with his dad being an actual doctor. But she knew Link wouldn't allow that. It was enough he was allowing her to see him in this state, though she didn't know why.

Every time he winced or jerked with pain, she'd shoot apologies and winced herself. Other than that, they didn't speak. Rory would open her mouth, but her words failed her. She knew he'd need a distraction from the pain, but she couldn't think of anything to say; she didn't want to dig too personal but asking about the weather seemed pathetic.

"So," she stared awkwardly. "Do you have female members?"

"What?" Link asked confusedly.

"You know—" Rory said. "—*Gods Among Kings*, like 'Goddess' Among Queens.' What if there's a non-binary member? Are they 'Deity Among Monarchs?' Is it a nine to five job? Like with a boss and an office?"

"Don't."

She gave him a quick confused glance through the mirror, "Don't what?"

"You know what," he said.

"Only trying to make conversation," she mumbled under her breath and continued to clean the wounds.

"No, you're not," he said. "You're trying to get information about the gang."

"I wasn't trying to—" Rory shook her head, "worth a shot."

Link's back was clear of blood and Rory could see how deep the cuts were. "OK, it doesn't look too bad—" She dumped the rag into the red-stained water, "—a lot of blood, but the cuts aren't too deep. I'll still disinfect them just in case."

Rory swore Link winced at just the thought. Clearly, he had been through this before and knew the next part was the worst. She opened the red box and pulled out a bottle of Dettol and a handful of gauzes.

Link watched as she unscrewed the cap and the strong sterile smell burned their noses. He was dreading this. When she cleaned his blood up, her small hands were as gentle as she could make them while applying pressure despite the roughness from the past few years of fixing the bar's machinery up. And he knew she was gentler than the boys would have been.

"I'm not going to tell you that this will hurt—" she started as she tipped a generous amount of the antiseptic onto a gauze "—because the look on your face tells me you already know, so I'm just going to apologise now and I'm going to give you time to get prepared for the—"

Rory cut her own sentence short as she pressed the gauze onto a cut and Link screamed out.

"That was for Abe," she mumbled. And Link gave her a 'really?' look through the mirror. The bench groaned under Links iron grip as she continued to clean some of the more minor cuts. Rory applied pressure to a larger and deeper wound and it burned his skin; eye-watering pain spread through Link's whole body and his hand flew from the wood to Rory's knee and squeezed it. His eyes shut tightly as he tried to keep his scream in.

"Was that for Davis?" he gritted out.

"No. Still for Abel."

Link lurched forward and tightened his grip on Rory's knee.

"I know, I know." She winced at the pain shooting up her knee. "Talk to me, Link."

The look that crossed his face wasn't pleasant.

"Talk to me, tell me something no one else knows," and again, he gave her the same look. "OK, too far." She removed the gauze from his back to apply antiseptic liquid onto a clean one; Link's fingers didn't ease up on her bare leg.

She muttered a warning before pressing on a spot on his back. "You said you went to Sinister South? You knew my father?" she rushed out, attempting to distract him from the pain.

He jerked forward but managed to hiss through gritted teeth, "Mr S—He would—Ahhh," he groaned out but tried his best to continue, "would wait with me after school for my bus, so I wasn't alone."

"That sounds like something he'd do. Was that the reason he was your favourite?"

"Among other re—reasons,"

"Yeah, like what?" It was working; Rory had moved to another gash and Link didn't jerk, only slightly hissing.

"Helped me with English—" Link managed a laugh, "—He was terrible with Math."

"Oh, believe me, I know." Rory rolled her eyes, "Nearly there, come on Link, what else?"

"Reported the Jacksons," Link spoke quietly and Rory knew this was getting too personal. She kept her mouth shut and bit on her lip as his grip tightened even more. "He had seen some bruises and promised to help."

By now, he had stopped reacting to the antiseptic, barely twitching but she was concerned the chemicals had gone to his head.

"Mr Scott said he would take me in himself, we had plans to meet outside a milkshake shop, but he didn't show—"

He stopped talking as it hit him. For the last seven years, Link had thought that Mr Scott had abandoned him—left him waiting on the sidewalk in front of the milkshake shop for hours, his backpack filled with the little possessions he owned. When 15 years old Link realised his teacher wasn't going to foster him—he ran away. Straight to Lenzo.

Mr Scott didn't abandon Link; he had died.

"How?" There was no commandment behind the word; it was so soft Rory could pretend she didn't hear it.

"That's the last one," she spoke.

Rory hadn't given much thought to her father surprising her with a trip to the milkshake shop one evening after school—it wasn't too uncommon for the pair to go out for a treat but, that night, it felt different. Excitement and slight fear when he had told her to put her coat and shoes on. As her father gripped her small hand tightly and walked with an urgency. It was that night. The night he had died. The night he was murdered.

Link made to get up, but Rory stopped him. "Woah." Her hands gripped his shoulders and tugged him back down. "You're going to want a bandage over them in case they start to bleed again."

Rory started to wrap Link's back and front up with a length of bandage with the gentleness she had used before. Starting from the bottom and working up. All the while studying his scars. Cold knuckles ran over a small circular scar on the corner of his abdomen on the right side. She wasn't stupid—she knew it was a bullet wound. And she knew the jagged line that ran under his left shoulder was from a blade. Rory took a deep breath and Link knew she was about to break the no questions asked pack.

"I'm not going to pretend to know a fraction of what's happening, with Abel and Davis and the gang—" Her voice was almost a whisper as she carried on wrapping him up. "—or assume that the same person who did this also caused the scars under them."

Link stared at her through the mirror, but she was focused on the white bandages. She tapped his arm and with difficulty—he raised them as high as he could. Hino's words had started playing in her head again.

'He has a code and a heart and a stubborn loyalty that protects everyone but himself.'

"But there is a line where loyalty becomes ownership. And in my experience, the toxic one always comes out on top."

In a low voice, Link asked, "What if I'm the toxic one?" These wounds, he was whipped, he was punished. Rory would bet based on Hino's words that it wasn't his punishment. "You're not toxic—not yet. Link, you're broken."

She ran the end of the bandage over his shoulder to secure it in place. She hummed when she was done and took in her work before packing away the first aid kit, still straddling the bench behind him. Link twisted in his seat to face her.

"There's a difference?"

Link knew he was broken and toxic. Everyone he knew ended up dead or hurt. His parents, his aunt, gang members he had lost out on the field.

"Yes—" her hands stopped fiddling with the red first aid box and she gave him her full attention. "Toxic people hurt others with actions that won't hurt themselves."

"Believe me, I've hurt people."

She sighed softly, "I believe you." Link sucked in a breath and dropped his eyes. "You—What I've heard and seen, you—you're protecting the ones you can in the only way you know how—only way you've been taught. You haven't had the chance to learn that this, there is more," Rory huffed, fumbling over words that weren't connecting to what she was trying to say.

"My father would have some philosophical speech on how you hurt Abel in a way that spared everyone but yourself an amount of pain. Even Abel. And I hate you for what you have done to Abe, but it counts for something. It has too."

Chapter Twenty-Four
No Curls!

"We've talked about this, Char," Rory groaned. The two were sitting at the bar, Rory next to Angel, who was winking at every man that went past and complained about it being a slow night. "I'm not flirting with a guy to get information!"

Chrissy had overheard parts of the plan and the Irish girl stood behind the bar, trying to convince Rory to go along with it. "Come on, Rory, get a few drinks in ya, dance where he can see ya and I'm sure he'll be begging at your feet!"

Rory found her straw with her tongue and sipped from her cocktail. The burn of the alcohol being soothed by the cherry's sweet taste and left her tongue deep red. She wasn't going through with their plans. As much as she wanted to help Abel. Rory was still trying to wrap her head around the information she had learned earlier.

Her father had taught Link, knew him. Enough to foster him. Bring him into their home that he shared with his wife and daughter. She idolised her father even after his death; he was her hero. In her eyes, he couldn't do no wrong, he couldn't be wrong. Her father clearly didn't think Link was dangerous or a threat. Link wasn't 15 anymore, though. She had no idea how long he had been in the gang and no idea what he had seen and did. If her father was still alive, would he take him in now?

Rory wished for Nia or one of the guys to join them and have her back. Charlotte and Chrissy banding together like best friends in school, convincing their shy friend to ask their crush out. They didn't understand half of it. Rory didn't understand half of it. She feared how lost out of the loop she was—how helpless she was.

"I'm not going to flirt with Link to get information!" she repeated for the tenth time in the space of an hour. "I don't have to smile, bat my eyelashes and shamelessly dance to get what I want!" she demanded.

"Of course, you don't," Chrissy threw the rag she had just used to clean the bar top over her shoulder, "but it's quicker and more fun."

Charlotte gave her a high-five over the bar and Rory didn't resist the urge to scowl.

"Besides," Rory emphasised. "Flirting with him? I don't know." She pulled a face. "I mean, it would be like flirting with Will, or Nicky."

Charlotte hummed and appeared to be considering something. "What about the blonde? He's always looking at you."

"That's because he wants to kill me."

"Why are you fighting this, Rory?"

"HE HAS A GU—he has a gun," she shouted a little too loudly and glanced around her, but the crowd was too busy dancing and lost in their alcohol to care. "What if I overstep with a question? What if I ask something that makes him angry? What if I make a fool out of myself? What if I—"

Chrissy cut her off, "You'll be fine! I promise! He's not going to shoot you; I'd bet my life on it," she said surely.

"Would you bet mine on it?" Rory's eyebrows went up, "Because that's what's on the line."

"Look, I appreciate the advice girls, but this isn't some spy movie where I flirt with the bad guy and he spills his secrets during an intense dance scene. This is real life, where I flirt with the bad guy and I end up dead in a ditch by the end of the night."

A customer came to order, saving Chrissy answering Rory. Chrissy still wasn't fully aware of the danger that the gang brought. Rory told Will to inform her more than just telling her to stay away. Of course, that caused an argument. And then Rory called him out for protecting Chrissy by shielding her from the danger. Which caused another argument—Will denying any feelings involving the newest bartender and Rory telling him that even Blind Roy (who would come in every Monday night for a scotch and peanuts) could see him pining.

Pushing the empty cocktail glass away, Rory sighed. For the first time in a month, she was in no mood to get drunk. She had already had 3 cocktails and a few shots.

Rory hadn't flirted with someone since high school and even back then, she was terrible at it. Nose stuck in her textbook long enough for her to miss out on learning the essentials like using what her mother gave her—in Rory's case, wasn't much—to her advantage. Rory envied the girls who could attract partners as easily as dancing in their eye view. So confident and powerful and comfortable in their body and mind. 4 years of her high school experience wasted for a career she dropped in one email.

Rory peeked over her shoulder to their booth, but only two were sitting there, Marius and Isao Hino. She didn't hate Marius ; he was polite enough when he ordered at the bar; she got the feeling that if she spoke to him, he wouldn't be as scary as he appeared. She was seriously considering employing him as security. Multiple times he had thrown someone out of the building because they got too rowdy. Gripping them by the back of their shirts and haling them out the door. But Marius and Will had a power feud—grunting and glaring at each other and as much as she and Will bickered—she'd back Will up in a heartbeat.

Ash and Link weren't at the booth, though. Hopefully, they had gone home; that way, she wouldn't have to entertain her friends with their impossible plan.

"Face it, Rory—" Charlotte took a sip of her drink. "You can't deny the curls."

Rory groaned loudly and rolled her neck, "I can deny the curls! "

"Whose curls?"

They spun in their chairs and Charlotte chocked on her drink, taking a napkin to wipe her chin clean. Link's eyes were on Rory as she gaped for something to say.

"His curls." Charlotte pointed her finger to Link's head and hid her face in her glass when Rory shot her a betrayed look.

"My curls?" Link had a playful mask on that suggested he already knew what they were talking about—Charlotte catching Rory and Link in the locker room, attempting to put Link into one of Will's shirts. The two fighting as Link's back was too sore to move his arms and not listening to Rory's directions.

"NO CURLS!" She shut them down, "No curls."

Link continued to stare at Rory with the same smirk Charlotte had when she walked in on them, excited to see how she would dig herself out of this. She opted for a subject change.

"If you're wanting to order, I'm off duty."

Ash made his presence known, "Clearly."

Neither Rory, or Charlotte missed the way Ash traced Rory's figure in the black dress. And Charlotte saw her opportunity to flirt for information.

"You know," She said, toying with her straw. "Rory was just telling me about how you guys are her favourite customers."

"I was?" She frowned.

Ash rolled his eyes, and Rory was content with the familiar response, glad he wasn't going to play along with Charlotte and humiliate her. "Is anyone actually working tonight? I need a drink."

Rory stood and squeezed between Link and Ash. "I need a drink too." She was going to make herself one when someone shouted Rory's name from the end of the bar.

"He's done it again!"

Chapter Twenty-Five
I'm Done

Rory wouldn't describe herself as an angry person; she didn't have a temper. James Scott had always been the patience parent, calm and collected. Taking control in a situation and ensuring it was diffused with as little to no raised voices. And as her role model, Rory always tried to be like her father. The years at the bar—fixing the machines, dealing with customers like Colonel and putting up with Davis had given her the perfect setting to practice her patience. There was only so much a person could take. Only so long a person could keep calm and collected. And recently—Rory had been running out of patience.

"Who's done what again?" Rory asked Will.

He made his way towards her—steam coming out from his ears and Rory straightened her back, preparing for the inevitable fight. Will and Rory were constantly bickering or fighting, usually over how the bar should be run. It wasn't uncommon for the pair to battle on a Saturday night in the middle of *Ethel's*. Nicky would force them to apologise. Otherwise, they'd have to forfeit the tips they had made that night. And they were suddenly best friends.

She wasn't the only one preparing to fight though, Link took a subtle step forward when Will reached Rory, ready to jump over the bar to step in between them. Rory didn't hold much up against Will. Smaller and less skilled in fighting.

"Davis—" he fumed and Rory's mind came up with one hundred reasons of what her boss could have done again and she couldn't pick which one she'd prefer to hear. "The bastard has cleared us out again!"

Rory's heart sank and her face paled. "When?"

"I don't know. The cash registers needed to be filled and when I went to get some bills, the only thing in the safe was paperwork."

Rory cursed loudly, "I'm going to kill him!"

She wasn't joking. Anger turned her vision red. The bar couldn't keep up with Davis's lifestyle, every time he cleared the money in the safe, the team got pay cuts and prices went up. "How did he even get in it?"

"I don't know, Aurora," Will hissed.

She widened her eyes at Will as he stood with his arms crossed over his puffed-out chest. "How is this my fault?" she argued back.

"I'm not blaming you."

"You only call me Aurora when you're accusing me of something," she testified.

"Well, when was the last time you checked the safe?"

Everyone held their breath; Charlotte had witnessed a fight like this before and knew not to get involved and say out of the crossfire. Her eyes searched the room for Nicky, but she couldn't spot him. Charlotte didn't think she would be able to stop the fight that was coming herself. Both sides looking as furious and deadly as the other. This could be catastrophic.

Chrissy had been attracted to the argument and approached the scene with care. "What's going on?" Charlotte tried to get her attention by waving her hand over her throat to tell her to stop.

"What's going on?" Rory echoed. "Apparently, what's going on is that I'm the only one who works here."

Will rolled his eyes at her dramatics and threw his hands up in frustration while Chrissy looked confused and slightly offended.

"I checked it this morning when I started, William." Her voice was getting louder and the customers who stood close to the bar had turned their attention to them. "When did you last check it?"

"Check what?" Chrissy asked. Her black spirals bounced as she shook her head in confusion and panic.

"The safe—" Will's shoulders that were knotted up loosened as he turned to Chrissy and it was Rory's turn to roll her eyes, "—Davis cleared the money in the safe and now we're short on bills for the register." He turned to Rory and he tensed again. "Hiding it in an empty locker wasn't safe enough; who would have thought, huh?"

Rory gritted her teeth. "Davis hasn't stepped foot inside the locker room. Ever. It was a great hiding spot!" Rory hated it.

Will had told her Davis would find it in the lockers when they had placed it there. And she swore he wouldn't. Which meant Will was right.

"Clearly, it wasn't!" he shouted, "because he found it!"

"Again. How is that my fault?"

"It's your job—"

"No, it's not actually!" Rory shouted, Will, shook his head and let out a cruel laugh. "Believe it or not, hiding a safe full of money from the alcoholic bar owner isn't in my job description!"

"Neither is playing boss, but you sure have fun doing that!" Will's go-to argument. No matter what they were fighting about.

"I play boss because someone has to!"

Chrissy was frozen, the first Will/Rory showdown she had witnessed and she wasn't enjoying it. Venom laced both their tones and the more comments Rory made—the more prominent the vein in Will's neck got.

Chrissy had asked Will after the fight with the gang members where he had learned to fight and Will told her that he would box in the gym down the block.

Before he had told his father, he had dropped out of school—Will would spend the days he was supposed to be in college boxing and working out. Will told Chrissy that the gym was where he had first met Marius and it was hate at first sight. They had competed against each other almost every chance they had and took turns winning—until a well-dressed man waltzed into the gym and asked to speak with their best fighters.

Will had heard of 'Gods Among Kings' before the boss had offered the small group of skilled boxers a chance to earn some cash. Will had denied the offer, not staying long enough to see Marius accept. Will had walked out of the gym and stopped by the run-down bar filled with drunk bikers and rockers—nobody was serving at the bar and the queue was growing anxious—so Will got behind the bar and served the line. Davis sent him home with a job.

Charlotte was frantically searching for Nicky or Nia, her head whipping around, but the crowd that had gathered to watch Will and Rory had made it impossible to spot them. Charlotte knew they couldn't be in the room—otherwise, they would have heard and broken it up already, but the panic had taken over and she was desperate.

"Maybe you both should take a breath, you know—" Charlotte's attempt to defuse the tension went unheard by both parties. She cast a desperate look at Link, but he was focussed on Will's threatening step closer to Rory.

"Just admit you messed up, Rory."

"I didn't mess up! This isn't my fault!"

"I told you he would find it."

Rory took a step forward, fists balled at her sides and her breathing was ridged. "And hiding it in one of the empty rooms was a better idea?"

"He doesn't go into them!"

"He doesn't go into the locker room either!"

They both took the final step forward and met each other in the middle—both moments away from jumping on the other and attacking. It wouldn't be the first time they had been pulled apart.

Charlotte and Chrissy's panic spiked, but it was the gang member that intervened.

"Take a step back, mate," he said roughly.

"Rory is a big girl; she can handle herself." Will didn't look at Ash as he spoke.

"I didn't say otherwise—but neither of you have a clear head right now and there are more important things to worry about," Ash reasoned from the other side of the bar—he handled the situation as if it was one of his friends who were facing off. Turn their focus from their anger towards each other to the real problem.

It worked. With less anger in his voice, Will asked, "What do we do?"

Rory took a deep breath to calm herself and she and Will turned to Charlotte with the same pleading expression.

"My keys to the 'All American' safe is at my apartment," she said helplessly. "Otherwise, I would have lent you some cash. Sorry."

"OK—" Rory's tone had calmed as she palmed her forehead. "—Round all products to the nearest dollar, encourage loose change and apologise for any inconvenience," she sighed and said reluctantly, "use the tip jar if you must and I'll take it from Davis's paycheck and share it between you all and add it to your next pay."

They did what she told them too without any complaints. Chrissy got to counting the jar and Will started to rewrite the price list.

"Let the twins know?" she asked Will and he nodded.

"What are you going to do?"

Rory didn't answer. Green eyes blazing as she headed for the door to the stairs. Rory was on the warpath.

Fists came down hard enough that they dented the old wood. Her hands ached, but Rory's anger and disappointment forced her to keep pounding on the office door. She shouted Davis's name repeatedly, but there was no answer though Rory knew he was in there. She rattled on the door handle, now smacking her palm against the door and demanded him to open up.

"Open the door, Davis!"

No answer.

"Open the damn door or I swear to God, I will take it off its hinges!"

She waited for a few more moments and got no response. "Fine," she huffed.

Marching back down the corridor to the locker room, she retrieved a screwdriver from her toolbox. With ease, she removed the four screws that attached the handle to the door. The metal dropped to the floor.

A scene too familiar was set up behind the door. Complete darkness, an intense fog of smoke and the stench of alcohol-induced vomit. Rory covered her nose in the crook of her elbow and felt around for the light switch. Davis was face first on his desk littered with empty bottles and crumpled paper and cigarette dumps—a lit one burning down on the desk.

Rory raced over to the desk, grabbed the burning stick with her thumb and index finger and put it out in the overfilled ashtray. Davis didn't move an inch. The only sign he was still breathing was the slurred snores that left his drooling mouth.

"Davis—" Rory placed her hand on her hips, "Davis," she chanted louder. But Davis hardly stirred.

Rory could see what was left from the safe. Crumpled bills scattered around the table. After the team had the cellar locks changed to stop him from helping himself to their stock—Davis turned to their safe. *Ethel's* couldn't afford another loan to cover the cost of Davis's actions. She was not looking forward to the brainstorming she and Emmitt would have to do in the morning to recover from this.

"Davis, get up," she said in a controlled tone. "Now."

Her palms came down hard on the table, startling the objects on it but not the man. Rory growled and dropped her head. She told herself to breathe her anger away. Count to 10 and deal with this as she usually would: Dunking water over Davis and pulling strings at the bank.

Counting halted at 6. Rory's eyes read red block letters under bills and envelopes. She tilted her head to the side and tried to read the words upside down. *FINAL WARNING.* Rory shifted the papers around it and snatched it up and held it to the light bulb for more light. It was from the bank. Rory collected the bank letters with the rest of the mail, always put to the side until she came in and sorted through them. She hadn't received a letter from the bank in a while—she should have known something was up.

Final warning. Final warning. Rory forced herself to read on despite the anxiety rising in her. She only caught a few words as she skimmed the page. "Collateral, failed payments."

"Son of a bitch," she whispered. "Son of a bitch."

Davis stirred and Rory watched with blazing eyes as he opened his eyes and sat up with a struggle, the chair groaning under his weight. His face was green and the whites of his eyes were yellow. They scanned the room and took a minute to register Rory standing in front of him.

"You awake?" the words came out through closed teeth. Davis made an incoherent sound, "Good."

"You put the bar up for collateral?" she bellowed. "For what, Davis? A house you don't live in. How many warnings, Davis? Why didn't you tell me? Emmitt could have helped; that was the whole point in the partnership!" Rory shouted, but Davis wasn't registering any of her cries. Too out of his mind to care or focus on anything.

"You are going to die, Davis," she said bluntly. "They will kill you and the housing dept and bar debt won't be your problem anymore—"

Davis struggled to keep his eyes open as Rory lectured him. His head swayed and he didn't have long before he would pass out again.

"—But what happens to us, Davis? We can't pay the debts that you'll leave behind. We can't afford to clean up your mess. I can't afford to clean up your mess." Rory was on the verge of crying now. Davis wasn't listening and that frustrated her even more.

"I'm nineteen, Davis!" her voice was hoarse from the shouting and she sounded broken. "The twins and Chrissy are twenty, Will is twenty-two. And I am nineteen. This was just a part-time job for us! We don't need—deserve—this stress! We can't do this anymore, Davis. You're drowning the bar and we can't swim!"

Tears fell. She didn't stop them. They ran hot down her face and left smudges of black mascara under her tired eyes.

"Dammit, Davis, say something!" she demanded through angry cries. Rage and frustration took over and she grabbed Davis's scotch glass and threw it behind him. It shattered as it hit the wall. Davis didn't flinch. He mumbled something that didn't sound like a language and Rory guessed he didn't just waste the money on alcohol.

She reached for a bottle and threw it in the same direction. Wanting to destroy and scream, anything to get Davis's attention. More bottles and glasses and his ashtray followed. All the mess and noise she caused did nothing.

"Fine, Davis—" she said through wrecked breathing. "You want to sit and wait to die in your own sick and piss, go ahead."

Rory pushed through the door to the bar. She didn't say anything as she handed Will the keys to the bar, adjusted the backpack on her shoulder and stormed out of *Ethel's*.

"Did Rory?—Did she?" Charlotte tried.

"She quit," Will finished.

Chapter Twenty-Six
Order 131

Heavens opened on Chicago and black skies made it impossible to see. A blurred figure came rushing out the door to *Ethel's* bar and tumbled onto the flooded streets. Ginger hair soaked instantly and stuck to her face. The girl stood on the street for 3 minutes, staring up and allowing the vicious rain to soak into her skin. Her dress becoming heavy as it absorbed the water. She didn't move out the way of the drunks stumbling from the bar or the people running up and down the street trying to escape the rain. She stood there for 3 minutes and then walked away.

The hooded figure watched from the dry cleaner's rooftop opposite the bar—for 5 hours, he waited. The rain had stopped an hour ago when the ex-boxer chucked the rest of the customers out and locked the door. A red truck registered under Charles Davis remained in the parking lot around the corner. Davis was still inside.

Three days was his time frame, but it had been a while since he had had a target. He got researching as soon as he hung up the phone. Charles Davis owned *Ethel's* bar. He had sold 35% to Amelia Sawyer's firm and was one financial crisis away from shutting down—Not even Amelia Sawyer could save that place. Charles Davis had a limited team, made up of 5. 3 dropouts and 2 college students. Only 1 of legal age, so he paid them under the table.

Charles Davis didn't have any family, no one to worry or call the authorities if he didn't return home that night. Charles Davis's office was on the second floor and at the end of the corridor. One door and one window. Dumpsters lined the back wall of the building that led up to one of the rooms on the second floor. Window open. No cameras faced any of the entries and exits. Nor covered inside the building.

This would be easy.

And it was. Within minutes, the hooded figure was standing outside Charles Davis's office door. No light in the building other than the dim yellow light coming from the broken door. Door handle lay at his feet and the figure laughed. One less thing for him to do. His gloved hand gently pushed open the door and it gave a quiet squeak. No movement lay inside and the figure thought someone had beat him to the target. Charles Davis lay on the desk. Bottom hanging off the chair. His balding head was flushed against the wood.

The figure turned his nose up at the stench, already as if someone had died in the room. He crept around the room with effortlessly sneaking that came naturally. Not as if any noise would startle the mindless man. The hooded figure bent down once he reached the side of the desk and shook his head at his target. Charles Davis wasn't asleep or passed out. His red eyes were slightly open though unfocused. Strung out on whatever he could get his hands on.

"Oh, Charles," the figure said disappointedly. This was going to be too easy; he was secretly hoping for his target to fight back or struggle, but the only thing he was going to get from tonight's mission was likely a disease from the rotting room. He let his eyes wander around the room and they spotted the mess of glass.

He assessed the pile of glass and ash on the carpet, he pulled his hood off his head. Brown hair pulled back into a bun, loose strands fell from the tie and lay at the sides of his head.

He hummed and stood up, dusting his hands on the back of his black trench coat. He stuck his hands inside the coat and pulled out a fixed blade. The silver freshly sharpened. He spun it multiple times with his index finger through the finger loop as he made his way around the room, searching for the logbook that Lincoln wanted.

Lincoln was the only member of 'Gods Among Kings' who contacted him. It was always a money issue with those guys. And the state of the bar, he guessed this time was no exception.

He had been doing his job for a year now and knew if someone dangerous like 'Gods Among Kings' wanted something to be found—it had to be important. And important things were usually hidden. He stood in the centre of the room, took a few moments to rock back and forth on his heels and began to sidestep around the room. Listening closely to the different creeks of the floorboards. And when one sounded hollow and loose—he bent down and lifted the damaged carpet. A small square cut out.

He pulled out a black notebook from the floorboard and blew off the dust and cobwebs. He flicked through—not having to worry about his target running away—and took his time reading the page from 20 May.

Harvard. J—Mrs Woodly, order #11
Cortland. A—Mr B Grey, order #12
Sawyer. A—Mr Hobbes, order #13

"Sawyer?" the figure mumbled to himself. He took the page and tore it out of the book and pocketed the paper. He placed the book back under the floor and stood up.

"Don't suppose you'll know why 'Gods Among Kings' want Sawyer's employment history?" he asked to Davis who hadn't moved an inch. "—I'm going to take a wild guess and say it has something to do with him being behind bars—" He was talking to himself now. "—It was back in May he was arrested. Maybe it's his alibi. Which means GAK set him up? Or he had joined them?—" He brainstormed. "—I guess you'll never know. Huh."

He tossed the blade around his finger with every step to the strung-out man. He poked him with the knife three times to make sure he wasn't going to get the pleasure of a fight. When he deemed the man clearly harmless—he got to work.

The silver blade sliced through his skin with ease. Red hot blood spilt down Charles Davis's neck, travelled down his brown shirt and covered his chest. The body stayed slouched back on the chair, eyes hardly open and mouth hung loose as if he was sleeping. Black gloved hands turned his face to the left and took the silver blade to his right cheek. Just like his neck, the blade cut into his cheek as if it was butter.

Charles Davis's killer took a step back; he pocketed the blade and took a burner phone out of his other pocket. He snapped a photo of his work and sent it to Lincoln, along with a message telling him that there was no logbook.

The assassin wore a smirk as he exited the building the way he had entered and strolled out to the empty street, breathing in the air after a downpour and set off down the street.

Chapter Twenty-Seven
Finally

"I brought sugary delights!" Charlotte's chirpy voice sounded through the near-empty bar.

Ethel's seemed to be taking the effects of Rory quitting. Everything that could have gone wrong—did. Nia called Chrissy for backup when the dishwasher had broken and then the soda guns started to malfunction. The two were soaked through with fizzy water and sat with miserable faces until Charlotte appeared with treats. Everyone had tried to contact Rory after she had walked away, but her phone was switched off and Charlotte told them to leave her to cool down. Hopefully, the bar would get over the loss of Rory and would stop attacking the remaining bartenders.

"Double chocolate muffin for Chrissy." Charlotte handed Chrissy her box and Chrissy didn't hesitate to rip the box open and tuck in.

"I'm a stress eater."

"And one strawberry pie for Nia." Charlotte slid the box to Nia on the bar top. Nia stopped the box and turned it around to read the sticky-label scribbled on the pink box. "Things are never as bad as they seem."

"Thank you," Nia said with a shy smile. Half because Charlotte remembered her studying 'To kill a mockingbird' and half because the quote fit the morning she was having. It felt as though Rory left months ago, all the broken things, the MIA boss who Nia didn't see come in that morning.

The stack of deadlines for paperwork she had no idea if Rory had handed them into their respective places (she most likely had). The girls sat in a grief silence as the bartenders ate their treats. JC sat at the end of the bar and a man on a laptop sat in one of the booths. No one talking, bad moods going around.

Charlotte tried to wrack her brain to think of anything to say to Nia to make her feel better. Nia looked as though she had taken Rory's leaving the hardest.

Black hair feral looking as if she hadn't had a chance to brush through it—though, with the soda gun incident, it wasn't her fault. For the first time—her big brown eyes weren't playfully glittering in Charlotte's direction. They were sad and tired and Charlotte hated how she couldn't help her.

The door opened and their delivery supply man entered, pulling a sack truck piled with brown boxes filled with various alcoholic products.

Nia made to get up, but Chrissy—who had finished her muffin—waved her off, "I'll get it—" She walked out from behind the door. "Order list?" she asked Nia.

"Rory keeps them in Davis's office," Nia told her through a mouthful of pie. Chrissy told the supply guy she'd be right back and headed up to the office.

Chrissy could see Davis's door ajar from the top of the hallway, handle on the floor. She slowed down her steps and debated whether to turn and go grab help. A growing feeling that something was wrong bubbled inside her. Her palms started to sweat as she pushed open the door. The young girl felt the scream rise inside her but didn't hear it. Everyone downstairs heard it, though. Nia and Charlotte came bursting down the hallway and pushed past a shaking Chrissy. Both took sharp gasps and Charlotte's hand grasped Nia's arm. Nia's own hand finding its way to cover Charlotte's.

Davis lay in his chair, head dropped back and the entire front of his body was drenched in blood. So much blood that they couldn't see the gaping slice in his neck that was the cause. His cheek, though—they could see clear as day. They had all watched the news segments and read the articles and overheard conversations in the bar. The Victim Counter. That's what everyone called them—the serial killer who left their victims with the murder count cut into their skin. The Victim Counter had struck at their bar. Davis was victim 17.

"Char—" Nia strained.

"I'll call the police." Charlotte removed her hand from Nia's arm and pulled her phone out.

Behind them—a green looking Chrissy barfed up the double chocolate muffin.

Charlotte gave the police *Ethel's* address and they instructed them not to let anyone leave the bar or in the room where the body was found. The three girls slowly backed out of the room and Nia volunteered to let JC and the man with the laptop know that the police were on their way and they had to remain at *Ethel's* and offered them free drinks while they waited.

"I've called Nicky and Will," Charlotte said as Nia came back from giving the man his drink; she slid onto the barstool in between Chrissy, who refused to drink anything in fear of bringing it back up and Charlotte, who was on her third shot. "—They're going to swing by Rory's and pick her up."

"Rory, Com' on kid—" Will said through the door, his voice raised so he could be heard through the wood. "—Open the door." He knocked a few times. He could feel Rory's neighbour, Ms Nealson, spy on him through the peek-hole on her own door from across the hall.

"Look, I know you're mad at me, but it's Davis; he's dead."

"Finally." He heard her muffled voice from inside her apartment and he sighed heavily.

"Chrissy found him."

Will heard movement from inside followed by a click of a lock. The door slowly opened and revealed a tired-looking Rory in some sweatpants and a jumper he recognised as Abel's. Her hair was in a low ponytail at the side of her head and her eyes were still red and puffy.

"Your eyes are bloodshot," Will stated dumbly and Rory rolled the bloodshot eyes.

"Yes. That tends to happen after crying in the shower." She took a shaky breath. "He's really dead?" she asked quietly.

"Yeah, he's really dead," Will confirmed softly. He stood awkwardly in her doorway; hands stuffed into his pockets. The pair hadn't apologised yet and they were both still angry at each other after their argument.

"And Chrissy found him?"

"Yep."

"Jesus—Poor girl."

Will studied Rory's face intensively like he wanted to ask her something but was trying to predict her reaction. "Did you do it?" he whispered quietly so Ms Nealson couldn't hear them.

Rory's mouth hung open and her face looked as if he had slapped her. "NO!"

"We'd give you an alibi, ya'know—"

"Will! I didn't kill Davis!"

"Right because you were with us the entire night," he said.

"William! I didn't kill him; he was strung out when I left him but alive."

"OK, OK." He put his hands up in defence.

Rory didn't think Will truly believe her and she didn't blame him. Rory left the bar abruptly and a mess. She cried out of anger and betrayal and tiredness all night and didn't manage to sleep until 3am. Rory had killed Davis in her mind so many times last night and when Will turned up and informed her of the passing of their boss, she was scared to admit that she wasn't sad or guilty or grieving.

She was relieved. Maybe GAK got to him finally—he had a three-week countdown, but it wouldn't surprise her if they sped up the process. Rory flashed back to the night before, Link on the phone and the joke about putting a hit out—or she thought it was a joke.

"Come on—" Will broke her thoughts. "—Nicky is waiting in the car."

Nicky had to park in the parking lot around the corner from the bar due to police cars and ambulances that blocked the street. People in white bodysuits and officers in uniform swarmed the street and entrance to *Ethel's* and it took Will, Rory and Nicky almost 5 minutes trying to push through the crowd to get into the bar. Will was arguing with the officer at the front door, adamant not to let them in.

"I get that it's a crime scene, but we work here," Will told the officer for the 10th time, but he shook his head and told the three that they couldn't enter.

"Sir—" Nicky started, but Nia appeared behind the officer and the three started shouting at her at the same time.

"Tell this idiot we work here!" Will shouted. And Nicky and Rory called something similar.

"They work here—let them in," Nia demanded and to their surprise, the officer stepped to the side and gave them access.

The three pushed into the bar at the same time and almost got stuck in the door. Nicky attacked Nia with a hug and Chrissy raced to Will's arms. Will pushed her away and searched her body for any sign of harm and pulled her back in when he was satisfied that she wasn't harmed physically. Charlotte remained in her stool at the bar and Rory slipped into the stool next to her.

"Are you OK?" Charlotte asked her and Rory sighed.

"No. Are you?"

"Nope," Charlotte popped and Rory noticed the whiskey in her hand.

"You don't drink whiskey."

“And you don’t work at *Ethel’s,* but here we are.”

Rory signed again and placed her arm around Charlotte’s shoulder and drew her in. Charlotte put her head on Rory’s shoulder.

“There was so much blood,” Charlotte whispered out, her eyes closing to stop the rising tears. Even with her eyes closed, she could still see Davis painted in red. She squeezed her eyes even tighter, but she couldn’t get rid of the image.

Rory placed a hand on Charlotte’s cheek and cupped it. “They’re going to find out who did it, Char—”

“No, they won’t—” Charlotte’s small voice cut Rory off and Rory hummed in question. “—It was the killer—the one who killed those people last year, the victim counter—Davis was seventeen.”

Rory faintly remembered studying the Victim counter at school when the killer had first struck. No one knew who it was, not an age, not a description. Just that they would carve the number of the victim on their cheeks. All they knew was that the victims weren’t random. Some were men, some we women and had a wide range of ages.

Though they all had one thing in common—they were marked. Some had the crown branded into their skin, but the officials couldn’t find a single piece of evidence to pin it on ‘Gods Among Kings’. Some had marks from other gangs, but they too were cleared. Rory didn’t doubt now that Link’s burner phone was the cause of Davis’s murder.

Nia came up from behind the two girls and rubbed Charlotte on the back in soothing motions. Nicky, Will and Chrissy following behind her—heads all hung low and grave faces.

“They want to talk to each of us alone,” she said softly and Rory nodded.

“If you’re underage—” she said loud enough her team—ex-team—to hear but low enough for the two detectives not to hear. “—You’re glass collectors and dishwashers.”

Chrissy leaned into the group and, as quietly and casually as she could, asked, “Do you think they’ll check my visa?”

The team nodded in agreement with Rory and waited for the two detectives to come over. Both were built the same, filling out their suits—the one with the trimmed beard had his suit jacket fastened and the button was hanging on its last thread. He reached into his coat and the team watched in anticipation—waiting for the straining button to pop. Instead, he pulled out a badge. His partner looked neither too young nor too old to be a detective. His wrinkled forehead and eyes showed a long, happy life, but his hair showed no sign of fading or greying—a healthy ash blonde.

"I'm detective freeman," the one with the darker hair introduced himself. "This is detective Altman."

The two showed their badges and waited for all of them to take a good look at the identification.

"We'll speak to you all individually so we can get a good idea of what you all know."

The bar team nodded in understanding.

"Who wants to go first?"

Chapter Twenty-Eight
Wouldn't Surprise Me

"I will." Will stepped forward, removed his arm from Chrissy's shoulders and led the detectives to a table. Freeman and Altman sat opposite Will and both pulled out a notepad and pen.

"We'll start with your name," Altman asked politely.

"William Morrison."

"And you work here?"

"Bartender yeh."

"Were you working last night?"

"I started at five and stayed until we closed—Davis was already in his office when I got to work and I didn't see him all shift."

Freeman hummed and scribbled Will's words on his paper and asked, "If you didn't see him, how did you know he was in?"

Will could taste the anger as he recalled the night before and he didn't try to keep it off his face or out of his tone. "Around eleven last night, I went to grab some notes from the safe, but it was empty—"

"You were robbed?" Altman but in.

"Does it count if it belonged to him—Davis cleared the safe again. He must have sneaked out around rush hour to blow it on alcohol."

"It's happened before?" asked Freeman.

"All the time."

"You don't seem happy? Did you confront him?" Freeman pried and Will considered what would happen if he threw Rory under the bus. She was underage and the last one to see Davis alive.

"Rory did—she left around eleven-thirty and there was a bar full of people who saw her leave."

"Right—" Freeman gave his partner a look that suggested they had found a lead in the case. But Will—and everyone else at *Ethel's*—would be ready with an alibi if needed.

"Your boss had a brand on his neck, a crown, identified with the gang 'Gods Among Kings'—Do you know anything about that?" Freeman quizzed.

Will gave them a shrug, "They come here sometimes—wouldn't surprise me if Davis owed them money."

"Would you like a drink?" Altman asked Chrissy, who had replaced Will in the hot seat. Her hands were clasped together to stop the shaking that had started when she had found Davis. "You're looking a little faint."

Chrissy nodded her head and looked away from her hands to the detective, who looked as if she was about to break.

"Water?" he asked.

"Vodka."

"Age?" Freeman had a less gentle approach than Altman and Chrissy forgot her shock and replaced it with annoyance.

"All morning, I've had machines and appliances attack me and then I found my boss horribly murdered by a serial killer that has been on the loose for over a year. I think I'm entitled to a drink."

"Not until you're twenty-one."

Chrissy huffed; she was tired—but couldn't close her eyes in fear of nightmares. She was hungry—but couldn't eat out of fear of bringing it back up. And the only thing she could do—she was too young to do it.

"Let's get to the questions, shall we." Altman tried to divert the tension. "Full name?"

"Christine Burke."

"Christine, you found the body, correct?"

"Yes," she whispered out—back to fighting with her hands.

"What prompted you to go into the office?" Freeman inquired.

"Um—" she struggled to recall. "—The supply guy came; Rory normally takes care of the orders, so I went to find the paperwork in Davis's office."

"And the door was open? Closed?" Alder prompted her to remember the details.

"Open—" she started but then shook her head. "—No, closed. But the doorknob was on the floor."

"Was that the only thing you noticed?"

Chrissy sighed roughly and blinked twice to get rid of the rising headache. "Just the handle."

Freeman took a quick glance at his notes, "You said Rory handles the orders?"

"Every Sunday."

"But not this Sunday?"

"She had the morning off."

Nicky and Nia's interviews were identical. Almost like they had rehearsed the answers beforehand. Which, of course, they did. Nicky was on dishwasher duty and Nia was on cleaning. Both had spent the shift in their respective area's and went home to their shared apartment and passed out eating leftover pizza and watching trashy TV. Both saw everyone in the team leave the building and didn't see Davis all night. Nicky made a point to mention a few of their friends who had stopped the night in case Rory needed an alibi.

Charlotte told the detectives that she had arrived at the bar around 7 and left not long before closing. The cameras outside her apartment building would confirm her story. Showing her enter the building last night and not going out until early this morning to open the cafe.

When the three were questioned about the *Gods Among king* brand, they all said the same as Will. Some members would occasionally drink there and with the financial holes Davis would dig himself into—it wouldn't surprise them if he had dug one in *Gods Among King's* backyard. Though none of them had ever seen them interact with Davis.

None of them wanted to be the one to rat the GAK boys out to the police. One member of *Ethel's* was already locked up; they didn't want anyone else behind bars or to end up like Davis because they opened their mouths to the police.

The last one to speak to the detectives was Rory and by now, they had already started to like her for the crime.

"Sorry about your wait," Altman apologised to her as she sat down and tucked her chair in.

Will and Chrissy both apologised to Rory, so she knew that they had mentioned her argument with Davis. She didn't know what exactly they had said, but she had to assume they knew everything.

"So, you're Rory? Full name?"

"Aurora James Scott."

Freeman hummed and took in her features, "You can't be more than twenty?"

Rory shook her head, "Nineteen."

"Let me guess," Freeman appeared annoyed and like he knew he had been lied to all morning. "Dishwasher?"

"Glass collector."

"Why is a glass collector handling the supply orders?" Freeman asked her and Rory identified him as the bad cop. He wasn't fooled by the group and his growing annoyance in his tone was giving it away.

"Someone has to do it."

"Tell us about last night. What happened when you confronted your boss about the money?"

"Will came and informed us about Davis clearing the safe out again, so I went up to speak to him."

"Speak to him? You must have been angry?" Altman finally asked a question.

"Understatement," she mumbled under her breath.

"Come again?" Freeman asked with a smirk and Rory had to remind herself that she couldn't reach across the table and smack the detective.

"I was angry, yes. But it doesn't mean I killed him."

"Why don't you tell us what happened then? Hmm?"

Rory heaved a sigh and rubbed the sweat from her forehead. "I went up to confront him, to sober him up enough to give him a lecture about being smart about spending money the bar doesn't have—"

Freeman interrupted her, "The bar is in dept?"

"Always has been, we thought that selling a percentage to Amelia Sawyer would help, but no amount of profit would save Davis. When I went up, his door was locked and he wouldn't answer, so I removed the door handle—"

"Removed the doorknob?" Altman sounded surprised.

"Screwdriver, though they're all old doors, it didn't take much force—"

“Is that where the bruises came from?” Freeman tilted his head to Rory’s hands; her knuckles were swollen and red.

“I kept banging on the door, but he wouldn’t answer.” She rubbed soothing circles on knuckles as she told them what happened. “He was spaced out and I couldn’t get anything out of him, so I threw some things around.”

“The broken glass, that was you?” Altman looked back through his notes and scribbled down on the paper.

“Yes. But then I quit and I packed my locker up and left. Everyone saw me leave and I spent the night in my shower crying. My neighbour has a hidden camera outside her door in her vase—the whole floor knows. Ms Nealson.”

Both men made a note of the neighbour’s name and Freeman asked the question that Rory had been dreading.

“Were you aware of Mr Davis’s involvement with the gang, ‘Gods Among Kings’?”

1. Confess everything: the branding, the ten grand and illegal alcohol. Tell them about the burner phone. Tell them about Abel being set up and branded. The police interview Link and Co and then they’ll get whatever informants in the force to tell them who sold them out so they can get revenge and Rory ends up dead in a ditch by the end of the day.
2. Deny everything and keep her life.

“No, I didn’t. Though he was in dept with everything, the bar, his house, the bank. It wouldn’t—”

“Surprise you if he was in dept with them too.” Freeman shut his notebook in defeat and leaned back in his chair before dismissing Rory.

The six sat on the bar stools with a bottle of vodka open and a shot glass each. Freeman and Altman had left after taking everyone’s information and contacts for alibis and a sly warning not to leave town. All the forensic vans and police cars had left not long after and the crowd that had gathered around the scene had gotten bored and disappeared. Leaving the team in silence at the bar.

“Did you all believe that I killed him?” Rory asked the silent group.

“Yes.” They all answered without a second to think. And Rory sighed.

She couldn’t blame them. Rory knew that Ms Nealson’s hiding camera would prove her innocence. Though the officials would want this case closed as fast as possible to spare them backlash from the public. Too long, the victim counter had been loose.

"Thank you," she said and took the bottle of vodka, filling her shot glass up, her friends sliding their own over for her to fill. "Now, I know I can trust you if I ever do kill someone," she joked, but the humour wasn't in her tone.

She passed the shots down the bar until everyone had one and Will cleared his throat.

"To Davis—" He swirled in his chair so he could see the bar floor and suited the ground. "—Rest well, you poor bastard."

Chapter Twenty-Nine
Pretty Attitude

Rory climbed the stairs to her apartment slower than she ever had before. Each step felt like she was adding three more to the journey to her bed. She was exhausted and drunk and all she wanted to do was climb into her covers with Caspian and sleep forever. She had called Emmitt on her way back from walking Charlotte home and saw her safe and settled. Emmitt suggested they'd shut the bar for a few days and regroup to see how to progress further.

Once she reached the fourth floor, she threw a finger to the broken elevator and headed down the narrow hallway that stretched longer in her vision. Two familiar-looking suited men stood at apartment 4C and were thanking Ms Nealson for her time. Rory groaned and tried to sober up as best as she could before the two men spotted her.

Detective Altman smiled warmly when his eyes landed on her and Rory sent a faint one back. Detective Freeman, on the other hand, looked angry. His eyes narrowed and he clicked his teeth.

"You got my alibi?" Rory managed to get out without slurring.

"Is the front door the only exit?" Freeman demanded an answer. In no mood to entertain.

"I take that as a yes," Rory bit. "There's the fire escape, but that stops fifteen-foot from the ground."

Freeman's face turned even sourer. "Right. Well, we still might need you to answer some questions so—"

"Don't skip town, I know." Rory pushed past them and didn't bother with goodbyes before unlocking her door and slipping inside her warm apartment.

She kicked her shoes off and threw her keys in the bowl but missed and the keys landed on the wood floor with a metal clang. "Oops."

Rory glared at the keys on the floor for a moment and a sense that something wasn't right spread through her. The apartment was an unsettling quiet. Rory quieted her breathing and her eyes scanned the room finding everything in place—nothing disturbed, nothing missing. *Caspian*. His bed was empty and the pup didn't come to greet her—or attack her with affection—like he always did. She couldn't hear the clicking of his nails on the wooden floor or his heavy snoring.

"Casp?" her voice rang out through the apartment and she waited, but he didn't come to her call.

"Caspian?"

This time it was louder and fear and worry laced her tone. Her head whipped to the side when she heard rusting from her bedroom doors—which she swore she had closed before she left that morning. Now they were slightly open and a light shone through. She reached down for her umbrella that was resting against the wall and grasped it like a bat, raising it above her head, ready to swing-out.

"I don't know who you are or what you want—" She took small steps towards the bedroom; her bare feet padded the floorboards softly. "—But I swear, if you hurt my dog, I will knock you into next century." Rory's hands tightened on the umbrella.

One.

She counted in her head as she reached the door, the rustling getting louder and a bark made her jump out of her skin.

Two

Her hand grasped the side of the door.

Three.

Rory slid the door open and swung blindly into the room. The weapon hit something hard and in a panic, she shut her eyes tight and swung again. Panic took over and all she could hear was Caspian's barking—louder now at the chaos. Rory was relentless with her attack, swatting the intruder over and over. Whatever whoever—she was hitting groaned loudly.

"Ow! Stop hitting me!" the intruder cried.

The sound cut through her panic and her eyes flew open to meet Link standing in her bedroom, rubbing his left arm where she had hit multiple times. Her mind took a minute to register the situation and she blinked numerous times.

"Where's my Dog and what are you doing in my bedroom?" she shot at him accusingly. "Or my apartment, for that matter?"

Link continued to rub his arm and with a dramatic tone, he said: "Your dog is in the bathroom. Your dog chased me into your bedroom and as for your apartment—" His rubbing had stopped as he finished, with a soft tone, "I came to check up on you."

Rory blinked twice. "Why is my dog in the bathroom?" She stepped around Link, not turning her back to him until she had reached the bathroom door—the umbrella remained in her hands, raised slightly. She could hear Caspian scratching the wood as she got closer.

"He chased me in here, so I shut him in the bathroom and I couldn't get the door open."

"Oh, the door gets stuck sometimes," she told him. "You have to turn the handle, push and lift." She did as she said and the door clicked open—A very mad looking Caspian raced out the room and started to nap at Link—who took refuge on her bed.

"Casp—here," Rory ordered and Caspian rushed to her feet—she bent down and scratched behind his ears. "Good boy," Rory praised. "Bed." Caspian obeyed and skipped to his bed in the living room—shooting Link a growl on his way.

Rory stood at the bathroom door. Her grip loosened on her weapon and her eyes sent death glares at Link, who sat at the edge of her bed—testing her mattress by patting and pushing the springs—watching as they bounce back up.

"What are you doing here?"

"I told you—" He twisted his head to look at her. "To check up on you."

"Why?"

"I heard about Davis." He shrugged. "Wanted to know if you were alright."

Rory wasn't buying his concern and raised an eyebrow. "You heard about Davis?"

He rolled his eyes, "Yes, I heard about Davis—" Link shook his head, "You know what? I came to check on you, I was nice and instead, I get assaulted and accused of murder."

Rory let out a noise in between a gasp and a laugh. "You didn't come to check up on me; you came to see if I told the police about you."

"If you had told them—" Link braced his hands on his knees as he stood up from the bed. In the early afternoon—her curtains parted slightly, allowing a small light from the low Autumn sun to golden her room. "—Neither of us would be stood here."

Rory caught the underlining threat, but the vodka and whiskey and annoyance in her system didn't. Defiance wrote all over her face. "I could have—Should have!"

Link took slow, haunting steps towards her and Rory planted her heels. She put the umbrella in front of her body as a shield.

"They want me for this, ya know? The detectives. If it wasn't for Ms Nealson's secret camera and a fifteen-foot drop—I would be in handcuffs right now. They know I fought with Davis; that doesn't look good. Detective dickhead wants someone pinned for this, Victim counter or nineteen-year-old dropout—they don't care!"

Link continued his advance on her. "Relax."

Rory's eyebrows shot up and her voice raised. "Relax? Relax? Did you not hear what I just said? I'm being questioned for murder because they can't get to their number one suspect!" She gestured to Link as he finally reached her. Standing a meter apart.

"Well, you're innocent, right?"

Her voice raised an octave or two. "Obviously!"

"Then you have nothing to worry about."

When Rory's face dropped—Link knew he had said the wrong thing. "My best friend is behind bars for a murder he didn't commit because of the flawed and corrupt justice system. Do not tell me to rely on it."

Rory's tone left no room for an argument that Link could win. She had studied the system and was let down by it. She was forced to stand back while Abel Sawyer was locked up because 'Gods Among Kings' had their hands wrapped around the justice system in Chicago. And though not every cop, detective and Judge in the town were on the gang's payroll—there was more that was.

"You're not going away for this, the shock from last night is making you overthink and panic." Link closed the distance and he lowered his tone. "Take a breath. They have nothing on you, you know it. You're smarter than this."

Rory did as told and closed her eyes and inhaled deeply and exhaling. Link was in such proximity that her breath fanned over his face. Link's eyebrows pulled together and he breathed in the bitter smell of alcohol.

"And you're drunk—" His dark eyes narrowed as they searched her own. Up close, he could see how bloodshot her eyes were. "—It's barely 5 o'clock, Aurora."

Rory's teenager kicked out and she pulled a sour face, "So What?" One hand went to her hip and Link rolled his eyes. "I think my boss getting murdered gives me an excuse to day drink just the once."

"Just the once? You're telling me that the day you saw Sawyer in prison, you didn't pop open a bottle?" Rory went to interject, but he wouldn't let her deny—or lie. "That night in the park—no way you were sober. And the fight at *Ethel's*?"

Rory felt her blood boil. Yes. When she got home after seeing her best friend rotting away in an orange jumpsuit, she had finished the tequila that Abe had left in her fridge and it might have been the fuel to her confidence—or stupidity—that drove her to confront Link in the park. And yes, she had taken multiple shots before her shift the night of the *Ethel's Vs GAK fight.*

"It's not like I'm relying on it to sleep, Link and besides, I've served you and your friends for over a year now—You want to talk about a drinking problem?"

"For now. You don't need it to sleep for now."

"I've had a pretty shitty month—" she defended, but it sounded more of an excuse than a reason. "—And I think you forget one common denominator."

"Don't," Link hissed out, the anger tugging on its leash, "I already have enough problems—don't project yours on me."

"I'm not projecting them on you!" she screeched in frustration. "YOU hurt Abel. YOU hurt Davis. I didn't ask for any of that!"

"Abel is an adult. Davis is an adult. Their actions lead them to their demise." Link wasn't shouting at Rory and she almost wished he would because this was more terrifying. "I told you to walk away from day one."

"How could I walk away from my friend's problems?!"

"Exactly!" Link exaggerated his voice, "Your friend's problems! Stop trying to fix everyone!" Rory was left speechless by Link's outburst, which invited him to go on.

"Fixing a dishwasher isn't the same as fixing a person, Aurora. Some people are too broken to be fixed! Focus on your own problems instead of putting yourself in danger to fix other's."

The umbrella dropped from Rory's grasp and clattered on the floor. "Now who's projecting."

"Do you know what you are?" Link smirked. "You're a rescuer."

"A rescuer?"

"Yes. You need to help people constantly while neglecting your own problems. Abel is your victim and you need him to depend on you to help—so you can be needed."

Rory seethed. "If I'm the rescuer. Then you're the persecutor. You blame the victim, criticise Abel in fear of being him!" She gave Link a pointed look. "Yeah. Dad taught me about the triangle of victimisation too."

The two stood in silence, Caspian's snoring filling the air softly and Rory envied the carefree dog. Sleeping away while the world burns around him. Link's chest was heaving and his face matched Rory's stunned one—embarrassed and shocked that their fatal flaws were out in the open. Rory was ignoring the little voice in the back of her head that whispered that the two weren't as unalike as she thought.

"I shouldn't have come—"

"How'd you come to that conclusion?"

"Pretty attitude."

"I try."

Link and Rory huffed simultaneously—neither having the energy to continue their fight. Both racking their brain to find something to say to break the defining silence. Fortunately—Rory's phone began to ring in her back pocket.

"If that's Detective Freeman calling to say they've got evidence against me and he's coming to arrest me—I'll set Caspian on you."

Rolling his eyes Link bit back, "Yes, because all murder suspects get a heads up before they're arrested."

Rory twisted her face at him but reached for her phone. Her heart stopped and the colour drained from her cheeks. "It's Chicago Prison," she whispered out. Link stopped examining the things on her bedside table and his eyebrows frowned. "Who's calling me from—" she mumbled.

"This is a call from MCC Chicago, Federal Bureau of Prison. To accept a call from Abel Patrick Sawyer press three."

Rory's fingers shook as she hit the number and pressed the phone back to her ear—scared of taking too long and missing the opportunity to talk to her best friend. A million thoughts ran through her head on why he was calling her—how he was calling her.

"Hey, AJ," Abel breathed out down the line—his voice rough and her heart jumped at the nickname he hadn't used in a long while.

"That's how you're starting this? Hey AJ?" Rory chuckled softly. The forgotten gang member frowned further as he strained to hear the conversation—which didn't sound much so far. "How are you even calling me? On a Sunday?"

"Perks of being a Sawyer," Abel joked though she could pick out the slight annoyance at the statement. "Emmitt pulled some strings, got me some phone time and your number is the only one I have memorised."

"Because you're terrible with numbers."

"You handle the Math and I handle the sarcastic comments. It's how we work."

Rory couldn't help the giggle that left her lips. Only Abel Sawyer could make someone laugh while on a phone call being recorded by the government.

"Abe—I have so much to ask you—"

"No." he said sternly and Rory groaned and almost stomped her foot. "I'm not calling to talk to Law school dropout Aurora James Scott. I want to talk to AJ, my best friend."

Rory chewed on her lip. "Abe," she whined. "I can't pretend that this is one if our normal phone calls. Secret Sawyer? Gangs?—"

"Please, AJ?"

"Alright."

She heard his relaxed sigh from down the phone. "Tell me about what I'm missing—How is Will and the Twins?"

"Nicky has just joined a band with some guys from college. He plays the bass, but he won't let us listen to them yet. Nia just passed a big exam with flying colours. And she's seeing someone I think, some chick with a lip ring."

"And Will?"

"Will is—Will."

"You two fighting again?"

"No, I'm not fighting with Will again."

Link snorted and Rory whirled around. Remembering that a gang member was still present and walking around her room—now, he was fussing over her bedroom window. She crossed her free hand over her chest and moved to the corner of her room—putting some distance between herself and Link.

"Maybe we're fighting."

She could practicality feel his eye roll. "What about now?"

The simple question triggered Rory's memories from the night before and that morning. She drew in a sharp breath. "Abe. I didn't want to tell you this over the phone, but—" Rory couldn't get the words to form in her mouth and they wouldn't leave her lips.

"What is it? Rory? Is it a bad fight?" Abel filled with worry and he straightened up from his position leaning against the dirty prison wall. "Did you two?—are you together—?"

Rory's empty stomach threatened to rise at the insinuation. Will was like her very annoying older brother, who would steal her toys and refuse to play with her. But he would be the first one at her side if she faced trouble.

"No. No. God no—" She waved the questions off with her hand. "We had a fight last night about Davis and well—" Rory closed her eyes and forced the words to come out. "Abe—Davis was killed last night. Davis is dead."

Abel's heart stopped; a wave of grief washed over him for a moment. "How?—Who?—What—"

"Chrissy found him this morning in his office—It was brutal," she whispered the last. Her back turned from Link and she could feel his narrowed eyes on the back of her head. "The detectives questioned us all this morning. I may be needing a tour inside soon; it's not looking good for me."

"You're not getting arrested."

"You're not getting arrested."

Link and Abel spoke simultaneously and Rory waved Link to be quiet, but Abel had heard Link.

"Rory, are you with someone?" It wasn't a question. She could hear it in his voice—he knew someone was there.

"No, It's nobody. It's the TV—ignore him-It. Ignore it." She cursed herself for slipping up and her face scrunched up. Prepared for a lecture by Abel.

"Put him on."

"No—"

"Now."

Rory groaned and the phone reluctantly slid from her ear and held it to Link. "He wants to speak to you."

Link smirked and took the phone from her. "Be nice." She mouthed but knew he would ignore her. Rory struggled to listen to what Abel was saying to Link, but she couldn't make anything out. Link's placid face remained for the few minutes Abel had spoken and Rory doubted he was even listening. Her fingers twisted together and she shifted from foot to foot, the unknowing conversation hitting every nerve. When Link would hum—Rory would shoot her eyebrows up and plead to know what was said. Link had to sidestep away when Rory tried to get closer to the phone and she huffed in irritation.

"I don't think you're in the position to demand anything, do you?" Link sassed.

"What demand?" Rory rushed. "What is he saying?" Link put his hand up to silence her and Rory blinked at the action. "Give me the phone."

Ignoring her, Link hummed. "And you're going to follow through with that threat how? Giving your current imprisonment and all."

Rory threw her arms up and they settled on her face, rubbing the frustration away. She had no idea how much phone time Abel had. The limited time they had and the pair were wasting it on threats and gods know what.

"Pretty big accusation you're making there, mate. Don't suppose you have any proof?" There was a moment of silence. "Didn't think so."

"Surely your mother taught you actions have consequences?"

"Your friends should consider that too."

"Are they? Then they have nothing to worry about."

"More threats?"

She was lost. Rory hadn't any idea what they were talking about. Only hearing one very vague end of the conversation left her in the dark. *Again*. And Link's mischievous smirk told her she wouldn't be finding out anytime soon. Her eyes fell to her clock—too much time had passed and she feared the call would end before she had a chance to talk to Abel again and it felt as though Link was dragging the conversation out on purpose.

"Who?"

Rory was pulled from watching the hands on the clock to the man in front of her. "Oh, her." His eyes twitched and her eyebrows drew together. Link ran his tongue over his bottom lip and she saw an idea flash over his face. "Can't promise that I'm afraid."

"Who?" she almost shouted. "Promise what?"

"And if I don't?"

"Careful." His expression wasn't smug anymore. Rory watched his fist at his side clench. Whatever Abel had said hit a nerve. "I don't need to remind you of what we're capable of."

"I can't take this," Rory stated and marched to Link, attempting to take the phone from his hand, but he shrugged her off easily. "Give me the phone or tell me what he's saying!"

"Wow, so demanding," Link commented and Abel spoke down the phone and Link took his attention from the struggling girl to the inmate. "I'll tell her you to say goodbye."

"Don't hang up—don't you dare—"

The phone went silent and Link finally pulled the phone from his ear and Rory snatched it and put it to her own—repeating Abel's name with no answer. She whirled to the gang member, resentment in her eyes.

"What did he say?" she hissed out deadly. And Link shrugged.

"Nothing important." As If the last five minutes hadn't had happened, as if he hadn't just stolen some of the limited contact she had with Abel Sawyer, as if he wasn't withholding information from her again. Link waltzed to her bedroom door and exited into her living room. "You should check the locks on your windows—easy access for someone dangerous."

Rory chased after him, but he had already shut her door and made his way down the corridor. She clutched her phone to her chest and told herself to breath. She'd speak to Abel again—he'd call again. The girl changed into nightwear and curled under her covers, the phone still held to her chest and the ringer as loud as it went.

Chapter Thirty
Bad News, Worse News, and Morally Grey News

"I told you this would happen," Hino sang. "Didn't I tell you this would happen?"

Ash sighed deeply and rubbed his temples, praying to God for patience. "Yes. You told us this would happen, but it's still better than being six feet under."

"It's really not," Marius said into his glass. The head of his beer formed poorly in the dirty glass, the bitter taste rotting his tongue and he wiped his mouth with a scowl.

After Order 131 was carried out a week ago, *Ethel's* had been closed. They were expecting some backlash from Davis's murder, maybe even a colder shoulder than they were already getting from the bar team. They didn't expect the shutters to be drawn when they went to cool off after a successful job on Tuesday. They weren't expecting it to be closed on Thursday either. They were sure by Saturday; the bar would be open and playing terrible music.

A week was more than enough time to mourn their shitty boss. Yet, here they were, Saturday night. Cramped around a tiny circle table, feeble wooden chairs almost overlapping each other. Drinking poor beer out of unwashed glasses and eating the stale peanuts that Marius had been overcharged for at the bar.

They had downgraded to 'The Two Sixes'—four blocks from their usual drinking ground. And right now, with the Football game aggravating one side and shady deals being made on the other. The boys wished they hadn't carried out Lenzo's orders. A bullet in the head for betrayal would be mercy.

"What did you say to Rory Scott when you went to see her last week?" Hino whined and Link shot his head to Marius, who suddenly decided that the drink wasn't that bad and hid behind his glass.

Link hadn't stated that Marius should keep Link's trip to the redhead a secret between the two, so Marius guessed Link wouldn't mind. The pair had walked by the bar on Friday morning just to check It out and then took refuge in 'All American' when the shutters of the bar locked them out in the rain. Rory and Nia sat in a booth, mumbling over some papers and books spread out over the table. Link ducked into a booth away from their eye view and Marius ordered coffee for them.

"Maybe we should ask when they're reopening?" Marius thought aloud and Link shot the idea down—filling his brother in on the events at Rory's apartment.

"I like that shithole, man."

Link followed Marius's eyes to the two girls, "Yeah, me too." His eyes were on the side of Rory's face, her hair like a ginger curtain as it fell over the side of her face as she leaned over the table to grab the book and opened to a page—showing it to her friend.

"You like the bar?—" Marius's eyes slid to Link and he had a sly smile, "—Or you like her?"

"Which one keeps her alive?"

Marius wore the expression he always wore when he would tune into big brother mode. Marius was brilliant, name a book—he had read it, name a language—he spoke it. He had a degree in English Literature, Art History and Architecture. And he was the groups therapist.

"I don't know what happened for you to fall into this life—but if you get a chance to get out, to live a normal life away from guns and branding—take it. You've sacrificed enough, kid."

"I can't—" Link didn't meet Marius's eyes, his voice barely a whisper and the tips of his fingers tapped his cup, "I can't get out—" He shook his head, "Not for a long time yet, I owe Lenzo."

"We all owe Lenzo; you've paid enough." Marius cut him off. It broke him to see his younger friend like this. Broken and tired and stuck with no way out. Sleep was supposed to be a way to rest and escape reality, but even Link's sleep was tainted with the harshness of his life.

Marius kept a consistent soft tone, "My brother, he got in an accident, he took some damage to his head—" Marius quietened and he sucked in a small breath, Link looked up to meet his eyes and they were glossy—the first time Link had seen his stronger older brother vulnerable. "—and I needed money for his medical treatments."

"So, you found Lenzo." Link tried to keep his voice as soft as Marius s, but his naturally rough accent wouldn't let him.

Marius nodded, "I was doing boxing at a gym to earn some cash and Lenzo showed up, offering triple the amount of money. Lenzo had me run some security jobs, mainly stand there to scare people—" He laughed lightly. "My brother, he took bad. A brain haemorrhage before I could pay for the treatment." "Marius didn't have to confirm the outcome for Link to know that his brother didn't make it."

Marius's shaking hands said it for him. "I'm not telling you this, so you'll share your trauma with me now. But you need to share it; you need to let go. Nothing Lenzo could have done for you is worth what he's doing to you now. See a chance to get out and take it. I'll be right behind you."

Link was snapped back to the present when a round of cheers shouted through the bar due to the football team scoring a goal.

"I was just checking if the detectives had anything on us." He knew they never had enough evidence (or balls) to go after the gang, anyways. He guessed he wanted a heads up before the order came in from Lenzo to take out the rats.

"You must have said something wrong," Hino whined again and Link scowled.

"Nothing I said was enough for her to close the bar for a week."

"So, you did say something; you should go apologies."

"Maybe the bar is closed because the owner is dead?" Link counter offered.

"Hino's right—" To everyone's surprise, it was Ash who spoke. "As much as I dislike *Ethel's*—I hate it here more." Ash turned his nose up at the room.

Link looked to Marius for backup, but Marius pulled a face. "Look, man, I agree with them—"

Link rolled his eyes and tried to lean back into his chair, but it made a straining sound, so he settled for an awkward angle. "I doubt the bar is closed because you accused Scott of becoming an alcoholic—"

"You what?" Ash and Hino cut Marius off. Ash heaved a sigh. "You are aware she poses a threat to the gang, right? Make her angry enough and she'll go to the Sawyers with whatever she knows. Which means we'll have to kill her."

Hino pulled a face. "You hate her. Shouldn't you want to kill her?"

"I don't hate her," Ash defended. "When have I ever said I hate her?"

"You hate everyone, I guess we all assumed—" Hino trailed off.

"But you should apologise; we all should. We've been expecting this for a while now. We got lucky that they even allowed us in after they found out about Sawyer. Their boss is dead because of his shitty habits and they blame us and I don't blame them," Marius finished.

A week after the death of their boss, *Ethel's* team were ready to open the bar and get back to work. The twins didn't like the idea of an empty bank account. Will needed work for parole and Chrissy, she wanted out of the house. The two detectives had paid her a visit for follow up questions and her grandparents (who she was living with) found out about Davis and they had smothered her for the whole week. Bringing her soup and milk while she lay in bed, trying not to think about Davis's blood while eating the tomato soup.

She couldn't breathe; getting back to *Ethel's*, back to normal, was the only thing on her mind. So, the four had contacted Emmitt and had planned to meet on Sunday morning at the 'All American' to discuss how to move forward. And with a lot of convincing—and baked goods on behalf of his partner, Khenan—Emmitt had managed to get Rory to agree to join them.

Rory shook off the October chill at 'All American's' door and scanned the room for her friends. Emmitt sat in a booth at the back, he was alone, but Charlotte was filling his cup up. Charlotte had come to Rory's and crawled into her bed on Wednesday and cried. Rory engulfed her in the blankets and let her friend let go of her emotions. Like Chrissy, Charlotte couldn't get Davis's body out of her memory. The night of crying and talking it out had helped a lot, but Rory could see that Charlotte was still shaken.

"Am I early?" Rory asked as she slid into the booth opposite Emmitt—Charlotte saying she'd grab Rory a cup of tea. Rory gave her friend a warm smile in greeting.

"Actually, I asked you here early."

"Oh?" Rory sounded slightly worried.

"I've got bad news, worse news and morally grey news."

"Mix them up and I'll guess which is which."

Emmitt braced himself with a sigh and said, "Abel won't see you anymore. My Mother is planning a surprise visit to determine whether *Ethel's* is worth the trouble it's caused and Davis left his share of the bar to you."

All the information hit Rory one after the other and didn't give her enough time to sink each one in. And she sat dumb as the news slowly, slowly—bounced off her brain.

"What?"

Emmitt repeated slowly.

"What?"

Emmitt sighed and sat back in the seat and Charlotte came over with Rory's drink. Rory looked up to her friend helplessly and Charlotte scrunched her nose up. "I know, sweetie, I heard this morning. Don't worry, though; Abel's stubborn, but he'll do anything for you—you know that. He'll be alright."

Abel didn't want to see her. What had he and Link spoken about on the phone? Whatever it was had Abel closing off again. Rory had waited all week with her phone in her hand, waiting for Abel to call. At this point, she would just be happy to hear his voice; she didn't need to press him for information or question him on the situation. She just needed to know he was alright.

Abel had called her and said it was the only number he had memorised, but she knew that was a lie. She knew he knew the bar's number and Will's number and Nicky's number. If Link had just kept quiet or if she had moved into another room or if she had refused to hand the phone over to Link or if she had—

"Don't worry about Abel," Emmitt blew on his cup but didn't take a drink, cutting Rory's self-blaming thoughts off. "I've managed to convince my mother to call in Mr Derry, one of our family defence lawyers, to look at the case. He may wish to speak to you, though. He knows Abel called you last week—so be on call."

Rory only nodded distantly.

"See, I told you, don't worry." Charlotte leaned into Rory. The Cafe was always empty on a Sunday morning and Charlotte could sit down with them. "It's the bar you have to worry about, though you do practically run it already."

Rory cursed. "This can't be legal?"

"You know it is," Emmitt said calmly. "You're nineteen; you're allowed to own a bar. Well, sixty-five percent."

"So, I'm not old enough to drink in a bar, but I'm old enough to run one," Rory stared at the cup and wished it was filled with something stronger. "This is just fantastic, absolutely fantastic. Will is going to love this."

"Oh, nice to grace us with your presence, Aurora." Will's remark made his, Nicky, Nia and Chrissy's presence knowing and Charlotte slid out the booth to get everyone a drink. They all shuffled into the booth tightly. "And I absolutely love this."

"I'm guessing the pale face means you've been told the good news?" Nicky said with a hint of amusement in his tone. "Congrats, boss."

Will said, "And Amelia Sawyer? What we going to do about her?"

"Could you refrain from referring to my mother like she's on your hit list, please?" Emmitt grimaced and Will apologised.

"I just mean, when she deems us unworthy, she'll back out, won't she?"

"Not if she doesn't deem you unworthy." Everyone looked at Emmitt like he had grown two heads. Chrissy let out a snort. Emmitt scrunched his face up. "It's not too bad if you get rid of the—"

"Smell?" Chrissy asked.

"Damp?" Nia said.

"Unidentifiable stains?" Nicky pulled a face.

"Gang members?" Will offered.

"Debt?" Rory breathed and everyone turned their attention to her. "Davis put the bar up for his ex' house. If we don't find the money for it, we're shut for good. I don't even think *A S Co* can help."

"How much?" Will asked like he didn't want to know the answer.

Rory told them and everyone's face drained of colour. Chrissy even mumbled, "We're screwed."

"There's no way we can get that much," Nicky chimed in.

Will saw it behind her green eyes. The idea that was forming. She started to chew the inside of her lip and her fingers played with her ear. "I know that look; it's normally followed by a crazy idea. What are you thinking, Ror?"

Rory stared at him while she was fishing the plan in her head. "I may have an idea."

Will rolled his eyes and sighed. "Does it involve robbery?"

"I guess since I own the bar—no."

"Does it involve gang members?"

"Kinda."

"Is it illegal?"

"Of Course."

Rory waited for Charlotte to join them again in the booth before diving into her plan. "You know how those detectives were asking about Davis and 'Gods Among Kings'?" She waited for everyone to confirm with a nod. "Well, he was involved with them," Nia mumbled 'shocker', but Rory ignored it.

"Davis borrowed money. Ten grand. From what I've worked out, he had promised to double it by what means I have no clue. He used it for bootlegged alcohol for the bar. Clearly sketchy. But he had me change the receipts, put them on different orders so if anyone came looking—"

"They wouldn't see he had used their money to buy knock-off booze that couldn't make a decent profit," Will finished and Rory confirmed with a slight nod. "Jesus Rory, do they know that you changed them?"

Though they hadn't apologised and they both still harboured anger towards each other—Rory was glad Will was here, not just at the meeting but with her. Beside her. And she knew she could count on him.

"No. I think they would have killed me by now if they knew. The alcohol, it's in a storage locker downtown. Maybe we could sell it all, we could get more than enough to pay the bank if we go to the right people and we should have some leftover to decorate the bar to impress Amelia Sawyer."

"Sell to whom?" Nia asked the important question.

"I'm hoping you could help with that part, Will. You have to know people?" Rory gave will her best puppy dog eyes hoping to fold him.

"I mean, maybe some bars, some old college mates with deep pockets and poor fake IDs." Rory lit up with hope and Will tried not to smile. "This may be your best idea yet Rory, it could work."

"Any idea when your mother Is going to surprise us?" Nia asked Emmitt.

"Most likely Halloween, to see how busy it gets on a popular night."

The group brainstormed ideas. From people and places who would buy their alcohol. Cheapest places to get decoration supplies such as paint and wooden flooring. Chrissy had mentioned that *Ethel's* was costing more to run during the day than it was making, so Rory decided to keep the bar closed during the days, opening at 5 in the afternoon until they were in a financial situation stable enough. The team also agreed on a uniform change, keeping the apron and name badges but swapping the impractical uniform to professional shirts printed with: *ETHEL'S 1984.*

“Two weeks, we have two weeks to sell fake booze, fix everything, paint and re-floor,” Will said, staring at the list of tasks they had written on an order paper Charlotte had given them. “Easy.”

Rory laughed lightly, “I’m going to need some help, an assistant or manager. Someone who can order stock in legally, someone I can trust to get things done when I can’t.” Her eyes were on Will and it took him a moment to figure out she meant him. His mouth opened slightly before shutting and he nodded firmly.

Chapter Thirty-One
It's Nothing

Will had called around some bars and friends after the cafe meeting and had managed to convince most of them into buying some crates for an unreasonable price. 'The Two Sixes' had agreed to take the spirits for way more than they were worth. Will claimed to know the manager from a gym they both were members of and Will warned Rory in the car on the way over that 'The Two Sixes' was also a hotspot for Chicago gangs and told her to stay close and keep her head down.

They were sat at a table for four, Will ordered them both sodas and when Rory went to take a sip, he covered the top of her glass and told her not to take a drink. It was an understatement by saying that Rory was uncomfortable. Will had spent the ride over telling her what to do and what not to do. And when Rory saw all the different characters, she understood why.

The group of bikers in one corner had stared at the two the moment they had walked in the bar (Rory recognised them as old *Ethel's* regulars before the college students found the bar and drove them out), eyeing up the crate Will had carried in—For Denny, the manager. On the other side of the bar were customers surrounded by smoke that burned Rory's lungs. Will had whispered to her once they had sat down that they were from a lower gang that dealt in street deals, lower than 'Gods Among Kings'. She wasn't to make contact with them.

"Why didn't you bring Nicky?" Rory asked and kept her eyes from trailing around the room.

"Because Nicolas will flirt."

"Is that a bad thing? We could use the money." Her voice was low.

"Oh and now you have no problem with flirting to get something?" Will teased and Rory's cheeks went red.

"Chrissy told you?"

Will nodded with a cheeky smile which dropped slowly and his eyes turned guilty. "Ror, I'm sorry for what I said, blaming you for Davis and the safe."

"Will, I should be the one apologising. I should have listened to you. You were right. I've been in a rotten mood since Abe has been away and I had no right to take it out on you—The bar, it would have sunk long ago without you and the twins and Chrissy. I rely on you all and I need to start realising it. You don't have to apologise."

"I do; it wasn't your fault or responsibility. I'm also sorry for keeping the secret about Abel. Everyone deserved to know I just didn't want to let him down. I should have told you sooner; maybe he would have agreed to a trial if you had gotten to him sooner."

"William—Abel being locked up isn't your fault and you know it. And he's coming out, I don't know how but he's coming home." Rory sensed the mood change and hated it. She had felt glum and miserable for so long and she didn't want to feel it anymore. "And when he's out, he'll kick your ass for bringing me here."

She managed to get a laugh out of him and it warmed her heart the slightest bit. His laughter died as the door chimed and heavy laughter sounded the room.

"Oh, you have got to be—"

"Morrison! Scott!" a familiar voice called out and Rory went red at the attention it attracted. "Fancy seeing the two of you here!"

"Isao. Hi," Rory greeted as he headed towards their table; everyone in the bar had lost interest very quickly and returned to their business. "Didn't take you lot long to move on; *Ethel's* has been closed for a week."

"A week and two days," Marius corrected, frowning at their surroundings. A silent plea to open *Ethel's* back up soon. "Gave up on the place?"

"We probably should have a long time ago," Will joked and took Rory back, her face physically showing confusion. He made a joke to members of 'Gods Among Kings' and to Marius of all people. They had permanent scowls whenever they saw each other. Everyone held their breath whenever Marius went to order and Will was serving, both one wrong look from jumping over the counter and attacking each other. And now he was joking with him?

Will must have surprised himself as well and frowned.

"But you're not?" Hino asked hopefully and Will shook his head.

"Nice collection," Link chimed in from behind his friends. He and Ash were hiding away in the back and hadn't greeted them yet. And after Link's comments the week before—He was lucky he was still standing.

"Thank you." Everyone sensed Rory's sassy comment coming. "Like you said, I can't get through an issue without it, so I thought I'd best have some with me at all times, you know, just in case." Her eyes narrowed at him.

"I didn't say that—"

"Hm, I think you did."

"I'm sorry," Link said almost silently.

"What?" Rory gapped in genuine disbelieve, thinking her ears were playing tricks on her.

Link heaved a sigh and painfully said. "I said I'm sorry."

"For?"

"Suggesting you have a drinking problem."

Rory raised an eyebrow, not satisfied.

"And for breaking into your apartment."

Eyebrow raised higher.

"And for locking your dog in the bathroom."

Even higher.

"For calling out your fatal flaw of needing others to need you so you can feel important and wanted all the while neglecting your own problems."

Marius took in a breath, Will slid away from Rory. Hino went pale and Ash looked at his brother, remembering the details of his face before the petite redhead destroyed him in the moments to come.

"For killing my boss and putting my best friend in jail would have sufficed, but now that you've brought it up, let's unpack—" Rory moved her hand in a circular motion around Link, "—All of that. How's your back?"

The boys all turned to Rory in confusion, but Link had a mix of dread and rage. "How's the self-deprecating?"

"Going down nicely with tequila. How's the daddy issues?"

"Fucking fabulous—How's yours?"

Rory's chest heaved. "How's the 'Yes man blind loyalty syndrome'?"

"How's the empty bank account?"

"How's the heavy conscience?"

The moment it came out, Rory regretted it. She heard Will suck in a breath and saw the pain in Link's eyes. She closed her own for a moment.

"Too far, I'm sorry."

"I started it," Link said softly.

Hino leaned into Marius and whispered, "What's happening?"

"I don't know, it's almost like they're—"

Will finished Marius's sentence. "Apologising sincerely?"

Rory went to scowl, but her phone started to vibrate on the table. Nia's caller ID came up. "Hello?" Rory answered the phone.

"The guy's here to inspect the damp," Nia started and Rory could hear the bad news in her voice. "He said it's worse than we thought and it's going to cost between five fifty and eight hundred."

"Five hundred and fifty dollars to fix damp?" Rory shouted down the phone and Nia mumbled in agreement. "Jesus, can you talk him down?"

"I did, from nine hundred."

Rory leaned her elbow on the table and rested her head in her hand, doing mental maths to work out how far the work would set them back. She could hear Will tell the gang—who still stood around their table awkwardly—about the damp in the cellar and along with one of the walls in the bar.

"It shouldn't be that much," Ash spoke up. Hino and Marius stepping aside so Rory and Will could see him clearly. "You're getting charged way too much; if it's the back wall and cellar, it should only be around three hundred."

Will and Rory frowned their eyes at Ash, who seemed to know what he was talking about. Will asked, "You've had damp? Who fixed it?"

"I didn't have damp. I did construction."

"You did construction?" Will and Rory said in unison.

Rory couldn't believe what she was hearing. Ash, constant sour face, so above the likes of *Ethel's* employee. Carried a gun everywhere and gave you the impression that he'd use it if you so much as looked at him wrongly. He had an education in a trade. Made a living doing something ordinary.

"Saw it all the time. A young girl would ring for an estimate and they'd assume she was stupid and gullible, so they'd exaggerate the damage, double the price. Poor girls would be scammed out of hundreds." Ash's voice filled with anger and bitterness the more he spoke. His arms threw up. "You know what, tell the guy it doesn't matter. I'll do it."

"Really?" Rory lit up.

"I'll have to have a look at the damage first, but I have the equipment already. How does two-fifty sound?"

"Deal! God, I could kiss you!"

"Please don't."

Rory went back to Nia on the phone and filled her in on the new plan before hanging up.

"I'll swing by *Ethel's* tomorrow to take a look," Ash told the two as he fished through his pockets, pulling out his wallet. "Here, text me a time."

He handed Rory a card. "You—you have a business card*?*"

With awkward waves, the four retreated away from the table to their own.

"Link—" Rory called and Link turned back, "—The drink isn't mine," she cleared, unsure why she felt the need to defend herself. Link looked at the crate and at Rory and gave her a nod in understanding.

"He broke into your apartment?" Will asked Rory.

"It was nothing, really."

"William Morrison!" For the second time, Will's name was called out, making everyone turn to the two. "I haven't seen you since your daddy caught us in the boathouse! God, I can still see your daddy's disappointment."

"What happened at the boathouse?" Rory asked with a smirk.

"It was nothing, really," Will repeated and Rory bumped his arm.

"And who is your clearly underage friend?"

Denny, Will's old friend, wasn't how Rory had pictured him. Will's friends were typically uptight, sauntered because their wallets dragged their weight down. Pristine hair and tucked their elbows in when they were at *Ethel's* as if they'd catch something if they relaxed. But Denny wore ripped jeans, dark vests and his goatee was wild. Despite the rough look, Denny had a warm smile, welcoming.

"This is Rory. Rory, this is Denny."

"Nice to meet you." Rory smiled politely, shaking his firm hand.

"So, you guys have something for me?" He slid into the booth and eyed up the crate of bottles.

Will leaned over the table to take a bottle out, "Tequila. Forty per cent on the label, twenty-five per cent in the bottle. The less percentage, the more time it'll take for your customers to get drunk, more they'll buy. Tastes the same."

Rory forced her face not to react to Will's lies. It didn't taste the same. It left a cheap, almost plastic, taste on your tongue if you drank it straight. But Will was lying so effortlessly, a true businessman.

“I’m sure you wouldn’t mind me trying it before I buy?” Denny requested and Rory froze up.

“Can I propose a blind trial?” Will surprised her again. “A shot of our tequila and a shot from your shelf. See if you can tell the difference?”

Denny seemed to like the idea as he called one of his barmaids to bring over a standard bottle and a few shot glasses over. “Of course, it’ll have to be bias—” he said and looked around the room. “Maddox, bro—Could I steal you for a second?” he shouted over to the only guy sitting at the bar counter.

His long hair was pushed off his face by a bandanna. Green eyes, almost like cat’s peered at the three of them.

“Yeah?” he asked, voice raspy like he had been smoking longer than he had been alive.

Denny straightened up, taking the bottle from his barmaid and setting the tray of shot glasses on the table. “Rory here—” He pointed to her and she sent Maddox a half-smile, “—Is going to pour us two shots each and we’re going to guess which is the sample and which is the real thing.”

“Sure.” That was all he said as he took place next to Denny. Will sent Rory a cautious look and Rory sent a panicked one back. She took the bottles and tray and moved to the empty table next to them; her back turned, so they didn’t see which shot was which.

She stared at the bottles and wrecked her brain for anything. Quickly she got to work on pouring the shots out. Looking up, she caught Ash staring at her as she carried out the plan. A hint of an impressed smile played at his lips.

“Enjoy,” Rory presented the boys with the shots. All but Rory took two and knocked them back as if they were water.

Will and Rory didn’t breathe as they waited for the verdict. Maddox spoke first.

“No difference.”

“I’ll have to agree, though the sample from *Ethel’s* bar burned just a little more.”

Bullshit.

Maddox’s ears picked up. “*Ethel’s* bar?” he asked and Will confirmed they worked there. “Hasn’t the owner just been killed or something?”

“Last week,” Will said.

“That’s rough,” he sighed. “I’m sure my friend used to go there all the time. Sawyer?”

Now Rory's ears picked up. "You know Abel Sawyer?" she asked.

"Aye. We went to school together, though I haven't heard from him in a while."

Will saw Rory gulp and stepped up to tell the story for her. Getting the hint, she didn't want to speak about it.

"Wow, if he didn't do it, wouldn't he have an alibi or something?"

Rory sighed and dropped into the booth. "That's the big question."

"Well, if he's innocent, something will work out. I'm sure."

"Enough of this Kid, let's talk about price." Denny smiled greedily.

Chapter Thirty-Two
If You're Sure He is Innocent

After selling the alcohol to multiple bars and frat houses, they had more than enough money to keep the bank happy and they had leftovers to buy paint, a new floor and a second-hand dishwasher. Nothing to fancy, but it worked. Ash had offered to lay the floor after he had damp proofed the place for an extra fifty dollars. Chrissy had turned out to be a math genius, better than Rory, so the two girls sat at the bar top, going through budgeting while Ash got to work lifting the sticky and stained floor that was placed down in the eighties. And the two girls almost had pitied him for him.

"Are you sure you want to do this?" Chrissy sounded from her place at the bar, thick black frames sliding down her nose and blue ink covering her fingers. "It doesn't look very safe."

Rory hummed in agreement, but Ash shook his head. The girls couldn't tell his expression with the mask that covered his mouth and nose. "If you get someone in to do this, not only will they overcharge you, but they'll also shut you down for being a hazard to health."

Nicky and Chrissy, who Rory had entrusted with choosing the décor, had gone with a dark tumbled laminated oak flooring, cheap, slip-resistance, waterproof and easy to clean. They had also bought several tins of paint—sage green to brighten the already dark room and Nicky had managed to score some vintage rock posters to replace the washed-out old ones.

Rory had planned to paint after Ash had finished his work on the walls, but the plaster hadn't dried yet, so she'd wait for him to lay the floor. He had been surprisingly kind enough to offer her some floor protectors to keep the new flooring safe from paint droplets.

"You know," Ash started, voice muffled through the mask, the girls just managing to understand him. "If you're getting new furniture, you should get some pads to stick on the bottom to protect the floor from scrapes and damage." All morning, Ash listened to the girl's planning and chipped in with ideas here and there. 'Warmer lights will set the tone better', 'Perhaps you could get a new karaoke machine—fun and brings in money'. 'Or you could start to rent the rooms upstairs'. 'Have you tried to hire bands for live music?'

Rory had told him that they had already thought of the room suggestion, but they couldn't afford the renovation until the bar brought in more money, which would be a long time from now. But they didn't rule out the karaoke and live music idea. Their machine was as old as the flooring Ash was lifting.

"If we stick with opening six on weekdays and five on weekends, we could replace the windows in around five weeks if we go to 'Bits and Bob's'," Chrissy told Rory, who was studying the equations Chrissy had presented her.

"Bobby's?" Ash snorted, pulling the mask down to rest under his chin.

"Who?" Rory asked, eyes still glued to the numbers and plans in front of her in fear of being caught staring at Ash and have to listen to Chrissy tease her for it.

"Bobby owns 'Bits and Bob's'," Ash sat up from the floor and brushed his hands on the dark blue overalls that were tied at his waist, leaving him in a black vest covering his chest. His bare arms covered in colourless tattoos of various objects, skulls, flowers, quotes in different languages, blades. He stretched his long limbs and Rory allowed herself to peek up at him. His muscles twitched as he rolled his stiff shoulders back.

Rory grabbed a soda for Ash from the only fridge that was switched on. They had decided to shut the bar for however long it took them to get ready to open again. Rory and Nia had drawn the short straws and spent the day before cleaning Davis's office, which took as long as they thought it would and now the room was bare, empty of everything, including the god-awful carpet.

"So, what's wrong with Bobby's?" she asked as Ash took the drink from her. "Other than the fact that you know him by name," she joked and Ash's lips lifted.

"Half his stock is stolen and the other half are illegally imported from England."

"Who illegally imports windows?" Chrissy pulled a face.

"You'd be surprised what's imported nowadays," Ash took a final drink and headed back over to where the floor was now lifted and began to open the new flooring packages up. "The far wall should be dried now, to paint."

Rory changed into joggers and an old college shirt that belonged to her father that was already stained with multicoloured paint. She was opening the paint tin when Chrissy spoke up about the busiest night of the year for *Ethel's*.

"So, Halloween? Do you guys do costumes?"

"Yes, we do a group costume; last year, it was the Scooby gang, the year before that, it was pirates," Rory explained and Chrissy tried to figure out who was who in the scooby gang. *Will was Fred.*

"Will wasn't Fred," Rory stated as if she was reading Chrissy's thoughts. "Nicky suggested zombies for this year but giving the past few weeks we've had—"

"—Not zombies!" Chrissy almost yelled out. A picture of Davis's mutilated body flashed in her memories. "How about Princes and princesses?"

"Write it down; we'll make a list—see what the others think," Rory dipped the brush into the green paint and started to coat the walls.

"We could do a gang group costume?" Rory teased, the purpose of winding Ash up, testing her luck. Since Davis's death, the gang members had been unusually amiable—offering help, apologising—so Rory was going to milk it and maybe, she'd get information on Abel.

"You do gang members and we'll do *Ethel's* members—try me," was his response—not looking from his work.

Chrissy didn't stay long after that conversation, promising she hadn't left to avoid decorating, just she had somewhere she was needed. The nerves of leaving Rory with a guy who had already been in a physical altercation with them before was evident in her persistence to get Rory to call her if she needed anything. Ash didn't dismiss her concerns, but Rory assured her friend that she'd be OK.

Ash had lain almost half of the floor and from the paint already on the walls—it looked good and Rory couldn't help the proud smile as she took in half of the improvements. The pair had taken a quick break and stood in uncomfortable silence while they drank their sodas.

"Can I ask you something personal?" Rory dared.

"No."

"I'm going to ask anyway—" Rory placed her drink on the bar and turned her body to face him fully. "—How did you end up here?" Ash frowned his eyebrows and Rory elaborated, "You're a professional constructor—you had a career in the business and you're good at it," Rory started. "So, how did you go from fixing damp walls to shooting people and framing people for murder?"

Ash looked around the bar as if to double-check no one was listening In. A hand gripped his drink tighter and he took a deep breath, Rory getting giddy at the new information she was about to learn and Ash said, "None of your business."

Rory deflated and a scowl took place on her face, "Fine, don't tell me. I'll just have to imagine."

"Please don't."

"Well, I wouldn't have to create stories if someone would just tell me something," she grumbled. Ash didn't catch onto her alter meaning and they fell back into silence.

It didn't take Ash long to finish the flooring and get packed up. The floor looking perfect and made the room ten times better already.

"Thank you, you've saved us a fortune!" Rory said as she handed Ash an envelope filled with cash.

"Anything to get this place open so we don't have to drink at 'The Two Sixes' anymore," he laughed though it wasn't a joke and then hesitated, looking towards the door. "Do you want a ride home? It's getting dark."

"Having one gang member knowing where I live is enough. I don't need more of you." Rory's turn to laugh without joking.

"All four of us know where you live."

"Concerning," Rory mumbled. "Can I ask you another personal question?" Ash hesitated at the door. In a quiet voice, Rory asked, "Do you miss it?"

"Miss what?" he matched her volume—goosebumps rose along his skin at the unfamiliar vibe that had settled between them and the empty bar.

"Life before the gang?"

That afternoon, the two had spent it civil, the odd question from Rory fishing for information regarding Abel Sawyer that he had easily dodged with a sarcastic remark or a raised eyebrow was the only reminder that Ash was in a gang.

For the first time since joining 'Gods Among Kings', Ash had spent the day not hating anyone or anything, he didn't have—or need—an ulterior motive behind his actions. Years of following orders, collecting checks, midnight meet ups in warehouses, all of the bullets and knives and threats. It had been that long, he couldn't remember, didn't know he was allowed to remember until Rory had asked.

He didn't understand why Link hadn't spilled his secrets to the bartender yet—the big question in the small voice. It was almost enough to fold him. Almost.

"For me to answer that question, I'd need to be very, very drunk."

Ash added before leaving. "You should get the gas pipes checked in the basement—they're looking a little rusty."

After painting, Rory had climbed on the bar top with her toolbox, fixing the fire alarm that took five minutes with the help of YouTube—the smoke stains from Coronal's cigars would be a task for another day, as would the new lights, even with the ladders, Rory was too small to reach the bulbs. She took a deep breath and sighed with content as she took in the view of her new bar.

The wooden flooring matches perfectly with the drying sage walls. The old booths and tables, though chipped and worn, had been cleaned and polished by Will the night before. All the old signs that read deals for college students and regulars were replaced with legitimate deals.

Rory's attention was drawn to the shadow that passed by the window. Rory tilted her head at the shuffling noises from the door. She guessed it was a customer who wasn't aware the bar was closed and hopped down from the bar. A white envelope was pushed under the door and Rory scrunched her face up, bending down to pick it up. *If you're sure he's innocent.*

She opened the envelope. A torn page slipped into her hand, she scanned the page, her breath froze for a second and then she rushed out the door and tumbled onto the empty street. Head snapping around, but she couldn't find who had slipped the paper under the door. She raced inside 'All American' and searched the room for the person. But the cafe was empty, apart from Charlotte and Nia sitting at a booth, Charlotte reading and Nia studying, books and papers spread out on the table. Both heads snapped up to paint-covered Rory, clutching a piece of paper in her hand and her eyes frantic.

"Rory?" Charlotte asked carefully.

"Did you see anyone go past the window?"

"When?" asked Nia.

"Just a second ago, did anyone walk past?"

Charlotte shook her head, "Sorry, sweetie. What's going on? What's that in your hand?"

Rory ran a hand through her hair and puffed out a breath.

"It's his alibi. It's Abel's alibi."

Chapter Thirty-Three
Come Home

"How old are you? "

Rory was sitting in Emmitt's living room. Despite the luxurious furniture and the spacious apartment, the apartment felt warm and cosy. The bookshelf fitted into the corner with a mix of different genres and the perfect reading armchair had Rory picturing Emmitt and Khenan curled into the chair while one read and the other gazed out into the night through the patio doors.

Rory couldn't help but imagine little feet running around the laminated flooring and helping a floured covered Khenan bake in the well-equipped kitchen, where he had retreated to make Rory some tea and a sandwich. Apparently, she looked more fatigued every time he saw her and a good BLT was her medicine.

The minute she confirmed that Abel Sawyer did deliver two kegs to a party on the 20th of May—and retrieving the security camera tape that caught Abel arriving and exiting the premises at the time of the murder—she contacted Emmitt—who after he calmed his laughter caused by Rory climbing over a ten-foot gate to get onto the party's host's property, contacted the Sawyer Lawyer. Emmitt had asked Rory to meet with the lawyer. The three spent a significant amount of time going over the case. Rory adding her inputs and impressing the lawyer.

Mr Derry was—what Rory could only describe as—scary. His face looked as if it had been stretched. He had hollow brown eyes that sunk into his head and his black suit hung on his bony body. Rory thought back to all the movies she had watched and cast him as Death in all of them. But Emmitt swore that Mr Derry was the best of the best and if anyone could help—he could.

"Nineteen, Sir," Rory answered stiffly.

"And you are studying Law?" he asked.

"No, Sir—" Rory tried to keep eye contact; she was too scared to come across as anything but respectful. "I did. I dropped out, Sir."

"College?"

"Law school—" Rory sensed his next question and answered it before he could ask, "—Skipped a few grades."

Mr Derry hummed and went to Rory's notes on Abel's case. Messy handwriting, but he could make out her logic and gave an impressed mumble. "And now?"

"Bar owner, Sir."

He hummed again, "We have some internships if you're still interested in the subject." Rory was slightly taken aback. "You could consider this case your application. I could put in a good word."

"Does this mean you'll take the case?" She couldn't help but ask, "Sir?"

Mr Derry chuckled. It was a strange sound, almost robotic. "I took the case the moment Miss Sawyer contacted me, Miss Scott."

"Thank you, Sir."

Mr Derry gave Rory a single nod and brought his attention to Emmitt, "The documents alone wouldn't be enough to build a case, but the footage evidence does help a great deal—"

"And the fibre evidence, it's class characteristics—" Rory cut him off with her rushed sentences "—it can't trace back to a single source."

"Yes and the trace evidence." He confirmed, "I'll arrange a visit with your brother after I speak to a judge—the sooner we put him in front of a judge, the sooner he can come home."

Emmitt and Mr Derry spoke in detail about the case, but Rory didn't take any of it in. Focused on the words. Abel was coming home. Finally, after weeks of searching and coming up empty, this was it. He was coming home.

"You should consider my offer, Miss Scott—" He handed Rory his business card as he rose from his seat and straightened his suit, "—You're a bright girl."

Rory leaned back on the couch and rubbed her face, causing it to redden. Her shoulders ached from the stiff posture she had held all meeting. Her stomach growled and as if Khenan had sensed it, he emerged from the kitchen with a large tray of sandwiches.

"I've got three BLT's and one without the tomato for Emm." Khenan placed the plate down, "I'll go grab the tea and mugs. Get eating!"

Rory didn't need to be told twice and grabbed half of her sandwich and shoved too much in her mouth, moaning at the soft bread. "Did you make the bread?" she muffled out to Khenan, who had returned with a pot of tea and three mugs.

"I didn't get any of that." He laughed as he filled her a cup.

Rory chewed a little until she was sure if she swallowed, she wouldn't choke. "Did you make the bread?"

"Yes, I did," he said proudly and took a seat opposite her, taking his own sandwich.

"Emmitt is just saying goodbye to Mr Derry and he'll be back in," Rory told him.

"How'd it go?"

"It's looking up. Mr Derry believes that we have a shot."

Khenan narrowed his eyes at Rory, examining her. "Then why do you look like you're the one behind bars?"

"I don't—"

Khenan raised a brow and Rory sighed, cupping her hand around her mug of tea. "I don't know—have you met Abel?" she asked him and Khenan told her he had a few times, but they didn't really speak much. "In the time he's been away, Abe's changed and that's expecting—it is prison, but when he gets out? I don't know what Emmitt has told you but, Abe is involved with the wrong people and he won't tell me anything about it and I don't know why or how deep or how to get him out or—"

"Why do you have to get him out?" Khenan asked calmly.

"Because he's innocent."

"Not prison, whatever he's gotten himself into," Khenan corrected and watched Rory come up with an answer, which was the rules of friendship. "Sticking through hardship is one thing. You and Emmitt, you want to save Abel. I do too, he is my future brother-in-law. The two of you can't fix his troubles if he isn't ready to fix himself."

His words hit Rory like a wake-up punch. "Have you ever felt like you're fighting your way to something and everything is just pushing you back?"

"You're asking me that question?"

Rory apologised profoundly.

"I understand though. I've witnessed Emmitt chase leads and fall flat for months now, this is a big break and you and Emm are waiting for it to fall through. Once Abel is out, he might open, he might tell you about the trouble he is in, but until he does, you can't do anything and you shouldn't continue to lose sleep over it."

"You could have said it nicer than that, but I think I agree," Emmitt sounded from the door, finally seeing Mr Derry off, swiping a sandwich from the plate and taking a seat next to Khenan, a hand slipping in between Khenan's legs and rested on his thigh.

Rory slumped back again, "If he would only just tell us!" she vented. "Abe has always been open about everything to me, well not about his family. But everything else. I know he doesn't like the gang, but what did he do to them that made them angry enough to frame him for murder? And since Abel didn't kill the cashier, who did? Was it Ash? He seems like an angry person. Or maybe it was whoever killed Davis? No—the cashier didn't have a number. Whoever killed the cashier was angry. The victim counter is swift and non-personal, like a hit."

Emmitt waited until he was sure Rory was done before speaking. "Mr Derry was serious about that internship, Rory."

Abel tried to refuse the visitor, Emmitt or Aurora and he didn't want to speak to either. Abel didn't sleep the night of their last visit. He couldn't get her broken look when he turned her away out of his head. Her green eyes watered up as she pleaded for him to say something, anything. To help her so she could help him. The night after was an anger filled sleepless one—the bar fighting with the gang. The reason he didn't tell them was to keep them from getting involved with 'Gods Among Kings'.

Abel thought Will would know better—would help him keep his secret. Abel saw Will at the station the night he was booked; guessed Will got himself in trouble before the gang could get to him; wrecking his father's car would put him away for a few months before Will's dad had decided Will had lean his lesson. Abel was glad Will was back at *Ethel's* so Rory wasn't alone, despite their constant bickering. And then he called her. And her voice was just as tired and light as ever and when she caught him up on how the twins had been doing, it was as if he was back at his apartment, having one of their goodnight calls.

Davis is dead. Abel couldn't help but think that Rory was responsible for a moment or two—she always had a strained relationship with her boss. Then he thought Will had killed him in the next moment—Rory mentioning they had argued over Davis the night he was murdered. The third moment was filled with a Will/Rory duo kill.

In his time away, Abel learned that if the guards wanted something—they got it. So, after they told him he couldn't turn away this visitor, Abel let them slap cuffs on his wrists and followed them. Though he didn't turn right to the visitor's room, he went straight on and then left to a room like the one he was interrogated in five months ago. He was led inside the room, a single metal table and two matching chairs on either side, loops for chains in the middle.

Abel identified the man sitting on one of the chairs as Mr Darry—the family lawyer. Mr Derry was always dressed like the dead. A plain black suit hung from his skeleton and his face was stuck in a long gloom.

"I don't recall asking for a Lawyer," Abel said stiffly.

"Mr Sawyer, I am your family lawyer—you should have asked for me the second they read you your rights," he scolded and Abel frowned as if he was getting told off by a parent. "Mr Sawyer, your mother contacted me. Your brother and friend, they've found something to shift the case in your favour—" Mr Darry pulled from his case a brown file and placed it in front of Abel, who stared down at it, making no move to reach for it.

"The case was closed five months ago. I've got no interest in opening it, thank you for your efforts, but it's a wasted trip."

"Open the file, Mr Sawyer." It wasn't a request and Abel knew that he couldn't argue with Mr Derry.

Abel tensely reached over for the file and opened it; flicking through the documents, he saw photos from a security tape, dated and timed. He cast a look at Mr Darry, who looked pleased with the paper and himself. Abel didn't know what to think. He held his get-out-of-jail card in his hands.

For a single moment—he felt relieved. Freedom, home, *Ethel's*—he had it in his hands, no more inedible food on metal trays or timed outside time. Then Abel remembered the gang. If he walked the streets, what was to stop them from putting him back in jail. Or Emmitt or Rory or Nicky or anyone he cared about. Abel decided the first time his cell door was locked, he was done with 'Gods Among Kings'.

If they wanted to make and deal fake money, recruit poor souls and carry out shady deals—they could—anything, so his friends didn't have to experience of freedom being taken away. Abel tore his eyes from the photo and looked in the file again. A folded lined paper peeked out from the file and Abel took it. A note—in Rory's messy handwriting:

Come home, Abe.
We need you.

Abel dragged his fingers over his cheek to get rid of stray tears. They needed him. Rory said that they needed him. Part of him could just imagine, back at *Ethel's* with a drink and bothering the bartenders while they worked. Back to walking Rory home, helping Nia with homework. Though another part imagined the four boys in the side booth, watching his back and waiting for him to slip so they could stick a knife in it. Or worse, in his friends back.

"This will work?"

Mr Darry nodded firmly.

"Thank you."

"Your brother and friend are the ones to thank Mr Sawyer. You'll be out in two weeks, one if the judge is feeling generous."

"I don't know what to say," Abel stuttered out. "I'm going home," Abel whispered, saying it out loud to help his mind come to terms with the news.

"You're going home."

Chapter Thirty-Four
MI5

"How am I re-enforcement?" Nicky wined as he sat atop the bar, watching Rory pace back and forth. When he received a phone call late last night, he didn't expect Rory to ask him to back her up at a gang deal with 'Gods Among Kings'. He hadn't slept all night, but he thought at least Will or even his sister and Chrissy had been called along too. But no. It was just him. And a tense Rory.

"Because you're big and good with people and you won't kill me for this."

Nicky mumbled he had made no promise to not kill her. Nicky hadn't decided if the idea she had manufactured was stupidly brilliant or brilliantly stupid. He sent a prayer up to the sky walking into the newly refurbished bar and took a few shots waiting for the four guys to turn up. Nicky knew that he could protect her if it came down to it, but he knew deep down that Rory didn't need just his strength. She required the familiarity and comfort of someone being there for what she was attempting to pull off.

Both heads snapped to the door and the four gang members stepped in from out the cold, shaking the bitterness off and welcoming the warm bar. All four stood in amazement at the bar that looked brand new. Will had placed the new lights and they cast a warm golden glow that illuminated the new flooring that Ash had lay.

"Looks great," Ash complimented.

"Well, you did all the heavy work," Rory told him and he smiled in return.

Marius gave Ash a clap on the shoulders and shook him slightly, "Nice, Ash! The bar looks amazing, Rory," he said to her and she flushed a proud smile.

"Almost ready to open for Saturday."

"Halloween? You're opening on Halloween?" Marius asked, stunned, excited to get back to his usual drinking ground and nervous for the bar opening on the busiest night of the year.

"Yeah and you have to wear a costume." Nicky made his presence known, hopped off the bar and stood next to Rory, legs open and shoulders back and arms crossed over his chest.

Ash sized him up. "Stand down; you called us."

Everyone turned to Rory and she rolled her shoulders back like Nicky. "I did—" She swallowed and remembered back to her classes on public speech and summoned her inner undergrad. "Feel free to take a seat and I'll explain why I asked you all here."

To no surprise, they had picked their usual table, which now had the number 7 engraved onto it—Charlotte had been giving a budget for the cafe to get new equipment and had gifted the bar some of the old set that still worked perfectly. Enough for *Ethel's* to add a snacks section on the menu, fries, pizzas, nachos and light dishes.

With the six of them, space was limited and they all touched shoulders. Marius was squished in the corner and part of his back was pressed against the cool window glass. Hino in the middle of him and Nicky. Rory between Ash and Link and could feel their guns against the side of both her legs. Everyone went back to staring at Rory and she was aware of how outnumbered she and Nicky were, but she didn't trust the others not to start a fight and she and Will had just made up. She really didn't want to fight again.

She demanded. "Guns away and out of reach." The four boys gave each other looks, but Link nodded and unclipped his gun from his waist, passing it to Marius to place them away on the booth behind him.

"To save time and energy and my sanity—" Rory started. "—Let's all stop pretending that the gang have nothing to do with Abel Sawyer and the reason he is in jail."

Rory carried on. "Let's say hypothetically that Sawyer is released and the charges are dropped. How would the gang react to that?"

Link took point to answer. "If someone poses as a threat, they'll be taking care of."

"How?" she pressed.

"However necessary."

"Who decides?"

Link gritted his teeth but said anyways. "The boss."

"If Sawyer were to be released, would he pose a threat?"

“Well, that all depends on Sawyer,” Marius spoke up. “If we were to have certainty, that he won’t be a problem. Then we won’t have reason to go after him.”

“Say we had something that could be within your interest. Would you exchange that for Sawyer’s safety?” Rory questioned and the four guys peeked up with curiosity.

“What could you offer?” Hino asked.

“It’ll be winter in a few weeks and it’s cold.”

“Yes, that tends to happen after Fall,” Ash quipped from beside her.

Rory’s cheeks heated up, “No, that’s not how I—What I meant—” she fumbled over her words. Nicky gave her an encouraging look from his space next to Hino. “I’m offering you a room.”

“I didn’t think *Ethel’s* did that anymore,” Hino said to himself.

Ignoring Hino, she said, “I’ve heard that you do deals and missions and—”

“Missions?” Link cut her off, “We’re gang members, not MI5.”

“Whatever you do,” she said, getting frustrated at how strong she had started and how badly it was heading. “I’ve heard you do it at the docks.” The four guys shared a look with each other, debating whether to confess anything to the girl. “Relax, I’m here to offer you a room for meetings and trades and other gang stuff. It’s warm, access to alcohol and private.”

Link straightened up and Ash’s ears perked up, interested in what she was saying. “You said that you weren’t ready to hire out the rooms yet. Not financially stable to renovate?”

“We’ve got a few rooms on the first floor empty and clean,” she explained, “there’s one with your name on it—if Sawyer’s target is removed. You don’t talk to him or look at him. If he’s sat at the bar, you go to the other end. If he’s in the bathroom, you hold it. You don’t think about him.”

Ash couldn’t hide his smirk. “You’re playing a dangerous game, Rory.”

Rory rotated her head by an inch and met with his face. Ash could read the determination in her blazing eyes; she wasn’t prepared to leave without a yes. “I’ve been playing the dangerous game for weeks—only now I’ve got a hand to deal.”

“Besides—” Rory moved her attention to the rest of the group. “—You’ve made it clear you don’t make the decision. I’m not asking you. I’m asking your boss.”

The morning after the meeting, the boys piled into Lenzo's office and retold him Rory's offer and he made approving sounds throughout.

"She's a smart one. What's her name?"

Marius, Ash and Hino didn't try to conceal the look they gave to Link, asking for permission to share the young bartender's name. "Aurora James," Link said.

"Cute—" Lenzo said without emotion, "and Aurora has taken over the bar?" The four boys confirmed and Lenzo sighed as he thought over the offer.

A private room would be ideal. That way, they wouldn't have to go to the freezing docks or the warehouses where there was too much risk of clients crossing paths with shipment and soon-to-be victims.

Over the five months of the Sawyer kid being behind bars and out of trouble—*Gods Among Kings* had acquired enough police officers on their payroll that it wouldn't be a worry if Abel Sawyer tried to interfere with their dealings again. Having a bar downstairs from a meeting room would come in handy with potential investors—alcohol at easy access to open everyone's minds and easily persuadable.

Lenzo thought back to the picture of Amelia Sawyer from the article. He knew she'd make a success out of herself, incredibly smart and pure. He had been told that Amelia Sawyer company had shares in every business in that neighbourhood—including the old brothel. And that both her sons had some influence in the bar. Would he dare cross over to her territory after their history?

He would.

"Only one condition she requested?" he asked them, rubbing his chin as if he hadn't made his mind up.

"Just to leave Abel Sawyer alone," Link confirmed.

Lenzo caught Link's bitter tone as he spoke, "What do you think I should do?" He pointed to Link.

"Can I answer freely?"

Lenzo motioned that the floor was his and Link took a breath and answered on the exhale.

"We're thriving, we have enough officers to start a force, Sawyer has been convicted of murder, served time and associates with a bar that is being run by a nineteen-year-old dropout and more staff are underage than of legal age—even if they can get him out—not one person is going to take whatever he claims seriously. Sawyer isn't a threat to 'Gods Among Kings', neither is the bar. Frostbite however, is."

Ice blue eyes radiated pride as Link made his case. Most of the points Lenzo had made himself. Link knew by Lenzo's nodding head and his pulled lips, not smirking, but approval, that it was a test—for what reason, he didn't know, but he knew he had passed when Lenzo leaned back into his seat, legs extended and crossed.

"Any meeting you four oversee will be held there."

Lenzo leaned his head back against the headrest of the chair and closed his eyes. Only a man like Lenzo could be in an open and vulnerable position and be anything but vulnerable. If someone was to attack, he'd wait until they were close enough to feel their shaking and stressed breaths on his face, he'd wait until the knife was pressed at his open throat—and then he'd strike, with the blade hidden under the arm of his chair. Taking them out before they saw him open his eyes.

"Honestly, I'm getting bored of this whole situation. Abel Sawyer is free. Tell the girl I accept her offer."

Chapter Thirty-Five
Melia

The building reeked of professionals with bottomless pockets and trust funds that aided as step ladders to private offices and iced coffees that interns spent their unpaid days cycling back and forth on company bikes to collect, all so they could say they got as far as to be a lackey at *Amelia Sawyer Co.*

Erik Lenzo strutted into the front reception through the double glass doors, brown oxfords clapped against the marble floor, one hand in his Cambridge grey suit pants and the other reached to his face to remove his sunglasses, pocketing them in his black suede trench coat. Though the well-dressed man—so used to eyes falling on him as he entered the room—wasn't the one who stopped the other well-dressed professionals in their expensive steps.

A step behind him—black unbrushed hair sprawled against Link's head. Getting a phone call from Lenzo at 8 in the morning wasn't his ideal way to wake up. And then to be told that he had to escort his boss to *A.S Co.* in an hour time wasn't how Link had planned to spend his rare day off, but Lenzo got what he wanted. Which was why Link was standing in one of Chicago's biggest and expensive building.

Black jeans and dirty boots attracting the eyes of the wealthy. He used the air-con in his Jeep to dry his hair and didn't have time to contain the wildness with a brush. Link was used to people staring and judging him, but he couldn't help the insecurities that filled his head. '*Am I dragging mud in from the street? Does my hair make me look homeless? Do I look like a charity case as much as I feel like one?*' His mind answered the questions for him: '*Yes. Yes. Even more so.*'

Lenzo swaggered to the front desk, straight through the metal detectors and ignoring the high alarms, as if they were expecting him—Link found that Lenzo walked into every room like everyone knew him and had been waiting for him to arrive so they could start their day.

Link had attracted two security guards when he entered and made their way over to the younger man. Faces set in seriousness and authority and Link stared back with boredom. Already knowing what they were going to say.

"Sir, do you have any weapons on your person?"

"Yes, it's loaded, yes it's registered and no—" Link said simply like he had done the dance a thousand times. "—I'm not handing it over."

The security made to argue, but Lenzo just waved the situation off. "Hand them your gun Lincoln, you won't be needing it."

The guards looked at Lenzo as if they understood his importance just by the way he commanded Link—who was grumbling while doing as he was told. Link handed over the weapon with a sarcastic smile. They muttered a thank you and Link sent them a finger behind their retreating backs.

Lenzo carried on his treck to the front desk and was greeted by a plastic grin from the red-headed receptionist. "I'm here to see Amelia Sawyer," he told her, not asked and she kept on her plastered smile.

"I'm sorry, but Miss Sawyer hasn't got any free spaces today? Could I take a message?" she asked sweetly and Link couldn't help but roll his eyes. The urge to stick his fingers down his throat was fought back.

"Oh, trust me—" Lenzo gave a scoff that had a hint of amusement, "Amelia Sawyer has time for me, tell her it's Erik."

Link had a few theories of why he was walking out of the elevator on the 10th floor and following Lenzo, who followed a young intern down the hallway, passing office after office, each one as big as the last. All the theories revolved around the other Sawyer's. Still, he couldn't figure out why Lenzo would be visiting his mother after striking a deal with Rory and *Ethel's* crew to leave Abel Sawyer alone. When he asked in the car, he received a 'no questions asked' look.

At the top of the hallway stood a woman in a business dress that matched Lenzo's grey suit. Her dusty hair pulled back from her face. Her rich olive arms were crossed over her chest as she studied the men heading her way. Her painted lips were pursed as if she was holding in a snarky remark. Sour, annoyed, aimed at his boss.

"Amelia Sawyer—" Lenzo said with open arms that Amelia Sawyer made no effort to run into. "—It's been a while."

"Twenty-five years." Her tone held no emotion though her eyes were filled with them. "Though I thought I had another thirty years before you'd come to pass judgement."

"I do love it when you compare me to God, Amelia."

"Actually, I always thought I'd end up downstairs, Mr Lenzo."

Link made a choking sound trying to hold in the laugh and sent Lenzo an apologetic look.

"You'll have to excuse Lincoln—" Lenzo started and Link had a feeling the following statement would be an insult. "—The boy isn't used to proper etiquette."

There it was.

"He does seem to appear out of place," she mused and gave him an obvious analytical look.

Taking in his washed-out jeans that were more grey than black. The black jacket was just as worn as his jeans. An old band shirt under his jacket. She hummed as if she was giving him a makeover in her mind. Chop his hair short, a tailored suit, navy blue to match his eyes. Link muttered an apology that had no meaning to it and Amelia stared at him like she knew it. Link regretted not wearing the new black suit Hino had tailored for him. Her eyes remained on Link long enough for Link to become uncomfortable and they eventually turned to Lenzo.

"What do you want, Erik?"

Link was slightly worried for Amelia Sawyer. To know Lenzo long enough to get the pleasure to call him by his first name was very rare. Only one or two people had the privilege.

"Your son—" Lenzo said and Amelia's stone posture cracked. "—Or should I say, sons."

Amelia dismissed the intern and told Erik to step into her office. Link didn't follow in and remained outside, taking one of the waiting seats.

Inside, the office was just like the rest of the building. Bare and bright. Not too much furniture to clutter the place. The matching glass office furniture had no objects on them and her desk was just as minimum as the rest. A photo frame of herself and a young boy, 7-year-old, ice eyes mirrored back at Lenzo's.

He held the frame up and Amelia rolled her shoulders back. "This must be Emmitt—interesting eyes, don't you think?" he spoke.

"No, I don't." Her jaw set as she held his eyes.

“Come on, Melia, I have no interest in the boy,” he simply said as he placed the frame back down—noting the lack of the second Sawyer in the office. “I heard about your youngest, Abel, isn’t it?”

“What about him,” she said dryly.

“Abel has always been a troubled one.”

“And Emmitt?”

“What do you want, Erik?”

“Your sons have been a problem to my business—”

“Business,” Amelia scoffed, but Erik ignored it.

“I’m sure you’re aware that Abel is getting released soon,” Amelia nodded and Erik carried on. “He’s free from us, so long as he and his friends stay out of my way. I suggest you do your job and make sure he stays out of trouble.”

Amelia’s eyebrows went up with disbelief. “You’re telling me to do my job. What job would that be? A parent?”

“You said it.”

“Actually, you said it. You don’t get to come in here twenty-five years later and tell me how to raise MY children!” Amelia’s voice raised enough for Link to hear from outside.

Erik licked his lips. “Oh, but that’s not true, is it, Amelia?” he said slyly. He sat up against the desk as she stood in front of him, arms crossed over her chest.

“If I recall it correctly. You—” He pointed to her, “—were the one to leave twenty-five years ago.”

“Do you blame me?”

“No. I don’t,” he spoke truthfully. “Though an heir would be ideal for the gang. But you made sure that didn’t happen.”

She took a deep breath and drew her emotions in. “You need to leave. Now.”

“Like I said, I’m not interested in the boy. I saw a picture—he’s too straight cut for a gang. Abel, however—” he joked, but Amelia didn’t care for it.

“Don’t.”

“My point, they’re both on thin ice with me, Amelia and I can extend only so much kindness. I promise to leave them be—but if they come to me—”

Amelia had always considered herself to have tight control over her emotions. A woman in a predominantly male career, Amelia had trained herself to stay calm and collected in situations where any slight sign of emotion could result in her employees or potential partners refer her to being ‘Too emotional’.

It had taking Amelia longer than she wanted to get where she was. Using her incredible intelligence, connections and—she wasn't ashamed to admit it—her beautiful looks. She built herself up and used every resource she needed to start *A S Co* and she was thriving. But if anyone could unravel that control—it would be Erik Lenzo.

"Kindness? You have extended kindness?" she laughed bitterly. "I didn't know that was part of your vocabulary." Lenzo grew an annoyed tight-lipped smile. "My son is behind bars, thanks to your kindness. He has your ugly scar on his neck, thanks to your kindness."

"I let him off easy—letting him off easy. If he was anyone else, I would have had my men gouge his eyes out for spying on my men at the docks. I would have had my men cut out his tongue for running his mouth to his friend. That was kindness."

"I'm going to say this once, Erik." Amelia's tone was deadly calm, the kind that a mother used to scorn her child after they had misbehaved. "Stay away from my sons. You do not get to touch them or look at them or breath near them."

Link—who wasn't listening in, just overhearing—couldn't help but think back to Rory's similar speech at the bar.

"Emmitt has told me only little about Abel's imprisonment and it stops there. You don't talk to him about it. He doesn't talk to you or any of your little followers about it. Am I clear?" she demanded an answer, but she knew Erik well enough to not get a straight one.

"You know—You're the second girl to order 'Gods Among Kings' to stay away from Abel Sawyer." Still leaning on the desk, he folded his arms and looked her up and down. "Though we get something out of her deal, what will you offer us, Amelia, to promise to turn them away if they approach my gang or me?" he asked suggestively and pouted his lips.

Face stormed and serious, Amelia said: "You're not the only one who can make people disappear, Erik. Don't touch my boys."

Before Erik could go into his usual 'I'm a God, I can't be touched' speech, a disturbance outside the room caused them both to head for the door. A muffled voice sounded out behind the closed door. "The hell I can't—it's my mother's office!"

"Trust me—you really don't want to go in there." Link had heard enough of the conversation to pick up the hints of the two elders shared child. He knew straight away that the child was Emmitt. The eyes he shared with Lenzo were bright enough to scream genetics. He also got the impression that Emmitt didn't know.

"What are you doing here anyway?" Emmitt fired at him.

"Thinking about a career in real estate." Link's skill to make sarcasm sound too real both impressed and irritated Emmitt.

"We had a deal," a female voice spoke out, one that neither Lenzo nor Amelia recognised. It was a calm voice compared to the boys.

"I don't see Abel anywhere. Do you?"

"No, but—"

"So, I'm sticking to the deal."

"Abel would hate this deal," Emmitt said like he to, hated the deal.

"Like I said—Abel isn't here."

"But you are. Why?" Emmitt demanded.

Link was spared from coming up with another lie or sarcastic remark as Amelia swung the door open behind him. Rory fought the urge to bow at the sight of the woman. She radiated so much power and grace that Rory forgot where she was for a moment.

"Do I need to remind you that the walls are not made out of lead and the whole floor—if not building—can hear your quibbling?"

Link and Emmitt visibly gulped and lowered their heads in shame. Link imagined this was what it felt like to have a mother be disappointed in him and didn't like the feeling at all.

"Mr Lenzo and Lincoln were just leaving," she told them, but Lenzo appeared at the door behind her.

"Melia and I have a few things to discuss, though you kids are more than welcome to join us," he spoke. Putting on a friendly tone that Link knew was anything but pleasant.

"*Melia*?" Emmitt asked defensively, looking between his mother's secret ridden eyes and Lenzo's bright blue ones that matched his own.

"Emmitt, go wait downstairs and I'll join you shortly," Amelia said.

Rory watched the interchange between her friend and the stranger, Mr Lenzo. Whose eyes weren't strangers at all. She turned her head to get a better look at Emmitt's and turned to Mr Lenzo and then back to Emmitt. Her mind drawing out all the similarities and racing for a conclusion.

Just before it hit, Link—who had watched Rory deduct—took a subtle step in front of Lenzo. "Sir, we really should be meeting with your 11 o'clock."

Lenzo checked his watch and sighed, "That's why I keep you around Lincoln," he praised with humour and turned Emmitt and Rory.

"You must be Emmitt Sawyer—I've heard a lot about you, son." He stuck his hand out to Emmitt and Emmitt took it firmly, staring intensity like a showdown. Amelia watching them both with careful eyes.

"I can't say the same about you."

Lenzo chuckled, "No, I didn't expect you to. I knew your mother a lifetime ago." He turned to Amelia, who was daring him to say any more, but she remained tight-lipped. Lenzo looked to Rory, she was holding a defence stance, as if she was protecting Emmitt. "And is this young lady your girlfriend?"

Rory snorted and gained everyone's attention. Rory wasn't in her work clothes—though if she knew she was going to meet Abel and Emmitt's mother, she would have chosen something classier than the washed-out band-tee. And as always, she was wearing her brown boots.

"Sorry." she mumbled; embarrassment spread through her.

"Rory Scott is a friend—I've recently gotten engaged."

"My apologies, I'm sure she's just as lovely."

"Oh, he's perfect."

"My apologies again; I'm sure he is." Lenzo said, "Rory, was it? Interesting name for a girl."

"Parents were positive I was going to be a boy." She gave him a tight-lipped smile. Rory didn't know who the man was, but the power he held, the way Link had reeled in when he stepped out of the office—like a soldier calling to attention.

Lenzo leaned forward on one foot and extended a hand for Rory to shake. She took small steps forward. Link's eyes were locked on Lenzo's. Trying to decide if he had it in him to step up to Lenzo if something were to happen. With her sleeves over her fist, she took his hand and shook it—holding her breath.

"My sons have spoken about you and that bar of yours." Amelia intervened.

Link caught Lenzo's side look.

"Emmitt has been keeping me informed with all the improvements you've done the past week. I must commend you on the affordable renovations and the new opening times; I'd be lying if I said I wasn't slightly impressed. Especially after the incident," she evaluated and Link started to sweat with the knowing tone. As if she knew who was responsible. Rory, however, blushed at the praises.

“I also hear that you’re the one to thank for my son’s release; you found his alibi?” Amelia said to her and Rory blushed even more at the attention.

“Not exactly, Ma’am. I just got it to Emmitt.,” Rory said quietly, aware of the gang members standing with them.

“No, but you climbed a ten-foot fence to confirm it,” Emmitt teased, still amused with Rory’s climbing ability and turned to his mother. “Mr Derry offered Rory a place in the law program.”

“Wow, Mr Derry doesn’t like anyone. It’s a great program and with Mr Derry approval, you could go far.”

“When does Abel get out?” Link filled the awkward silence that settled between them.

Emmitt answered him. “By Saturday with the best team—and our team are the best.”

The silence filled again.

“I just came to drop off a few forms for the bar—I really should be going, though,” she announced uncomfortably. “It was really nice to meet you both, but I’ve really got to be going now.” She pointed behind her, already taking steps back. “Miss Sawyer, Mr Lenzo, Emm—” She bid an awkward goodbye to them. Her face turned bitter towards Link and he shared an equally childish look.

“Oh, Emmitt,” Rory started. “I may need you on the first of November—someone is coming out to check the gas pipes in the cellar.”

“I’ll be there.”

Lenzo grilled Link in the car on their way to his eleven o’clock meeting and Link had no choice but to tell him the truth. There was no point in lying. Amelia Sawyer had given away Rory’s name and importance to the bar and the Sawyer situation. So, Link told him.

“You assured me that the bartenders wouldn’t be an issue,” Lenzo commented from the back seat of Link’s Jeep and Link peaked into the rear-view mirror to get a sense of Lenzo’s emotions, but his eyes were glued to his phone screen and Link couldn’t get a reading.

He sucked in. “We handled it.” His eyes fixed on the road.

"Rory Scott," Lenzo tasted the name on his tongue, "Aurora James Scott. Didn't you know a James Scott, a teacher?"

Of course, Lenzo knew he was right, he was testing Link as always and Link knew it. He also knew that Lenzo had already given an order to gather any information on the girl and undoubtedly the rest of the team.

"Yes. Her father was my teacher."

"Ah!" Lenzo said as if he didn't already know. "Is she aware?"

"Yes."

Lenzo hummed and followed it with a sign, looking at Link's tense shoulders.

"Poor girl. The horror she witnessed at such a young age," Lenzo said with such fake sympathy and he watched as Link's fist gripped the gear stick tighter. Link's hand on the steering wheel tightening too. Lenzo had the report up on his phone, familiarising himself with the old case. When young Lincoln joined the gang seven years ago, he had run a background check and the murder of his teacher that he was supposed to move in with flagged his interest.

It was a classic robbery gone wrong. Three thugs had hung around the corner all night, waiting for someone who looked like they had a heavy wallet. A schoolteacher taking his daughter out for milkshakes had appeared to be a great target and the group of young men had overpowered the man and his small daughter and pushed them into the dark alley.

His daughter recalled in her police statement that the men repeatedly demanded that her father emptied his pockets and they didn't seem pleased with the contents of the wallet. One of the men had spotted the girls clutch and when they reached to grab it—her father stood in the way. She recounted a vague struggle and then her father was on the ground—the men frantically grabbing his wallet, her bag and exiting the ally and disappearing into the street.

The file Lenzo had fished up on his phone had the girl's statement and the physical description of the attackers. The three sketches looked the same and they looked like every other male in Chicago. One of the reasons why the case was unsolved. Lenzo scrolled down to the anonymous phone call script made by a boy who reported hearing screams and cries from the street and had seen three men running from the same street they had been stalking all night.

"Does Aurora know you placed the call?"

Link hadn't connected the robbery he had overheard while waiting for Mr Scott on the sidewalk outside the milkshake shop and Mr Scott's death. Rory hadn't mentioned a single thing regarding her father's death and Link felt his stomach churn as he drove his boss around Chicago while he read out the statements from that night.

"No. She doesn't."

As if Lenzo could read Link's thoughts, he gasped in mock. "You didn't know either."

"You know I didn't," Link said dryly.

Clicking his tongue. "They never found the men who were responsible."

Lenzo drew his eyes from his screen and they took in Chicago passing by the window. Keeping Link in the dark about that night had been on purpose on Lenzo's behalf. Lincoln was a delinquent 15-year-old run away with anger and authority issues, already unpredictable. If he had found out that his schoolteacher that he latched onto had been murdered a few feet from him? Lenzo couldn't risk losing an asset like Lincoln.

"I've sent you the case report," Lenzo said. "Do with it as you will."

Chapter Thirty-Six
History

It wasn't a first for Lincoln to forget his homework. Even his Geology teacher had stopped asking for it. His homework would constantly be shoved into his backpack and in the trash the moment he reached home. He didn't have time for homework, straight onto chores that would last well into the night or he was too busy patching up cuts and bruises—forgetting about the homework.

History, though, he would attempt his homework. Lincoln never got full marks, always stuck between a C and a B. But he tried, answering every question on the sheet to his best ability. Even when Mrs Jackson had smashed his hand in the fridge door for breaking some dishes, Lincoln had stayed up until the early hours of the morning, writing messily with his left hand. Mr S had always handed his homework back with a positive comment and a comment on how to improve—a comment Lincoln would keep in mind when he did his next lot of homework.

For the full year, Lincoln had handed in his homework without fail. So, when Mr S had stopped at Lincoln's desk requesting this week's homework—his ginger hair just as wild as Lincoln's black hair, lying over the top of his thin-rimmed glasses—Lincoln couldn't face his disappointed teacher.

The bell sounded the end of the class and the end of the day and like most students at Sinister South, Lincoln wasn't in a rush to leave school and return to his foster parent's home. As slowly as he could without appearing to be stalling—Lincoln packed his backpack, the only one left in the room other than Mr S.

"Lincoln?" Mr Scott's gentle tone called across the room. He was sat at his messy desk—a cold coffee cup, paperwork that was stacked so high they had falling and an over stacked pen pot—Lincoln raised his head, but his eyes didn't meet his teacher. "Would you mind if I spoke to you for a few minutes?"

Lincoln nodded his head, already prepared for the 'disappointed in you' speech. Lincoln knew that if he had shaken his head and walked out of the room, Mr S wouldn't stop him. It was what Lincoln liked most about his History teacher—Mr S understood his students. He knew the slight fear, panic, that would dawn on Lincoln whenever someone in authority would speak to him privately. Mr S knew that Lincoln would pick his brain trying to remember something he could have done to result in a punishment that was bound to come.

Mr Scott looked in his coffee mug and grimaced at the hours-old coffee, causing the ends of Lincoln's lips to tug up slightly. "I won't keep you long, son," Mr S said. Lincoln was stood in front of his desk, hands playing with the straps of his bag.

"I wanted to check in with you—"

"You want to know why I didn't do the homework," Lincoln clarified but regretted it instantly. Mr S didn't appear to be upset with Lincoln's bluntness, but he couldn't help the guilt that flooded him.

Mr Scott smiled softly at Lincoln, a smile that he gave Lincoln whenever he would have an outburst of anger or frustration, whether caused by other students teasing him or losing patience over his schoolwork. A smile that said he understood that everything would be alright no matter how bad it seemed.

"Lincoln," Mr S sighed, "I'm not going to write you up for not handing in homework one time. I would, however, like to know why you hadn't?"

Lincoln contemplated spilling the truth, telling Mr S every punishment, every punch, every kick, every missed meal. The Jacksons were the worst family he had been with and Lincoln went to bed every night wondering why a family would foster children just to treat them like animals. What was the point of taking in life and not loving it or caring for it? It was the money, he concluded.

Lincoln knew that Mr S would believe him and attempt to help him and he so desperately wanted to crumble into his teacher's arms and sob into his tweed blazer. But he also knew he'd still have to go back to the Jacksons and if they had found out—

"I lost it."

Mr S gave him a look that screamed he knew it was a lie.

"I'm sorry if I—I—Could have another copy—I promise I'll not lose—I must have dropped it or—" Mr Scott stood from his chair and sat on the lip of the desk in front of Lincoln, his hands in his trouser pockets and his feet crossed. He took Lincoln in, the dark half-moons under his tired eyes, the raised collar doing a poor job to conceal the blue and red patches. His nails bit down and his hands too overworked for a schoolboy.

"I received a phone call from my daughter's school last night," Mr S started; Lincoln didn't know why he was being told this but knowing Mr Scott, it was relevant. "She's just a little younger than you. And she's incredibly smart—"

"I don't have time for a tutor, Mr Scott," Lincoln huffed, not too pleased with the idea of someone younger than him teaching him.

Mr S laughed warmly, "Oh no, Son that wasn't my point. Though an interaction between the two of you would be interesting. No, I was informed by one of her teachers yesterday that several students have submitted work that holds a similarity to her own. I spoke to her last night and asked her for her side of the story."

Lincoln couldn't help the jealously and longing he had felt. Mr Scott's first reaction to his daughter being accused of helping other students cheat wasn't harmful. He hadn't gone home that night and shouted at her or locked her in the outhouse in the freezing cold until she had confessed. He had asked her for her side. Gave her a chance to explain.

"Of course, she denied the whole thing and had no Knowledge of the work in question. Though it didn't take long for her to cave, guilt lying heavy in her stomach and she confessed to charging the older students' money and she'd complete their homework in return. She even handed in the cash she had earned."

"Smart girl," Lincoln commented.

Mr Scott looked at Lincoln through the top of his glasses, "I know you didn't lose your homework, Lincoln. Do you know how I know?"

Lincoln knew there was no point in denying it again. He had an idea that Mr Scott's daughter had caved because her father had a face so gentle and comforting and gave you the impression that you could confess your deepest darkest secrets to him and he'd have the solution. Lincoln shrugged a shoulder.

"Because you're wearing the same expression that my daughter wore last night. Your teeth are clenched, looking through your eyebrows yet not making eye contact. What happened, Son?"

"I tried to do it; I swear—" Lincoln rushed out. "I was to do my chores and then my homework, but I—I messed up and Mrs—Mrs Jackson—She—It was my fault, really, but I was—just—tired—I'm just so tired," Lincoln stammered; his head hung in shame.

"Thank you for telling me, Lincoln," Mr S said softly and Lincoln was grateful that pity and anger didn't underline it. "Have you told anyone else about the situation?"

"Will anyone care?"

Mr S sucked in a harsh breath. "Somebody always cares, Lincoln. You must believe that someone will care or you won't care yourself." The teacher moved around his desk and scribbled on the back of a report card—handing it to Lincoln. "That's my number. I trust that you'll use this whenever you need to talk or you need help. I care, Lincoln."

Chapter Thirty-Seven
Too Warm for October

The air was warm. Too warm for October. Rory's hair stuck to her forehead and she had to peel her jacket from her arms as she stepped inside Ethel's. The electric fans were switched on before anything else and Rory stood in front of the biggest one behind the bar—following the rotation and savouring the breeze and trying not to think about how hot and stuffy the room would get in a few hours when it was overfilled with customers on opening night.

The afternoon sun cast a soft gold light around the middle of the room—the top of the room left in darkness where Rory and Nicky had built a small stage for live performers. The black curtain to the left was draped back, but the right hung loose. Rory sighed and dragged herself away from the cool air to fix it. Rory was stopped in her steps when she heard a faint noise coming from the curtain.

Pushing her feet to move, her breathing became shallow, the golden hew grew duller and her arms began to chill. The closer she got to the curtain, the more audible the sound was—choking, coughing. A sound that was too familiar to her, but she couldn't place it—nor could she explain the fear that grew inside her as her hand reached the curtain and drew it back in a swift motion.

Her knees hit the wood stage with an echoing thud. Her father lay on the stage—his teaching suit stained a deep red. One of the lenses of his glasses were cracked and the blood that had pooled from his wound had leaked into his already bright red hair—matting it up. She crawled towards him and put a shaking hand on his forehead.

"Daddy?" she whispered voice younger than it should have been. "Dad?" she pleaded.

His gaze fixed up to the ceiling. Her hand ran through his hair and blood transferred to her hand. "Somebody help."

Though she watched her father bleed out—Rory felt as if the world was moving in slow motion. Her voice was quieter than she wanted. Her head scanned the room for one second and when they returned to her dying father—it wasn't her father.

Ginger hair replaced by blonde curls. Now with the lighter hair, she could see just how much blood coated it. Chocking and gurgling snapped her eyes from the stained hair to the lips. His lips. Abel's lips. A squirt of blood came from them as he tried to speak, but Rory shushed him—a comforting hand resting on his cheek.

Sobs broke from her and her free hand placed pressure on his chest, feeling the rigid skin where the knife had punctured through. She tried to hold as much blood in, but Abel's face had already lost its colour. His eyes locked wide on her face and more blood filled his mouth, spilling down his chin instead of the words he was trying so desperately to get out.

"Don't try to talk," Rory soothed, "you're going to be OK, I'm here, you're going to be OK." She didn't know if she was trying to convince Abel or herself.

A loud rapping on the door shook through her and she tore her eyes from Abel, shouting for the person to come in and help. "Somebody is here, Abel; they'll help—"

When Rory looked back at him—he was gone. The blood was gone from the floor, from her hands. She was alone on the stage, kneeling on the ground. No trace of her father or Abel. Her tears were freezing cold on her face and she could see her breaths. The knocking on the door echoed in her head and shook the walls around her.

A faint continuous barking sounded miles away. She stood and took small steps to the door, the shadow behind the glass unmoving despite the constant knocking. The door handle was burning hot and sizzled when her cold hand made contact. She counted down from three and swung the door open—

Rory's eyes snapped open and darted around her dark room, noticing all the familiar furniture that surrounded her like a security blanket, reminding her that she was in her apartment and safe. Caspian was standing over her with panicked eyes and with his nose, he nudged at her arms.

She wrapped her arms around him and took comfort in his fur. Trying to copy his breathing to calm herself down. He jolted up at the knocking at her door and Rory swung her legs off her bed. The knocking was less forceful than her nightmare but was just as urgent and to save herself from Ms Nealson nagging her in the morning about making a racket, she rushed to open it, not taking a minute to look through the peephole.

Leaning on her door frame was Link, dressed in grey sweats and a black hoodie. His hair was sticking to his forehead though the open window blowing her curtains with a light breeze told her it wasn't raining. His breathing was as wild as hers had been just moments before. He took in her appearance—hair tied in a low pony, a plain green t-shirt and dark bottoms with orange pumpkins and grey skeletons decorating them. Her eyes were a dull green and they couldn't seem to settle on one thing. Rory peered around the door frame on both sides and ushered Link into her apartment before Ms Nealson appeared.

"What took you so long to answer?" he quizzed, slight worry underlining his tone.

"Heavy sleeper," she mumbled, adrenalin from the nightmare wearing off and exhaustion slowly taking over.

"What are you doing here? At—" She peered at the clock hung on the wall. "—2 AM?"

"I was out for a run," Link said, now just realising how strange it was to bang on her door in the early hours of the morning.

Going for runs through the night was Marius's idea. It would help him release stress and give him time to think. Tonight, it was the file. After driving Lenzo around all day, he had returned home and read through the file Lenzo had emailed him. Mr Scott's cold case. There wasn't much to it, but it had brought up old memories chasing away his sleep away. Link had planned to do laps around the park until he passed out, but his legs brought him through the park and towards Rory's apartment.

"I was there when it happened."

"You were where?" Rory asked in confusion.

Link stood in her living room; hands stuffed in the pockets of his hoodie. His head dipped, but Rory could see the guilt anyways. "The night your father was killed." Rory's eyes widened but she remained silent. "I was waiting for him that night; he told me to wait outside of a milkshake shop. I went straight home, packed my backpack. I was three hours early and just sat on the pavement waiting. I was going to meet his family—You." Link corrected himself and tried to picture the 12-year-old girl he imagined while he sat and waited for Mr Scott.

The girl had reddish hair like Mr Scott, she'd be small and innocent looking, she had glasses that were too big for her face because all the smart kids had worn glasses—and she had the biggest smile.

"I didn't see them grab you, but I saw the three men shifting around the street all night. I heard the girl shouting and crying for help, but I didn't—I couldn't have—If the police came, they'd take me back—And I couldn't go back. Not there."

He was practicality pleading his case, but Rory was still, brain racing to process the new information. Rory remembered wishing for rain (it always rained in the movies when something life-changing happened). Instead, the air was hot and stuffy—too warm for October. Her jacket tied at her waist and left her shirt vulnerable to the blood that would stain it.

Rory would never forget her father's smile when she knelt over his body, gravel digging into her knees, the one he wore whenever things were tough or at rock bottom. The smile was wider on the right side than the left and creased his cheeks. The smile that made everything better. Including his own death. She remembered his forehead being cold on her hand as she smoothed the hair from his eyes. She remembered her small voice telling him he had broken his glasses.

"It was me—" The same small voice cut through Link's sniffles; she hadn't noticed him starting to cry. "—I was the girl screaming and crying."

Link dropped to the couch, his head in his hands. "I crossed the street and called the cops and waited on the other side for your father to show. I had no idea that across the road—the ambulance—I didn't know it was for—"

"Lincoln—You couldn't have—"

"Why are you so placate about all of this?" Link almost shouted at her. His head had snapped up and Rory couldn't believe the tears she was watching roll down his face. "They're still out there. The men. Free and unpunished."

Slight frustration grew and Rory sat next to him on her couch. "It was almost eight years ago; I've moved on. I don't want to spend the rest of my life being angry at the world."

"You should be!" he snapped. "I'm sorry," Link apologised, using his sleeve to wipe at the tears on his cheeks and chin. Emotions he hadn't allowed anyone to see in too long.

"Don't apologise," Rory said firmly, "I've had eight years to move on. For you, Link—" Link caught her eyes and she held him there with so much power and he saw Mr Scott in her. So sure and intense, faith in themselves that spread out to their subject. He pulled a small card from his pocket and his fingers fidgeted with the warn corners subconsciously.

"For you, it's been days. You didn't know that he was killed; you didn't know that my father was dead. You can be angry and upset and depressed and cheated. But you can't be sorry. What you're feeling now—Hey—"

Link had turned away from her, but her hand caught his chin and she lightly forced him to face her.

"What you're feeling now, I felt that when I was twelve. I felt anger and pain and murderous. I wanted them gone and I wanted them to feel a fraction of hurt that they caused me." Rory's voice softened but held the same amount of sureness and confidence. Not ashamed of how vulnerable or weak she may appear by sharing her darkest time.

"Then I felt sad and lonely and I wished to God that I could join him and be with him, went as far as to prey for a parent swap. Hated my mother for just being there; how could my hero be ripped away from the world he had such an impact on and she was just there."

"I chose to move on. My father wouldn't want me to be angry and resentful and lonely. I find it difficult and painful to recall that night, but I have hundreds of much better memories and moments that I choose to look back on."

Link's nose and eyes were bright red as if the tears caused him physical pain. Rory's hand had dropped from his chin and she could feel the tears that had wet her fingers. She reached up to wipe the remaining tears from his face but again, another loud rapping sounded from her door—this time, drunk cheering accompanied it.

Rory recognised the voices straight away. The twins shouted in unison through the door ordering her to open up. "Come on, Rory!" Nicky sang, "don't be boring and open up!"

Her eyebrows frowned to apologise to Link, who had wiped away his tears and replaced his vulnerable face with a stone mask.

"I'll go out the window." He was already at the open window before Rory had clicked what he had said.

"Wait—" she called. "It's a fifteen-foot drop."

Link had climbed out onto the fire escape without answering Rory, making his way down until the stairs stopped. Bracing himself, he leapt off the railing and landed skilfully on the pavement. Looking up, he could see Rory's outline peering over the railing, watching after him.

Once she was sure Link wasn't splattered at the bottom of her ally, she had removed any traces of Link (straightening the cushions that gave away someone had sat on them) and let the group of chaotic friends into her home.

Nia and Nicky stumbled forward as Rory opened the door they were using as a support to stand and Will and Chrissy stepped over them, Chrissy carrying a bottle of unlabelled alcohol and Will shot her an apology and stating he was forced to tag along. The small apartment filled quickly, Nia and Will taking each side of the small sofa—Chrissy almost on Will's lap. Nicky took one of the blue armchairs and his sister had sat hugging Caspian in his bed.

"Uh—" Rory said to get everyone's attention. She closed the door and made sure to lock it, "What are we celebrating?"

Nicky took a swig of his bottle—Rory had noticed everyone had their own and started to regret pouring every drop of alcohol down the sink in temper after Link had accused her of depending on the substance—"Davis dying. Abel's trial. *Ethel's* reopening. Your birthday. Take your pick."

Chapter Thirty-Eight
Halloween

Abel was home. He had bid goodbye to the orange jumpsuit and white canvas shoes. Abel was home. His trial was quick and the jury had found Abel Patrick Sawyer innocent; Rory and Will had both cried when the text message from Emmitt had come through, confirming that Abel was free.

Rory wanted to be there, to stand at the gate while Abe was being released, wanting to see him without the weight of prison guards watching their every move under artificial lights. But She had work, the bar was opening again to the public—on Halloween—she needed to be there. Emmitt went to welcome his brother back to freedom at 1 PM and told Rory and the team not to worry. And at 4:45 PM, 15 minutes before opening, she was very worried without a word from the bothers.

Everything was set for opening night, fridges were stocked, cash registers were filled with cash and change and the dishwasher was working. So, the bar team retreated to their locker room to get ready for the big night. It was a costume night only and the bar was decked out in fake cobwebs and fake police tape and hanging monster signs. All that was left was for the team to get into their group costumes. They couldn't decide which bartender would we which 'Power Ranger' and only 2 agreed with Nicky's idea of '*Ethel's* Employees from the 80s'. After rock paper scissors, gang members beat princes and princesses.

"They're going to hate this," Chrissy complained but carried on fixing the black fedora on her head twisting, thick curls out to frame her face—the hat matching the rest of the team so they could watch for each other throughout the night. "—Ash said—"

"Well, if the twins didn't fight each other on everything, we could have been 'Power Rangers'!" Rory huffed from the bench, lacing up her boots, like Nia and

Will; her white button-up shirt was ripped at the sleeves. Rory had left three buttons undone, her black tank top underneath.

"I look better in yellow." The twins defended at the same time.

"Everyone ready?" Will asked with a heavy sigh.

A string of agreement sounded and they all stood in formation in front of the mirror. All wearing matching white shirts with *Ethel's* ironed on the back thanks to Nia. Fake bruises on Nicky's, Rory's and Chrissy's face and Nia wore fake tattoos. Will's bare arms let his real ones complete the look. Everyone wore black suspenders, the girls wearing high-waisted jeans (Chrissy in flared trousers) and the boys in black suit pants.

"We look like—" Chrissy stopped to think of a word that best described their makeshift 1920s Gangster Halloween costumes.

"Idiots," Rory stated. "We look like idiots. Let's do this."

They filtered out the room, but Will stopped Rory at the back of the group and asked her cautiously, "Any news?"

With a sad smile, Rory shook her head. "Not yet, though it's only been a few hours."

"True—I just hate waiting to know that he's OK."

"I'm sure Emmitt's got it handled. Abe's probably passed out on his sofa." She laughed and felt lighter when Will laughed lightly too. "If we don't hear anything tonight, we'll pop by tomorrow, yeah?"

Will nodded his head and let Rory step around him out of the room.

"Oh, Rory!" he stopped her again, this time with a smile. He fished out a badge from his pocket and started to pin it to her shirt. "Happy birthday, kid."

The night was going off with a hit. Every customer had worn amazing costumes and the team had received many compliments on their own. Rory and Chrissy were working the floor and the two boys and Nia manned the bar and the line of customers. Chrissy was stuck in a conversation with Coronal (who switched his old force uniform to a black cape and a white button-up). Rory was running backwards and forwards with empty glasses while collecting birthday tips.

Rory watched the group sit down at their booth and casually made her way over. "Sign on the door says costumes only," she reprimanded.

Now in front of them, Rory could see Link had tried. Under his eyes was smudged red and two red smudged lines on either side of his lips. And a trail of fake blood ran from two circles on the neck and down under his black dress shirt.

“That is not how we dress,” Link smirked. And Rory scoffed.

“I’ve seen Ash wear a pinstripe suit multiple time.”

Hino smiled brightly at her and said proudly, “I am wearing a costume!” Dressed in the same black dress shirt as Link’s and his spiked hair was messily curled as best as the short strands could. Rory struggled to identify his costume and the confusion was evident on her face. Link was looking annoyed.

“He’s me.”

Rory gave Hino an approved smile. “Lincoln,” she pointed to Hino, “vampire,” *Link.* She turned to Marius and Ash. “We have witches hats spare. You’re going to have to wear one to stay.”

Marius laughed, “You’re telling me that everyone in here is wearing a costume?”

“Even JC is wearing a witch’s hat.” She nodded and the boys looked towards JC at the bar with a purple pointy hat on top of his grey hair. (Will had placed it on his head when he had sat down.)

Ash sat up in his seat and cleared his throat. “I’m actually wearing a costume.” His voice was hesitant as if he was nervous and awkwardly shook his jacket off, revealing a plain black shirt with a white label that reads: *‘RORY’.* “Like I said, you dress like us; we’ll dress like you.”

Rory dipped her head in respect.

“And I also have a costume—” Marius unzipped his coat that was too thick to be suitable for the indoor bar, a red body warmer underneath.

Rory’s eyebrows raised. “Marty McFly?”

“Ah. Great Scott!”

“Heavy.”

Hino leaned into Ash and whispered. “What’s happening?”

“This girl has great taste in movies, that’s what!” Marius said and Rory beamed with pride.

“Back to the future references aside—I do have to ask you all to behave tonight. Amelia Sawyer may be stopping by to check on the bar and we need it to go well,” Rory asked heartily and the boys nodded.

Marius hummed, “We’ve got you—Don’t want you guys to close again, especially on your birthday.”

“Thanks,” she smiled.

Will thought that working, making himself busy with glass collecting and cleaning, would ease his mind and take his thoughts from his best friend. But the more he threw himself into conversations with customers, the more Abel nagged in the back of his head. Why hadn't he called? Why hadn't he stopped by *Ethel's*? Why hadn't Emmitt called? Why hadn't Emmitt stopped by *Ethel's*? It made perfect sense to anyone else.

After spending six months wrongfully locked up in prison, all someone would want would be to be at home sleeping without fear of inmates or guards. But Abel wasn't just anyone, *Ethel's* was his home and the team was his safety. His worries only worsened when he had reached booth 7. Will began placing their empty bottles on his tray full of beer bottles and shot glasses, ignoring the occupants. Who wasn't ignoring him.

"So, Sawyer's out?" Link asked him and Will's hand paused on the bottle he had picked up.

"Yes."

"And will he be here tonight?"

"Not sure. Don't blame him if he doesn't, though," Will lied without effort with a shrug.

Link took a swig of his beer, "We have an agreement, we won't touch him—"

"Your agreement means nothing to us—"

"—It means something to Rory and Emmitt—"

"Because they're blinded with need—" Marius, Hino and Ash watched the exchange, heads whipping back to forth like a tennis match, as one interrupted the other, leaving a broken sentence argument.

"—And you need him back?"

"Of course, I do. We all do. But I know you. And I know that your word means nothing."

"If there's one thing my boy's value—" a honeyed voice stated behind Will. The four boys sat up and placed their drinks on the table. Eyes shifted to each other in shock and looking for explanations as to why he was here. Will turned to face the unknown man. Suit too pricey and shoulders too proud for the bar. "—It's their word. Lenzo." He stuck his hand out to Will and Will turned his nose up at it. "You must be?"

"William Morrison," Ash answered.

Lenzo sized Will up and put the face to the stories like he had with Rory. Lenzo vaguely remembering coming across William years back at a gym he had been recruiting at. "No need to be hostile, William, I am here to have a drink with my boys. Do I order—"

William cut him off—all the reasons to be hostile listed in his head. "At the bar."

"Of course. Do you have any recommendations?"

Arsenic. "We have a wide range of scotch. Your boys can help you choose."

Will left the four boys with Lenzo, who oozed smugness. It was a confidence that came with knowing you had power and with that power, he had hurt his friend. Will was just starting to tolerate the gang members being in *Ethel's* by ignoring them. Which was how he was dealing with Rory's arrangement with them.

"Well, it's less shitty than I imagined. They sure turned it around after Davis," Lenzo said. "It's almost professional." None of the boys said anything as if a switch had flicked in them, they were no longer mates having a drink on Halloween. They were gang members, ready and sober for orders.

"I'll have a Manhattan," A redhead ordered at the bar. Her friends and herself had been regulars. *Ethel's* was the only place that accepted their IDs and with a heavy heart, Rory asked to see it. The girl was taken aback for a moment and then her face turned sour.

"Can I see yours?"

Rory's face dropped. "One Manhattan coming up."

Nicky gave Rory a look as she handed over the drink and she flipped him off.

"I hope you don't need to see my ID." The following customer joked, but Rory didn't laugh. Lenzo stood In front of her and Rory had never been more thankful for the bar between them. "I'll take whatever my boys drink. And I'll take the room."

Rory signalled for Chrissy to take her place serving and Lenzo signalled the boys to follow them. Will hot on their tails on behalf of Rory.

The room was the second largest on the first floor, the locker room taking the number one spot. Will had chosen the room, said the size and the controllable entry and exit points would appeal to them. Two adjoining rooms that could only opened from this room.

The room was painted a dark blue and in the middle sat a 16-seater table that Nicky had somehow stolen from his college. They filtered into the room and Rory and Will stood awkwardly at the door while the guys checked it out. Murmuring the approval. The tension in Rory's shoulders not settling, though.

"I expected less if I'm frank, you surprise me, Rory," Lenzo praised, his hands gripping the chair at the top of the table.

With a small voice and even smaller confidence, Rory said, "I have some conditions." She held her breath as Lenzo pulled the chair out.

"If everyone would take a seat. We have a business to discuss."

Nicky, Nia and Chrissy shared worried glances across the bar. Will and Rory had been upstairs with 'Gods Among Kings' for at least half an hour. Nia had taken up five bottles of beer and a glass of water ten minutes ago and had told Nicky and Chrissy they were discussing the terms and conditions of the deal. Catching Rory mention a 'no killing rule'. Their helplessness worries only increased with the arrival of the Sawyer brothers and an older woman they guessed was Amelia Sawyer.

Nicky and Nia stared doubtfully at Abel. Rory had told them of Abel's disorientating state in prison but even fresh shaving and showered, he looked different. His hair was not far from touching his shoulders and looked malnourished—the shine was gone. He was thinner too—Abel wasn't a guy built on muscle to begin with, but now he looked as if they hugged him; he would snap in half.

With a cautious smile, he stared at the twins, trying to decide whether he would say something sassy or cry. Nicky's own tears brought Abel's out and they crashed into a spine crushing hug. Tears damped Abel's hair and Nicky's shoulder. "Welcome home. brother," Nicky whispered in his ear and a fresh set of tears fell again.

They pulled apart and Nia, with shiny eyes, took small steps to him. He opened his arms and Nia lifted her hand up and slapped him. Hard on the cheek, Abel's head snapped to the side. "I've missed you too," he groaned and Nia almost knocked him off his feet with a tight embrace. Confusing Abel with the Spanish insults she was ranting in his ear.

"You must be Chrissy," Abel said to Chrissy, who was feeling left out of the family reunion. "Rory has told me a lot about you."

She blushed. "Good things, I'm hoping."

“Yes. Good things.” He looked around, searching for something. Someone. “Where is she? And Will?”

Thc twins frozc. If Abel knew, he’d get himself thrown back in prison. Part of the deal was that he’d leave them alone and if he knew Rory was upstairs in a meeting with the gang, he’d break that part of the deal.

Amelia Sawyer took a step forward. “I would like to speak to her too—for what I’ve seen so far, the bar looks,” she paused and looked around the busy and happy room. “Better.”

Nicky thought quickly, “She’s fixing the kegs in the basement. She shouldn’t be too long.” *That sounded believable.*

“She fixed the kegs yesterday—I know that because she had me on speaker while she swore at them for not working,” Emmitt started with a questionable look.

Nicky suppressed a groan and Amelia and Abel looked at him for an answer. Chrissy was biting her lip, the truth wanting to blurt out. Will and Rory could be in danger. They could help. Someone should help. Nia looking just as guilty as Nicky.

“Nicky,” Voice low, Abel took a step forward. “Where is she.”

Chapter Thirty-Nine
Not Your Bitch

"Not happening." Rory stood her ground. Furious at the conditions being made. She had stressed her own: no killing, a heads up before a meeting, no gang activity downstairs. Now it was Lenzo's turn to name his own. So far, they were easy: no questions asked, no communication with the police. But his last one was out of the question. "I'm not putting my team at risk just so you guys don't have to walk up and down some stairs. We're not your bitch."

Lenzo—sat at the top of the table—shook his head, "You already are risking them by having us here. So why not get them to do their jobs and serve us? They only need to bring drinks up every half hour. That way, we also obey your condition, no activity downstairs."

She couldn't help but give in to his words. He was correct. It was the smartest and easiest option. It was worth it. The money, the safety of Abel. 'For Abel'. She had been repeating those words all throughout the meeting. "You open a tab before the meeting starts and pay it once it's over. Nicky or I will come up every half hour. We'll be your bitch."

Marius pulled a face, "Why you and Nicky?"

"Nia would likely start a fight. Chrissy has been through too much already and Will—"

"Will isn't your bitch," Will finished for her.

Rory nudged his leg with her own under the table. Next to her was Hino. Ash, Link and Marius opposite them. Lenzo must have found Will's spirit amusing as he let out a deep chuckle, claiming he 'liked this one'.

"So, do we have a deal?" Rory asked, hopeful for the ending of this meeting that had her hands clammy and mouth dry—her hands shaking under the table too much to reach for her water. The awareness of the guns they all carried was now permanently in her mind and she regretted not asking them to remove them before she sat down.

"No, you don't."

Ash, Marius, Hino and Link shot out of their seats and their guns pointed at the party standing in the doorway. Lenzo remained seated and eyes fixated on Amelia. Who looked almost bored by the four guns pointing at her and her sons.

Sons.

Rory stood slowly from her seat. Mouth slightly parted but eyes wide and glossy. A million things ran through her head, how he had changed since her last prison visit. Cleaner. Taller without the chains shackling him down. No more orange. Now in a blue denim jacket and dark jeans with a belt to fit his slimmer waist.

No guards were stalking the walls and no one would stop her from reaching for him. She wanted to run to him, touch him, to check he was real. Embrace him in a hug that would likely break the pair of them. She'd slap him for his lack of help in the early stages of his imprisonment. She wanted to push him for keeping secrets and not trusting her. She wanted him. And no one would stop her. Yet her feet dug deeper into the ground. And instead of running to him, she dropped back into the chair.

Will was the one to make a move, almost running around the table to greet his friend in a hug attack. "Secret brother, rich mother, prison. You've got a lot to make up for, Bro!"

Abel's arms tightened around Will's waist and squeezed him hard. "I know. I know. I'm sorry."

"Well, doesn't this just warm your heart!" Lenzo clapped his hands and the attention went from the two brothers to Lenzo.

Amelia rolled her eyes. "Put your toys away, boys, before you hurt yourself." With a motion from Lenzo, they placed their guns back at their waists. "Kids, go wait downstairs. We have some things to discuss."

"No," said the kids all at once.

Like parents, Lenzo and Amelia both raised bold brows. "I beg your pardon?" Amelia asked, daring someone to answer.

"I'm not leaving you alone," Emmitt dared.

"I'm not leaving Emmitt," said Abel.

"I'm not leaving Abel," Rory said.

"I'm not leaving Rory," Will said.

"We don't take orders from you," Ash spoke out.

Amelia narrowed her eyes, "Don't get involved."

Rory scoffed and for a slight moment, she felt fear for disrespecting Amelia Sawyer. "It's too late for that. My bar. My rules. Now someone tell me what the hell is going on."

Lenzo, still looking entertained, stood up and gestured to the empty seats. "You heard the boss. Time for truths."

She hadn't thought this through. Everyone sat at the table. Amelia took the top spot at the table opposite Lenzo (a power move or to put as much distance between them, Rory didn't know). Abel had taken Will's seat with Emmitt next to him. Will on the opposite side, closest to Amelia. No one spoke, but everyone sized each other up. Hino muttered something about truths being more fun with shots and Link muttering he'd be happy to shoot him. All the questions Rory had kept for weeks, she didn't know where to start. She blew air out of her mouth.

"Why go after Abel?" she asked no one in particular and Emmitt spoke about wanting to know too.

Lenzo gave Ash permission to speak with a simple nod. "He saw something and couldn't be trusted to keep his mouth shut."

Will scrunched his face. "Abel told me what he saw at the docks, the plates and recruitment. Why didn't you go after me?"

"You took care of yourself and crashed your daddy's car before we could confirm what you knew," Marius had explained and Will scowled at him.

"So, you killed a cashier to frame me?" Abel asked though it sounded as if saying it out loud was helping him piece together the information.

Link spoke this time. "No. That wasn't part of the plan. It was supposed to be a simple robbery. Go in, shake the place up a bit. Plant the gun with your fingerprints. The Cashier—he fought back."

"Who killed him?" Abel inquired. He had lost the past five months to this incident. He deserved to know.

"Me."

Ash and Link had spoken.

"Who really killed him?" she asked them. Getting stuck in a stare off with Link.

A long moment passed. "I did."

Rory broke the stare off and spun to her right. "You?" she whispered.

Hino refused to look into her eyes. "Yes, me," Hino confessed. "I had turned my back for two seconds and he made a break for the door. He fought back and I had to keep him quiet. Our orders were to frame Sawyer and if he had managed to get the police there earlier—So, I hit him and he started a fuss again. So, I hit again and kept until he stopped."

Hino's voice was ice cool and it reminded Rory of that day in Davis's office. Where this all started. Where she first (poorly) stood up against them. Based on the photos in the report, Rory had guessed Ash, it took strength—or anger. A morbid anger. But Isao Hino? Hino gave them kind smiles and told them shameless jokes that made them giggle and snort.

He attended Halloween nights dressed as his best friend. Not brutishly murder an innocent. Would he really do—that. They all would, she reminded herself. They're part of the 'Gods Among Kings'. They were ruthless. They were powerful. Rory had got so caught up with them the past few weeks. She had fought them, made deals with them, decorated and laughed with them. Cried with him. They had killed her boss and hurt her best friend. At what point had she got to know them enough to be—disappointed in them.

She wasn't the only one stunned by the news. Lenzo rubbed his chin. "I had bet it was Ash. Not you, Hino. Didn't know you had it in you."

He clapped him on the back, but Hino didn't appreciate it. His face was hard and his knuckles were white. Rory tried to look for a hint for remorse, a sign of regret or guilt or something that resembled a human emotion.

Nothing.

An awkward silence had filled the room though Abel was always able to fill the silence. "Why didn't you just kill me? Surely it would be less hassle to throw me into the river than to send me to jail."

"Abel Patrick," Amelia said level, but the threat was clear.

Lenzo seemed to like the question and he leaned forward, his forearms on the table and grinning like the Cheshire cat at Amelia. "Your last name, kid. That's what saved you."

"Because I'm a Sawyer?"

"Because he has a history with Mum," Emmitt said. "History, I'm very interested in hearing."

Rory and Link caught each other's eyes and Amelia visibly gulped. Lenzo still enjoying the opportunity to toy with Amelia. "Do you want to tell him the story, Melia or should I?"

“We knew each other a long time ago,” was all she offered through gritted teeth.

“How long would you say, Melia?” Lenzo forced the story from her.

She sent him a distasteful glare. “I don’t quite remember.”

With a wicked smile drunk on power, Lenzo asked, “Emmitt, how old are you now?”

“Twenty-four,” Emmitt said slowly. Mind connecting the hints and teases. He didn’t know how it had taken him this long to realise. The eyes, the bone structure. The way he had called him Son and how Amelia would flinch and become defensive whenever he’d bring that day in the office up.

“Were you with him? With the gang?”

“No.”

“Yes. You were my best girl. No one did negotiations like you did. It tore me when you left, no note, no explanation.” Despite him recounting his most negative memories, Lenzo’s tone was light and cheerful.

Entertained by bring up the past and tormenting Amelia. “It wasn’t until my boys came to me with a story about Sawyer having an older brother that I figured out why you left me all those years ago. You did always close up whenever we talked about having an heir.”

There it was. Lenzo had confirmed what most had already guessed and Rory suddenly felt guilty for forcing them to stay and play truths. Emmitt went pale and Amelia looked defeated. Abel in total shock.

“Emmitt I—” Amelia tried, but Emmitt held his hand up to stop her. “I only lied to protect you—”

“Shut up—” Emmitt shot, his head hung and Amelia turned furious at her son; before she could ground the adult for disrespecting her, Emmitt’s head shot up. “Does anyone else smell smoke?”

Everyone smelt the air. Distant smells of smoke filled their noses and panic rose quickly. As they all came to the realisation that something was on fire—the fire alarms had gone off.

Jumping up—everyone headed for the door at one time and down the stairs to the smoke-filled bar. Rory couldn’t see any flames. She couldn’t see anything. Smoke filled her nose and throat and her eyes began to sting unbearably. Dazed, she stood in her spot as dark figures rushed around her. Lists of names in her head formed, regulars she had seen earlier that would have to be accounted for. Rory watched the smoke cover the tables and she could see footprints staining her new floor. Hands gripped her shoulders and shook her harshly from behind. A voice in her ear telling her to move. To get out. She turned to face Link.

"It's coming from the basement, I think. We need to go." His hand moved to her elbow and gripped it hard, pulling her away, but she broke free.

"I have to make sure everyone is out!"

"What—" Link spluttered out. "—It's too dangerous!"

Ignoring him, she ran towards the toilet doors and began shouting. Girls came running out of the toilets and headed for the door in the thick smoke. By now, the flames had appeared in the doorway to the basement. The doorknob had already started to melt in the heat and Rory watching helplessly. She was watching the bar burn around her, the fresh sage walls were coated in soot, posters that Nicky had hung were curling at the edges.

Bottles that Chrissy had stocked were shattered on the floor. Her work was burning and then she was swept off her feet harshly and thrown over a shoulder, her stomach digging into the broad shoulders, no doubt leaving a bruise and she gripped at the shirt. She was carried out the building and dropped onto the road, lungs burning at the fresh air and she began coughing uncontrollably. The person who had carried her out—Ash—also started to cough in a fit.

"Thank you." She got out between coughs. The street had filled with customers and on goers, watching the smoke filter out the building. Rory searched the crowd and swore when she spotted the twins. She rushed as best as she could to them. "Chrissy?"

"Here," she called and pushed through a group of bikers, still holding their glasses of beers and smoking their cigars.

"Will?"

"I'm here."

"JC? Angel? Coronal?"

"I saw Angel pull Coronal out," Nicky confirmed.

"No JC?"

Nicky shook his head and Rory swore. "Your friends?" she asked Ash.

"They got out."

"Abel? Emmitt and Amelia?"

"We're here!" Emmitt shouted. His mother hugged him. "We thought Abe was with you."

Rory's heart stopped, she shook her head and without hesitation, took off back into the bar. An arm swung around her and flung her back into their chest—Nicky.

"Abel, he's in there! He's still in there!" she screamed and it broke Nicky's heart to tighten his grip around her. Rory kicked and scratched up his arms. "I just got him back, Nicky. Let me go! I have to get him."

Will and Link shared a look that called a truce in their feud.

"I'll take upstairs," Link said and the pair raced into the building. Causing the rest of the group to shout and fuss.

Link took the stairs two at a time in search of Abel. The building was mainly smoke, but flames were rising and he had already begun to sweat. He screamed for Abel though they were cushioned by the thin layer of smoke and roaring flames downstairs. Link didn't hear the arguing in the meeting room.

"You ruined my life," Abel screamed. A gun shaking in his hand.

Abel kept a gun in his drawers before he was locked away; he lived in a bad neighbourhood in Chicago, it was protection. And when Emmitt suggested a trip to *Ethel's* to see his friends. Abel craved protection. So, he stuffed the gun under his t-shirt. The fire had caused everyone to panic and disband. No one noticed Abel hold Lenzo back in the room. The gun was loaded and the safety had been off all night. Smoke filled his lungs and he was struggling to breathe. The gun pointed at Lenzo's chest and for once in his life, Lenzo was slightly afraid. In the panic, Abel had taken Lenzo's gun and he was left defenceless.

"You must be stupid, boy!" he barked as more and more smoke filled the air. "The longer we stand here, the more smoke we're inhaling!"

"I don't care! I haven't been able to breathe in months!" Abel screamed. "You ruined my life! You have no idea what it's like. To be locked up for something you didn't do! Not daring to sleep because you don't know what will come for you if you close your eyes. To be forced to pretend that you are that monster, a murderer, for so long it starts to sound believable! I'm free, yet I can't do anything! I can't breathe or sleep or have drinks with my friends! You took that from me! You took everything. You killed me!"

Link didn't hear the arguing. But he heard the gunshot loud and clear.

The twins, Chrissy and Rory, curled up against each other on the road. The Fire service had arrived and were assessing the best way to deal with the situation. Emmitt had a tight hold on Amelia. Ash and Hino held Marius back, screaming and fighting to go after Lincoln. They had been in there for 6 minutes.

Too long to be in there with the smoke. Ash fell over the crowd like snow and their Halloween costumes were wrecked in the panic and chaos. The fire services were just about to enter the building when two figures slowly struggled out of the building. Link and Will. Each bridal carrying a body.

Link handed the body he was carrying to the group of paramedics that rushed to him. And it wasn't until the stretcher went past that they recognised the dead body as JC.

Rory jumped up and took in the unmoving body that Will had in his arms. Tears-stained Will's cheek and left marks where they had washed away the ash. His guilty and destroyed gaze locked on Rory as if the sight of her kept him up and moving. Broken. Will looked broken and with a shake of his head. Rory broke too.

There was a scream—herself or Amelia. Rory didn't know. But there was a scream, the kind that shattered through everyone's hearts. That had the whole crowd grieving for someone they didn't know. Paramedics tried to take Abel's body from Will, but he refused to let him go, turning away and holding his brother tight to his chest. Marius, who had calmed at the sight of Link still breathing, reached for Will's shoulder and told him that Abel would be safe with the paramedics and they'd take care of him.

Chapter Forty
He Knew

The ground and first floor were ruined. The basement wasn't accessible to anyone who valued their life. Rory had been told that the fire was a simple gas leak from the pipes in the cellar. It took two days for them to be allowed into the bar. The ceiling was black. The walls were charcoal and the ground was covered in ash. Half the bar counter was gone, melted remains stuck to the floor. It was midday, but the room was cast in a black shadow.

"You're insured. You can fix it if that's what you desire," Emmitt spoke softly to Rory, who was lifting the counter lid to get behind the bar. All the fridges were melted and ruined. "It'll take a while, but it can be done."

Six days. Six days since Abel and JC had died in the fire. Six days since they had got Abel back. Six days since they had lost him again. Forever. Emmitt took the days off and spent it curled up with Khenan, crying, screaming, breaking things and eating everything. Today he was back in a suit and back at work. Rory had done a similar thing. But instead of curling up with a hot baker fiancé, she curled up with Caspian and Will. Taking turns with a baseball bat and objects on the roof of her building. A body had been found on the first floor—burned severely but still identifiable as Erik Lenzo.

"Maybe," she replied. But Emmitt knew she hadn't heard what he had suggested.

"Aurora," he sighed and got her actual attention. "Abe—he left a will and he made you his next of kin." Rory tried to blink back the tears. "That means his funeral—it's up to—you get the final say. And we don't know what he wanted. But you knew him more than anyone."

"He never liked the idea of being buried," she heaved a heavy sigh and her voice wavered. "He used to say, If he were to die—always if because we had yet to prove he wasn't immortal—" She laughed at the memory of Abel, tipsy, dancing around her living room, making even death sound like an adventure.

"I should have done it," she breathed out like it had been a weight on her chest. "Back in the meeting room. I wanted to run to him and I didn't. He sat next to me and I still didn't touch him. The last time I touched him. He was being pulled away by guards. I should have—I didn't even say hello or welcome back. I—he didn't know how much I wanted him back—" Her voice broke and she sobbed into her hand. "—And God, do I want him back."

"He knew," Emmitt said sternly. "The note you put in the file. He had it in his hand at the trial and he had kissed it when they read the verdict. He had it in his hand when they let him out of the gate and Abel kept it close to his chest the whole ride home. When I had asked him what he was holding—a promise that he had a home."

Tears streamed from her face and she used the back of her sleeve to wipe her nose. Her sobbing had only increased.

"He knew."

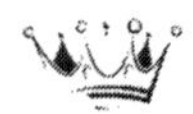

Chrissy. Will. Emmitt. Khenan. Amelia. Nicky. Charlotte. Nia. Rory. Angel. Coronal. Caspian. Maddox. Regulars from *Ethel's*. Old school friends.

No less than forty people lined the shore. Crying, holding hands with strangers and cuddling their loved ones. Swapping stories and tales about their mutual friend. Times he had made them laugh and times he had made them so angry they could scream. Making promises to meet up soon for coffee because life was too short and unpredictable.

That would never happen because they lived different lives with busy schedules but right now, standing at the shore, it didn't matter because they had reunited at that moment. Because right now, no less than forty people had reunited to say goodbye. No less than forty people lined the shore for one reason.

To say goodbye to Abel Patrick Sawyer.

Amelia held a metal jar. Clutching it to her chest. Rory on one side and Emmitt on the other, holding her up as she wept.

"He liked the beach."

She unscrewed the lid and let it fall to where the sand and water met.

He would wake us up and make us drive to the beach to just stand there and watch the waves. No matter the time or weather.

Taking a handful of the ashes, she sobbed loudly and it hit Rory and Will and Emmitt, all wrecks from continuous crying.

He would say the shore was like a door—gate—to the world. The ocean connected us to the rest of the world. If we ever needed an adventure, we would just have to stand at the shore, close our eyes and imagine.

The waves crashed against their feet and Amelia flew the ashes towards the water. The wind picking them up and carrying them out to the ocean. Rory and Emmitt both took a handful of ashes. And let them go out to sea.

"Goodbye, my son."

"Goodbye, my brother."

"Goodbye, my Abel—"

That's where he would want to be. At the shore, so he could have thousands of adventures. He'd want us to close our eyes and imagine the biggest adventure we could. And then imagine a little more.

"—And live. Go live your adventures," Rory whispered to the wind.

"Boss wants to see you three."

Marius, Hino and Ash stood up from the uncomfortable chairs and made their way into the bare office. They stood in a line in front of the desk while they waited for their boss to turn and address them: shoulders back, chins high and hands behind their back.

"Come on, guys—" Their boss said as he turned around and took the scene in front of him in. "You don't have to act like that."

Lincoln kicked his feet up on the desk. "It's just me."